W9-AWH-052

BOTH OF ME

Other books by Jonathan Friesen

The Last Martin

Aldo's Fantastical Movie Palace

Aquifer

JONATHAN FRIESEN

BOTH OF ME

BLINK

To Siobhan, a very savvy Londoner.

BLINK

Both of Me
Copyright © 2014 by Jonathan Friesen

This title is also available as a Blink ebook.
Visit www.zondervan.com/ebooks.

This title is also available in a Blink audio edition.
Visit www.zondervan.fm.

Requests for information should be addressed to:
Blink, 3900 *Sparks Drive SE, Grand Rapids, Michigan 49546*

Library of Congress Cataloging-in-Publication Data
Friesen, Jonathan.
    Both of me / Jonathan Friesen.
      pages cm
      Summary: "When her carry-on bag is accidentally switched with Elias's identical pack, Clara uses the luggage tag to track down her things. At that address she discovers there is not one Elias Phinn, but two." — Provided by publisher.
      ISBN 978-0-310-73188-7 (hardback) — ISBN 978-0-310-73187-0 (softcover) — ISBN 978-0-310-73189-4 (epub) — ISBN 978-0-310-73190-0 (epub)
      1. Multiple personality—Fiction. 2. Dissociative disorders—Fiction. 3. Artists—Fiction. 4. Voyages and travels—Fiction. 5. Love—Fiction. 6. Christian life—Fiction. I. Title.
    PZ7.F91661Bot 2014
    [Fic]—dc23   2014031382

Any Internet addresses (websites, blogs, etc.) and telephone numbers in this book are offered as a resource. They are not intended in any way to be or imply an endorsement by the publisher, nor does the publisher vouch for the content of these sites and numbers for the life of this book.

Cover design: *Brand Navigation*
Interior design and composition: *Greg Johnson/Textbook Perfect*

Printed in the United States of America

---

14 15 16 17 18 19 20 /DCI/ 20 19 18 17 16 15 14 13 12 11 10 9 8 7 6 5 4 3 2 1

PROLOGUE

At what moment does your life become your own?

At birth? No, you are owned and helpless, unwitting and unaware. Life is food and sleep. But you are listening, listening to and learning from Dad and Mum. Your 'rents, they make you.

And if your dad strikes a copper and ends up in the slammer, well, that's stirred into your pot.

School arrives, but you are not free. Once again, you are owned, this time by teachers who have heard of your rep and know of your dad and decide without cause that remedial work is your lot.

They don't see into your flat. They don't see the angelic faces of Marna or Teeter, your sibs who had no dad or mum to learn from because Mum spent her days weeping and her final nights little more than a zombie at the factory. But even then, I suppose, they were watching, learning that our brief lives are never our own, and the future is as murky as the London sky.

Mercifully, your final term ends. Exams show you to be equal parts unemployable and incorrigible, but it doesn't matter, as that is how they show everyone to be.

And for the first time, you have a choice.

You tuck a blanket over your last memories with Mum, remembering her fitful sleep and her cold face stained with tears. You listen to your brother and sister—children you've raised— arguing in front of the telly, and wonder what you've done.

When will you be more than a sum total of your 'rents' many mistakes ...

And your one large one.

When does your life start?

And in a fit, you rummage beneath your bed, retrieve your passport and all the savings you own, and stare into the mirror.

Nobody stares back.

"Clara?"

Teeter's call acts like a vise, and the squeeze is unbearable.

"Clara!"

You repeat your name. "Clara." A whisper that gains strength. "Clara." Because unlike your life, your name cannot be lifted from you. Friends, family, teachers—thieves all—have taken everything else, but they grudgingly agree; the name is yours. Even to the swine, it is sacred.

You stare at that name in your passport and look out over Marbury Street, at the buses that run the same routes, at the same times, carrying the same blokes. They've given up, traded teachers for bosses, and will live the rest of their lives in responsible agony. And you vow you will never be like them.

"I'm hungry, Clara!"

"On the hob! Start without me."

You stroke the world map, yellowed and torn ... together with a Celtic cross and journal, they are the few pieces of Dad you've allowed to remain. One hundred red tacks supposedly mark one hundred selfless acts Dad performed for strangers across the globe.

At least that's what Mum used to say ... and maybe she was right, but ...

There is no tack in London.

Now, tomorrow, he is coming home.

According to the warder, Dad's incarceration was the result of "extraordinary circumstance," and Mum's recent death qualifies him for early release. He will return to your flat, to Marna, an eight-year-old he has never met, and to Teeter, a thirteen he will not want to.

He will not return from prison to you.

Not when your actions had a hand in sending him there.

"Clara!" Marna calls. "The wash wasn't started."

"No, it wasn't." You remove Dad's weathered leather journal from the trunk in the closet, the volume entitled *1995*.

You quietly fill a bag — one is enough, because at eighteen years old there's little to remember — and wait for night to fall, and for unfamiliar stars to call you far away.

And you never look back.

PART 1

CLARA

CHAPTER 1

The accent. Tell me where you're from." The young fool crumpled his McDonald's bag and leaned over the table. "I could listen to that all day."

I took aim and lobbed a chip at his nose. It bounced off his eyelid, and still he smiled. Quite the idiot. "It's the little things you miss, really. Little, like chips and a shake. Nepal had neither." I stuffed my mouth and eased back. "Is it cold in here? I'm thinner than when I left home, and it seems I'm always cold." I glanced around the terminal — after eight months and hundreds of layovers, they all looked the same. Even the faces blurred. Travelers, different only in age and size. Their voices long ago faded to white noise.

They drifted by me harmlessly, like so many clouds . . .

Then he walked by, and my gaze fixed on him.

He walked between his 'rents. His proud dad. His watchful mum, eyes darting for lanes through the bustle.

The child carried a little Superman bag, and from the look on his face, he was happy. So happy he didn't notice the stuffed bear poking out his bag's zip. So happy he didn't notice the bear fall.

"One minute." I grabbed my own bag, jumped up, and joined the fray, weaving through the crowd. I reached the fallen bear, and a well-dressed loser distracted by his mobile stepped on the toy. I shoved him, and he stumbled and cursed, but he no longer existed to me. I bent down and gently picked up the loved animal, with its patchy fur and one eye.

Little T owned a bear like this.

I pushed forward. Toward the boy. He would want this, need this. I reached the family and placed my hand on Mum's shoulder. She reached for her son's hand and spun around.

"Yes?"

"Your son. He dropped his bear."

The boy's smile widened, and I swallowed hard.

"This nice young lady found Pooh!" Mum knelt beside him, rounding his shoulder with her arm. "What do you say?"

He said nothing, but rather reached out his hands, and I placed the bear inside them. He squeezed the bear and I wanted to squeeze the boy. His almond-shaped eyes, the muted features. He had Down syndrome, and he was perfect.

I backed up slowly. "I just wanted to reunite the two of you. I once had a brother who loved a bear like yours." I turned and walked slowly back toward my new mate. A hundred nobodies parted around me.

Reaching the table, I slumped down into my seat and stroked the tiny number 3 tattooed between my left thumb and pointer.

"What was that about?"

I shook my head. The little boy had looked happy.

"Now, then. What were you saying? Oh, yes. London," I said quietly, glancing at the bloke across the table. "Born in London. Seems forever ago."

"Clara, it's been almost a year, right? I know we just met, so you can take this or leave it, but, nobody wanders forever. You've got to go home sometime."

I leaned back, and stared upward. "I know a man who never did. He was brilliant. His 'rents put him through university, and he became the most sought-after architect in his class. He had job offers across the United States. But one month before graduation, he packed his bags, left school, left his family and his country. He never went back. He wandered the world digging wells for the poor, building hospitals, churches. I carry a record of his route."

"So you're following in this guy's footsteps."

"No." I took a deep breath. "I don't dig. I don't build, and I will not rot penniless in prison. But his path keeps me safe. People remember him, help me on my way." I scooted nearer. "Have you ever followed what you're running from?"

"Last call, Flight 302 departing for Minneapolis."

"That's me." I rose, reached down, and gathered my bag. "Thanks for the meal. It has earned you a place in my diary, though I've quite forgotten your name. How would you like to be remembered?"

Young fool jumped up and grabbed my wrist. "Take the next flight, Clara. Let me show you New York City. Honest, if you'd just get to know me ..."

I pried loose his fingers, and patted his cheek. "We've already met. In Paris and Pakistan and Brazil. Accommodating lads like you are everywhere. If there's one thing I've learned these last eight months, it's this ... involvements equal pain." My voice fell. "Not that I've always remembered the equation."

I hoisted the strap over my shoulder. "And I've a mate waiting on the far end of this flight."

The last passengers boarded, and I sauntered toward the gate agent. She left her desk and moved toward the gate door. I raised my ticket high.

I would not jog. I would not shout. Those actions belonged to the responsible, to those who cared. The memory of my first flight returned and tugged at the corners of my lips. How early I had arrived. For five hours, I sat nervously inside Heathrow, checking and rechecking my flight's status. But that was before. Before the world reminded me there was always another plane, and revealed to me the wild joys of plan B, the spontaneous path the punctual never travel.

I peeked over my shoulder, blew a kiss to the young fool still watching from a distance.

He would certainly take me in if the agent would not.

She gave a final glance about the gate and our eyes met. She beckoned wildly.

"You on this flight? Get a move on, girl. You came mighty close to missin' the plane."

"Yes, I suppose I did."

She swiped my ticket and I wandered into the tunnel. Tunnels were the Great In-Between. Tucked between the leaving and the arriving, these bridges, these portals, existed on every continent. Inside, I always pictured myself back in London, slogging toward a bus. The same bus. Stuck in the middle.

I hated tunnels, but they were a necessary evil.

Planes — now, they were different. They held mystery and promise, and over the course of my Third World travels, a chicken or two. They also held the very real possibility of death.

I ducked inside and paused in first class, surveying my travel mates. The red-eye from New York to Minneapolis held nothing but the comatose. Self-satisfied businessmen, ties loosened and shirts untucked, returning to knackered wives. Beyond, a sea of the ragged and unwashed. My world.

I greeted the stewardess and slipped toward the rear of the plane, toward the one empty seat, a middle. I opened the overhead and pressed my bag into the compartment, and then paused to analyse my neighbours.

On the aisle, a tall, bald man. He winced and groaned, undoubtedly wishing for hinges with which to fold up his legs. His knees barricaded my row, but he quickly dislodged and stood, likely grateful for one last stretch. Beyond him, tucked into the window seat, sat a good-looking lad with a serious face, his gaze locked in a sketch-book and his pencil working feverishly. He was so absent, he almost blended into the plane.

I eased down in-between.

Neither spoke. I could do worse.

I removed Dad's journal from my jacket pouch, tracing the numbers 1–9–9–5 and the cross on its cover. I removed his shredded map from inside it and a marker from my pocket, and dotted Nepal yellow. A quick count: Eighty stars across five continents.

Dad, I will soon have you beat.

Minutes later, the plane taxied away from LaGuardia. Some-day, I would experience New York, but not with an idiot I met at McDonald's. The cabin lights went dark. I yawned and Aisle Man groaned, but Window Boy reached franticly for his reading beam. He managed to turn on all three vents and hit and cancel the stew-ardess call twice, but his flummoxed fingers could not locate the light. Sweat formed on his temple, and he muttered about an immi-nent attack and a lethal threat and an insidious enemy.

All very poor word choices when seated on an aeroplane.

"Hush. Let me help." I reached up and flicked on his beam.

He peeked at me, and as our gazes met, I assigned to him, as was my habit with all handsome blokes, a Possibility of Entanglement score — POE for short. This involved four questions worth three points each, the outcome scored like a football match. The lower the score, the safer for me.

Has he shown himself to be needy? Yes. Three points.

Does he remind you of anyone from London? Oh, the eyes of Jordy Waltham. Three points.

Does he show any interest in you? No. Three points.

Is he an original?

Window Boy dug in his pocket and extracted a tiny pencil sharpener and a baggie filled with shavings. He popped the plastic sharpener lid and picked out three shavings, whispering as he went along, "One, two, three." He placed each minute fleck into the bag, one by one, as if handling the sacred, again whispering the count. Then he carefully sealed the bag, fought it back into his pocket, and gave his pencil precisely three turns inside the sharpener.

I frowned. Is he an original? Yes. Three points.

Total POE score: 12

I exhaled slowly.

I haven't met a twelve in months.

"What's your name, then?" I asked.

His jaw tensed, but he neither glanced up nor spoke.

"Right. Heading home or away?"

This time his hand paused and he double clutched his pencil. He wasn't answering, but he was hearing. An unusual lad.

"I've never been to Minneapolis." I leaned into his shoulder and felt him flinch. "Tell me about it."

"You talk too much."

Direct, emotionless ... flipping fascinating. I shifted in my seat. He was right, and I couldn't help but smile.

"Yes, I do. And you practice eye contact far too little."

"I look at visitors when I need to, and since I don't need to, and I already know what you want, I will ignore you."

"And what is it that I want?"

"Secrets."

Here, on the outbound from New York, I had happened upon the most interesting bloke yet—a glorious breeze following five parched continents.

"Yes." I licked my lips, my goal only to extract him from his sketchbook. "I do want your secrets. Every single one—and since we have the time, let's start with your name."

His face tightened. "My name is *not* a secret. Elias. Elias Phinn."

"Hmm. A perfectly sensible name."

"Now you're trying to put me at ease with compliments." Elias stared down at the lights of the city. "Many stars fell tonight. But" — his voice hardened — "just like my name is no secret, it's also no compliment. Your schemes won't work." He paused. "I know where you're from."

"Horrid for me. You've uncovered my clandestine programme, and you know where I'm from. This places me at a slight disadvantage." I craned my neck to see what precious thing he could be sketching, but he raised the book's back cover and blocked my view.

He returned to drawing, and I bit my lip. I couldn't lose him, or this conversation. Though I had to act utterly dim, this nonsense was addictive.

"Did my accent give me away?"

"Your accent." He thought, and shrugged. "You're probably pretending to have an accent. Your dad doesn't have an accent."

I pressed back into my seat. He was right again, depending on perspective. My father, American by birth, never sounded like a Londoner. But Elias's guess on that point was the least of my worries. How had we traversed so much ground? Dad was a topic reserved for my inner circle. Elias was not in that queue.

"You know nothing of the man," I said quietly.

Elias slammed his book shut with a flourish, and stared into me. He was angry, or not — his face gave away so little. Suddenly, I felt very small.

"He's only the most dishonest, selfish, ruthless man in your entire nation. And don't try to deny it. His disgrace is the reason you're here."

I had wriggled free from many scrapes during the course of my adventures; I had only to be quick and clever. But Truth is inescapable.

"How do you know this?"

"You're not the first one he's sent. There was Kayla and Tessa.

Both tried to seduce me with their words and discover what I know." He paused. "I never thought Rupert would risk his own daughter in this cover-up."

Rupert? Dad's name was Sean. Okay, Window Boy was certifiably deranged. But he had also come close, too close. I'd matched wits with blokes all over the world, and been jolted by a lad who belonged in a mad house.

Time soon took its toll, and Elias gave in to sleep. He clutched his sketchbook, clearly as dear to him as my diary was to me, against his chest. With a sudden and large slump, he melted against the window, arms limp at his sides, his holy book slipping to his lap.

I stared at his prize. Certifiable or not, Elias had pricked me, as nobody in eight months had. He had no business poking into my family, or dredging up pain from the deep. I decided to poke back.

Gently, I lifted the sketchbook from his thighs, took one peek at Elias, and opened to the first page.

"Not possible."

CHAPTER 2

"Miss, you really need to exit the aircraft."

Fifteen minutes had passed since I eased the sketchbook back onto Elias's lap, since Elias woke and grabbed his bag and pushed his way off the plane.

My gaze roamed the face of the stewardess, but it was the pictures from the sketchbook that remained, impressed in my memory.

Page one: A factory. Not maybe a factory, positively a factory, drawn from the inside, from the floor, where huge looms pumped and pumped the cloth. Workers bent, weary looks on their faces. They worked too hard, too long. Just like Mum.

Page four: A prison. Drawn from inside the cell. Through the eyes of a prisoner. To the right, a cell wall, scratched and worn by a million hopeless moments. And at the bottom, hands—guilty hands—upturned. As a younger man, these palms gloried in strength and promise. Now, weathered and wrinkled, they'd taken too much. A murderer's hands? A rapist's hands? A fighter's?

Dad's?

Page seven: Me. Not resembling me, or me from a distance. Me, up close and peeking around a corner. Hesitant. Running from something. Elias reflected my gaze, my vacant mirror gaze. He captured my longing.

These were no abstract drawings. Elias drew with firm, perfect strokes. More telling than a photo. More, just more.

"Miss, are you all right?" The stewardess laid her hand on my shoulder. I stared at her fingers.

"No."

I rose, squeezed into the aisle, and reached for my bag. It felt heavy slung over my shoulder. For the first time in months I felt weak and crumpled against a seat.

"How did that bloke know my life? In his sketchbook, how could he know it?" I asked, and glanced at the stewardess. "Did you tell him? Wait, how would you know?"

"Do I need to call someone for you?" She stepped out of the aisle to let me pass. "I was supposed to keep a watchful eye on Elias throughout the flight, but maybe you need—"

"A bit of sleep and I'll—I'll be fine."

I wandered off the plane and into a vacant airport.

He's gone. My chest loosened. *A random meeting with a paranoid mentalist. Disturbing, but random nonetheless.*

"All right, Clara. Gather yourself."

Money. It would be good to check on where I stood with that. I threw my bag onto a blue plastic seat, tugged on the zip, and took a deep breath.

My bag was not my bag.

"Stop!" I screamed, and raced back down the tunnel. I burst back into the plane and grabbed my stewardess mate. "My dad's journal!" Every caution and tip and all his contacts! Not to mention my own diary. Eight months of everything. Every thought. And photos, of Teeter and Marna and Mum. "This isn't happening!" Together, we executed a frantic search.

"I'm so sorry." She glanced at her watch. "You can fill out a report, and if your backpack turns up . . ."

I would not fill out a report. Not when every moment spent with pen and paper was another moment farther from my bag. No, there would be no report. No paper trail. I would find the idiot who lifted my bag and make the criminal pay.

I hurried back into the terminal and spread the contents of not-my-bag out on the floor.

Men's clothing, bundled and balled on top. This, I expected. I was the only female thief I'd encountered thus far. Beneath the clothing, some personal effects and two medications.

Risperidone and Melatonin. Thieves are always blasted.

I set the drugs aside, and peered into the bottom of the bag.

Paper. Reams of it. Paper laying loose; paper gathered into tablets. Paper in sketchbooks.

"Oh no," I groaned.

And crumpled among the pages of drawings I dared not examine was a small slip, worn and creased.

Contents of this backpack belong to Elias Phinn.
If found, please contact Guinevere Phinn at:
Phinn's Bed and Breakfast
1 Loring Parkway
Minneapolis, Minnesota
(612) 555-0177

Guinevere. So be it. I will not deal with Window Boy. I will sort this out with Guinevere and retrieve my diary and forget this flight.

My stewardess shut down the gate area and joined me.

"Find what you need?"

I held up the address. "Loring Parkway. Is that near?"

She nodded. "Twenty minutes. None too far. It's in the heart of downtown." She started to walk away, and then turned. "Nice thing you're doing, returning it yourself. It might even be fate you wound up with that bag. My dad, he took the wrong bus somewhere in

England after the war, and my mom was on it. That's how they met. It turned out that there was a reason for hopping on that wrong bus."

"Thanks, but every bus in England is the wrong bus." I slowly reached for Elias's shirt, flattened it and folded it. Then another, and another. My heartbeat slowed. Left sock, right sock. I lined up the seams of denims, set the folded clothes aside, and gently stacked the papers. Finally, I lifted the items back into the bag.

My mind clear, I hoisted the bag over my shoulder. I would locate Loring Parkway, but now, with my blasted laptop in Elias's possession, I had a greater need . . .

• • • • •

Help Support Children of Incarcerated Parents
500 Days of Wandering, 500 Days of Hope

I hated blogging from my phone, and I hated being rushed. But tucked inside my diary, £3,000 in bills found its way into Window Boy's hands, and his bag didn't return the favor.

Bottom line: I needed money, and for that, my site needed attention. Compose. Click.

Day 240

I realise, now that I am well into this adventure, just how I long for home, for my precious England. But the need is great, and so is my resolve. (Here, I paused to cough, and continued.) Presently, I find myself in . . .

I stepped onto the people mover, glanced about, and shrugged. I'd only posted a handful of fictional entries, but I needed money, and I'd learned elegance was key.

New Zealand, a beautiful country; in Christchurch, a lovely city. Surrounded by mountains and waterfalls, stretches of plains, and deep-cut valley. These are the views that children of incarcerated parents will never glimpse. This is the air that the incarcerated long to breathe. These hardened ones at least remember freedom. But their unfortunate children languish like downed kites. They are abandoned, unless you, dear reader, act.

Will you lift the wings of a poor child today?

Will you donate to the Children of Incarcerated Parents Fund?

Friends, together we have reached thirty percent of our £500,000 goal.

One hundred percent of your gift goes toward the support of one of these children, a child who has just lost everything.

"At least that line's the truth," I said, and finished my entry:

Give generously. Give now.

I posted the blog and waited. They would give. Incredible that over ten thousand people, a small cult following, discovered and subscribed to my blog. More incredible still that a tenth of them financially supported my global trek. Yes, they believed they were giving to needy children. That occasionally—like today—I fabricated even my location, always gave me pause. But there was no other way. Their charity alone kept me traveling, and by the time I reached ticketing, £400 had been given.

"Well, all right then." I pocketed my phone and grimaced. "We live to lie another day."

CHAPTER 3

"What took you so long?"

The beautiful girl slammed her car door and slowly walked toward the curb where I stood. She offered her infectious smirk and we embraced.

"There was trouble on the flight. Trouble with a boy." I pulled free and shook my head. "But you, Kira, you haven't changed a bit."

Again, she smirked.

It was that knowing look that first intrigued me years ago. Her father had moved their family into a neighbouring flat for a six-month stint in London. He was a traveling contractor, and Kira's mum an excessive shopper, which left the two of us with time to make plans in secret. Our most ambitious scheme: One day I would visit America.

"Looks are deceiving." Kira unlatched her car's boot and hoisted my bag inside. She pounded the lid down with a flourish and threw back her hair. "For me, there is no more mom, no more dad. I haven't seen them in a year. Oh ... I'm really sorry about your mom. She didn't look too bad when we were there. What was it?"

"Cirrhosis."

"What is that?"

"Drink ate her insides."

Kira nodded. "Wow. Well, like I was saying, I live with three

24

roommates on the university campus." She paused. "You've been all over the world, but I bet you've never experienced the kind of craziness I'm about to show you."

From anyone else, an insensitive ignorance of Mum's fate. But Kira's shallowness was more than her greatest weakness, it was an enviable strength.

She never had to feel.

"Not so fast," I said. "I need to collect an item first. Can you take me to this addy?"

I handed her the slip.

"Who do you know in Loring Park?"

"Elias."

"You two hooked up on the plane?"

"He lifted my bag from the plane."

Again, the smirk. "Sounds promising. Hop in."

I suppose it might have been the evening's flight, or a fret about my bag, but listening to Kira spout on about her exploits, both wild and domestic, held no fascination. Her excitable voice faded into white noise, and I rested my head against the window, forcing smiles and nods but hearing little.

No, I decided, Kira had not changed. But I had. In London, I was her little disciple, following the whims of an older, bellicose American. She had been my first exposure to an untamed world beyond Marbury Street, and what a thrilling picture she'd painted.

Now my eyes had seen that world. They'd seen brilliant northern lights over Iceland, washing the night sky in pinks and greens. They'd seen those same colours alive and vibrant in the fish and corral of Australia's Great Barrier Reef.

But they'd also seen death, from dysentery and dengue fever. Dad's journal had taken me on lonely dirt paths in West Africa and through jungles of Nicaragua, where I'd wished like anything that I could hear my sibs argue again.

Family. You should not so flippantly toss them aside. Like Kira had.

I pinched my forehead between thumb and forefinger.

Like I had.

"... the partying each night is insane, and my parents would never forgive me if they knew ..."

But I had no choice. The shame of our family's Greatest Undoing was mine alone to bear. For years, the event's bubbling panic would not ease. I had needed to stay in London, to give up my childhood and become parent. I owed Dad that much. But just as I'd needed to stay, I'd also needed to flee, to keep moving, to keep traveling. I could not face him upon his release.

I balled my fists. Little Thomas, he hadn't needed to die. These hands could have prevented it. My capable hands. My competent hands. Dad and Mum trusted me, and I failed and fled and watched my precious brother bleed. I bowed my head.

There was no forgiveness for that.

"... Elias."

The name jarred me aright.

"I'm sorry, it's late and I drifted. What did you say?"

Kira eased onto a windy lane and pointed toward a sign.

Phinn's Bed and Breakfast
Est. 1914

"We're at the address. Let's see this, Elias!"

"No, Kira, let me sort it on my own. Wait here."

Kira accelerated, her tires squealing around each corner. "I did not drive this far only to be denied a peek at your criminal. It's important to know what type you like."

"We aren't a pair. The bloke's a most unsettling thief. I simply need my bag."

"And you and your proper English shall get it."

Kira's Fiat screeched into the roundabout and came to a halt in front of the porch. From somewhere in the night, a siren blared, and several upstairs windows filled with light.

"Oh, well done." I pushed out of the car. "Open the latch."

I retrieved the bag and paused. It was a beautiful B & B. Several stories high, and constructed from white clapboard, it looked a place that belonged in a quaint coastal town. The inn stood unique among neighbouring apartment buildings, with its lawns that stretched out in manicured green, and two fountains that graced the yard.

The dog stopped barking.

"Onward," I said.

I approached the door, and raised my hand to knock.

Kira honked her horn, and I startled, spun, and frowned. She smiled and waved, and when next I turned toward the inn, the door stood open, and Elias stood in it.

His blond hair was disheveled, which was irritatingly pleasant, but otherwise he seemed the same lad I'd met on the plane. Save for the eyes. They were calmer, a cool brown peering out in place of his earlier paranoid gaze. His hands were busy clicking a pen, a pen that looked suspiciously like mine.

Neither of us spoke for several moments.

Another honk.

Elias glanced over my shoulder, and then quickly back to me.

"You took my bag." I slipped out of the shoulder strap and let his thud to the ground.

"When did I take your bag?" He appeared genuinely befuddled.

"On the flight." I eyed my pen. "Have you not noticed the contents are not your own?"

He licked his lips, stepped out, and stroked the returned. "We have the same pack."

"Yes, and I came to recover mine."

Elias stood, and backed into the inn. "Don't worry. I won't take it."

"You already took it!" I pushed my hand through my hair.

"Elias Phinn, do you recall nothing of the flight? You accused me of secrets. You spoke of my fath—You drew me. I'm on page seven. You took the wrong bag when you left the plane, which I will not hold against you, as long as you return mine to me ..." I snatched the pen from his hands and raised it in front of his nose. "With all contents intact." I grabbed a quick breath. "And kindly explain those sketches. If you think I'm leaving before you clear up how you were able to draw certain ... elements of my past, you're mistaken. Was that just a series of fortunate guesses or ..."

He stared at the pen. "I'm sorry, but the B & B is full."

The door slammed in my face.

I did not travel this far for a pen!

I pounded with both fists, and again the door swung open. This time, the tired body of a woman filled its frame. Elias's mum, I was certain of it.

I opened my mouth and waited for words to spill out, angry words. I expected to spew a list of ways that Elias had slowed my progress. The entire Minneapolis trip was already a personal detour from Dad's path.

But angry words did not come. This woman reminded me too much of Mum.

She smiled and stepped out, slowly unzipping the bag and offering a long sigh. "My name is Guinevere Phinn, and my guess is that my son took the wrong bag off the plane and you, being very kind, came to return it."

"Yes, to the botched bag deduction. Perhaps not so much to the kindness."

"Come in."

I grabbed Elias's bag and stepped into the foyer, a beautiful space lit by a dim chandelier. I was surrounded by framed drawings I recognized immediately to be Elias's handiwork. I peeked to make certain neither I nor any other member of my family hung on the walls, and quickly relaxed. The majority were landscapes. Mountains and seas, seagulls and ships, harbours and islands. Hanging between were sketches of Orion, its position tilted and stretched in twenty different angles.

Spiral stairs with ornate handrails rose on either side of the foyer. I turned from them in time to see Elias disappear into a room down the hall.

"I don't mean to trouble you further," I said. "I just want what's mine."

"Yes, I imagine you do." Guinevere glanced toward the closed door and winced. "Here is my dilemma. Not knowing that Elias had your backpack, I allowed him to bring it into his room."

I nodded. "Understandable."

Guinevere forced a smile. "Yes, well, not ten minutes ago, Elias woke me to say that he had finished cataloging his new belongings. I was so tired, I thought little of it—"

"His new belongings? My belongings? He's been cataloging my belongings? What does that even mean?"

"Don't worry, everything is fine. It's just—"

"Just ..."

"Elias will have placed everything in your pack in order. Usually from lightest weight to heaviest. They will be spread out in his room."

I raised my arms and let them flop. "So we enter and gather and all will be spot on—"

"And if we do, there may be a whirlwind. He will not sleep. I will not sleep. My guests will not sleep. He doesn't do well with late-evening changes."

"I don't do well without my diary!"

There was a heavy silence, and Guinevere placed her hand on my shoulder. "An idea. In the morning, we will get your things. I promise. But tonight, please, you and your friend stay in the guest room. Would you do that for me?"

No. The word sounded in my mind. This was a deviation. And while I'd welcomed many deviations, this deviation need not be. My bag and my diary and my computer were twenty feet away. Kira waited outside.

No. I will not do this for you.

"What's wrong with him?" I quietly asked.

She didn't answer.

"But there is something? Something in the mind?"

Again, no reply.

I peeked back toward the door. "Fine, then."

I spun around and exited the inn. Kira's fingers worked an anxious rap on the wheel.

"Well, that took long enough." She craned her neck. "Your bag?"

"It's inside. I can't collect it until tomorrow."

"They're holding your backpack hostage? They can't do that." She grabbed her mobile. "We can call someone."

"No. I'll get it tomorrow. I'm going to stay here tonight. There's room for you too, so I suggest we catch up inside."

"Right." Kira turned the key and the Fiat roared to life. "I have places to be. No, not true. I had places for *us* to be. You know, I—I was really looking forward to you being here. There are things to talk about. But I get it. Guys and backpacks over friends, right?"

I straightened and spoke to the sky, "Something's odd about him. I mean, he reminds me of . . . I don't have a choice."

"You once told me there's always a choice."

Kira's car jerked forward and she sped away into the night. I listened until I could hear her car no longer, until the sounds of crickets and horns and shouts from surrounding flats took its place.

I slowly climbed the porch steps while wondering, what exactly did Elias know about my life in London; what precisely was wrong with his mind . . .

And what was the heaviest item in my bag?

CHAPTER 4

"H uh!"

My breath caught in my throat, and I risked a second opening of my eyes.

The walls — they still stared at me.

Last night, I had fallen quickly to sleep. Without toothbrush or change of clothes, I'd opened the door to the guest room and collapsed onto the bed in the dark. Now, with light streaming in, I glanced about me.

"That will wake you up," I muttered.

Each of the four walls was covered by a photograph — no, a drawing — of an eight-foot-tall, six-foot-wide face. The same face. A huge, gawking, forty-year-old man captured from the neck up. His four gazes held me however I moved about the room. Depending on which direction I glanced, the man laughed, smiled gently, or gazed proudly. All pleasant enough. Except for face four, the one on the room's east side. His dark, clouded eyes stared, plotting and sinister. That face unnerved even me, and I searched for a bathroom door.

No bathroom. No mirror. Charming.

"All of you blokes; close your eyes."

I removed my outershirt, undershirt, and bra, balled up the middle layer, and put the rest back on.

Until a proper change at Kira's, it will have to do.

It was time to leave. Time … my last months taught me to live without concern for it. I rose when my body was jolly well ready. I peeked again at face four. Ready I was. I grabbed my mobile off the bedside table.

Now would be a good time for Kira to collect me.

I texted.

And waited.

Nothing. Kira would wait long enough to let me know I had committed a sizable injustice. Yes, she would wait, but just as assuredly she would soon text back. She was like fireworks; she burned hot and colourful, but the display never lasted long.

Kira's little drama would give me time to collect my things.

I opened the door and listened. The distant sound of voices, punctuated with the clink of dishes and silver, and the tinkle of glass. Warm smells of cinnamon filled the hall, and I toyed with my hair and moved toward the source.

I reached the foyer, moved through it, and stopped in the double doors.

The dining room was alive. Ten tables dotted the room, and this morning all but two were filled. It was a joyful scene, definitely not an inn scene.

A family scene. I stepped back from view and entered a memory.

The third of March. It had been my dad's idea. Before Mum lost her smile. Before Dad disappeared.

Before the Great Undoing.

There was the third of March, the Blythe Family Holiday. Nothing of note had ever happened on the third, or on any adjacent day, which is why Dad chose it for our annual celebration. For me, it trumped Christmas and New Year's all rolled together, and I longed for it like no other day.

We ate and we laughed and laughed and ate, and always our flat filled with the warm smell of cinnamon.

I rubbed my face hard. Elias, and everything about him, was a memory cancer, spreading and aching and reminding of all that was. I straightened and marched into the dining room.

Slowly, heads turned toward me and voices trailed off. I succeeded in sucking all joy from the family table.

Typical.

"Clara. You're up. I didn't know when to wake you." Guinevere rose from her table, and the room once again filled with conversation. Apparently, I had been accepted into the tribe. She walked toward me and hugged me deeply. She stepped back. "Oh, you *are* beautiful. Come join us."

I shook my head.

"Ah, your things. Yes. I've, uh, partially taken care of that." She winced and glanced toward the fireplace.

Eight feet up, a ridiculous moose head poked its antlers into the room, and hanging from the right antler was my bag.

"We'll fix the situation, but at least allow me to feed you." She leaned over and whispered into my ear. "This is good practice for Elias."

I stared at that moose and hated it.

She grabbed my hand and led me to the table by the fireplace. Elias sketched on a napkin, and did not look up to greet me.

"Elias? Elias. We have a visitor. I believe you know her."

"I know her," he said. "Why is she here?"

"Pencil, Elias." Guinevere pointed at a chair and we both sat down. "Remember the pencil—guest rule."

Elias lifted the tip off the napkin. It quavered within his hands, not unlike it had on the plane. He finally set it down and peeked up toward me. "Welcome." He clenched his teeth. "I'm glad you're here."

There was no softening. No now-it's-your-turn in his gaze. His face remained fixed and intense, as if he was reciting, not speaking.

"I said," he repeated, "welcome! I'm glad you're here!"

I peeked at the moose, cleared my throat, and stood. I rounded the table, grabbed Elias's chair with both hands, and yanked. Elias tumbled, and I carried the chair to the fireplace wall.

I climbed on top of the chair and reached for my bag. Three inches. Three inches too short. I tugged at my bag and finally gave a mighty pull. The entire moose head broke free, falling, narrowly missing my noggin and crashing to the floor.

Nobody moved or spoke as I calmly extracted the strap from the antlers and unzipped the bag.

And thought of many curses.

I carried my empty bag to the table, bent to the ground, and jammed it onto his still-prone belly, and then retook my seat.

The room remained silent.

Elias rose, walked to the chair, and with visible effort hoisted the moose head back over the bracket. It hung cocked and dented, and he stroked the creature's face.

"Elias, please, come down and sit." Guinevere exhaled.

He returned, walked behind me, and next I knew I was bum to the floor. He took a seat on my chair as Guinevere retrieved his for me.

I glared at Elias, and he at me. I wanted to hate him, as I did that grotty moose. But I couldn't. Don't know why, but I couldn't.

I hinted a smile, which made him frown all the more, which forced me into a bigger smile.

"Well then, I hear you organised my items last night."

He stiffened.

"Catalogued was, I believe, your mum's word."

"I did."

"And what did you find?"

He glanced toward his mum and back to me. "I didn't find anything. It was already there."

"Yes ... technically yes, I know." I thought a moment. "What did you find to be the heaviest item?"

"The jeans."

I nodded, and placed my napkin on my lap. Elias watched me and did the same.

"I thought it would be the jeans. And what was the lightest?"

Elias squinted. "I'm not sure what they are." He dug in his pocket, and soon a pair of black underwear lay on the butter dish. I tongued the inside of my cheek. Guinevere burst into laughter.

I slowly reached for the gift received, unbidden, many months ago from another POE twelve. There was good reason to exercise caution around young men with such elevated scores.

"You really don't know what these are?" I asked.

"I thought I did, but I think I'm wrong. There's not enough to them."

"Very good." I cleared my throat and reclaimed my garment, stuffing it in a pocket. "So, is there a menu about?"

"I'll get it." Elias pushed back and quickly disappeared into the kitchen.

His mum stared at me. "Where are you from, Clara?"

"Would you believe Mississippi?" I waited, and sighed. "England. London, to be precise."

"I've always wanted to visit England. Buckingham Palace, the Changing of the Guard, Westminster Abbey, Piccadilly—"

"Right. I understand."

Guinevere took a long sip from her water glass. "But clearly those places aren't that impressive to you."

I quieted. "They are impressive, just familiar."

"Do you live here now?"

I looked off and shook my head. "Nowhere, actually."

"Because you're very good with Elias. He doesn't ... he doesn't get menus for anyone."

"Is that his job?"

"No, but that proves my point."

Elias returned, and set the menu upside down before me. "I can take your order too."

"As you are being a gentleman thief, I would have coffee, black, and one of the cinnamon rolls I'm smelling." I handed him back the menu.

He closed his eyes, and I could see his lips moving. "Okay, I think I can do that."

Again, Elias disappeared into the kitchen, and I glanced up at the moose. "He seems to have rediscovered his manners."

Another young man approached our table. He, too, was handsome, his skin a lovely shade—perhaps Hispanic—with teeth so white I licked my own. I prepared to deal with the bloke.

He likely saw the underwear on the butter dish.

It was best to deal with these hounds proactively.

I shifted in my seat. "If you are looking for anything beyond the salt and pepper, I suggest returning to wherever you came from."

He ignored me completely and bent down toward Guinevere. "Señor Tilson texted. He wants me to do his lawn perfect for tonight's dinner party. Today, I can't take Elias. I'm sorry."

Guinevere slowly nodded. "I really need him back in after-school remedial. And Lord knows, he needs some normalcy after a week with his grandfather. But I understand. Go, Juan."

"Thank you, Ms. Phinn. Thank you. Count on me for tomorrow."

I watched Juan leave without so much as glancing my way. I must truly look hideous.

"What to do ... what to do," Guinevere muttered. "How to get Elias to remedials. I can't leave the guests. I can't leave ..." She stared at me. "The guests."

"No." I raised both hands. "You're not ... no. I stayed for my bag. You have already experienced more generosity in a day than I thought I owned. I am not a cabby."

"I'm in a bind. I'll pay you." She scooted her chair closer. "He knows you from the plane, and despite what you say, only a girl with good character stays overnight to keep the peace." Guinevere placed her hand on my forearm. "You're so good with him. It's a ten-mile drive. Take my car and head out right when he gets home from school. It won't take long, and I'll ask nothing more."

"You don't know me. Really, you don't. If you did, maybe you wouldn't trust me with him. I don't ... I haven't always been trust-worthy when it comes to people who are ... special."

"Nonsense. Special or not, we're all God's children, and I can't imagine you treating anyone otherwise."

I thought of Little T and winced. *If you only knew ...*

Elias returned with my coffee and one of the largest rolls I'd ever seen. He set them down before me, and straightened.

"I did well, didn't I, Clara?" His eyes were eager.

I looked from him to Guinevere, sitting with raised brows, and back again.

"Breakfast is impressive." And to his mum, "Fifty dollars. One day."

Guinevere mouthed "thank you," and I quickly finished and exited the dining room. This would give me one more chance to ask Elias about the sketchings; was it paranormal knowledge or an elaborate parlour trick? I felt a vibration while in the foyer and dug for my mobile.

As planned your bank acct set up. Need 2 w8 3 days for your website $ 2 flow in. B redy in 15. OMW. K

I rolled my eyes and returned a sticky-finger text:

Thanks for setting up current account. Need to stay a bit longer. Apologies.

What was I doing? Elias was a black hole, sucking me deeper into responsibility, the one thing I'd been slogging away from. For Guinevere, I was now back on a clock, back on a job, meeting another's obligations, and losing a mate in the process.

I could have done all this in London.

• • • • •

"Lottery! Lottery!"

I peeked out of my room and down the hall. The call, punctuated by the clang of a large bell, rang out through the first floor, up the stairs, and throughout the rooms above. "Lottery!"

I crept back into the foyer and listened as a stampede of footsteps stilled above my head. I ascended quietly and walked toward the gathering of voices.

They sat in front of a fireplace in a cozy meeting room, about fifteen people in all. Old and young, all chatted happily. I recognized many of them from the dining hall. Once again, I had stumbled upon a family gathering.

I stood inside the doorframe. "There was a bell . . . Is this something I should know about?"

The looks I received from the other boarders spanned from embarrassment to frustration, and I raised my hands. "I guess not. I'll leave you to your . . . lottery."

"The young lady can watch if she likes," said an older gentleman. "Take a seat—your name will probably be added soon, so you might as well see how this works."

"Non! We have too many names as it is! Too few moments each with him. Last year there were ten, now fifteen people? Sixteen is too much."

"It's all right, Doucette." The gentleman turned back toward me. "Please, have a seat."

Kira had yet to text back or make any sort of appearance. As a result, waiting at the B & B for Elias to return from school had slowed the day to a crawl, and I had no desire to return to the four-face room. "If you're sure." I slowly approached and joined their large circle, and for the next ten minutes I listened to stories of health and the weather, the little things that mean everything. This family was already complete. It needed no one else, and I decided to leave.

"We may as well get started." A young lady beat me to my feet, and walked toward the closet, returning with an oversized bingo tumbler filled with table tennis balls, each marked with a number.

"Before we draw," she said, placing the contraption on the table, "I must say that Doucette and I had little time with him last week. As you know, Elias was out of town and we were not able to get the five hours we had coming to us."

The gentleman spoke softly. "Last week was unusual, Roseau—"

"Yes, Jakob is telling the truth. He and I had less than one hour with Elias in Salem." The woman seated next to Jakob placed her hand on his forearm. He patted her wrist and pulled away.

"Let's begin." Jakob turned the handle on the tumbler. "Juan had to leave early, and he asked me to pull a number for him. Does anyone object?"

No one spoke.

"Very well. This first pull will be for Juan. Bette, will you keep track?"

The woman at his side nodded and picked up a pen. She poised it over a sheet, and the entire group leaned in as Jakob opened the tumbler door, closed his eyes, and extracted a ball. He held it up for the group to see.

"Five. Juan has five hours this week with Elias."

"That is not fair on two counts!" Doucette jumped up, her arms flailing. "One, he is not here. His turn should be forfeited. Two, he drives Elias to school every day. He already gets more time than the rest of us!"

"Not every day," I said quietly. "Not today."

I had no idea what was going on in the room—no idea what the lottery meant—but it seemed important, and Juan was not here to defend himself.

"You are driving him?" Doucette quieted, and nodded at me. "Then you will soon be joining us in the lottery. We may as well be friends." She bent down and kissed me on the cheek, before returning to her seat.

The lottery continued until everyone except me had selected.

Juan—5

Doucette—3

Roseau—1

Jakob—2

Bette—6, but she said she would trade four of her hours to anyone but Jakob.

The tumbler was stowed away in the closet, and slowly the room emptied.

"Doucette," I called, and she stopped near the door. "What just happened?"

"You are new here, but you'll see. Elias has only so much time in Salem. We meet here each week to decide how many hours each of us will get with him while he is there."

"Salem ... Where is Salem?" I asked.

"You don't know?" She pointed to her head. "It is in his mind."

"So, it's imaginary ..."

"Imaginary? I would not say that. Believe me, when you're there, no place could be more real. What makes any country real? Memories and history and people ... Salem has all of them."

I gave an exaggerated nod. "Right." This inn was populated with the mad and deranged. I'd just witnessed a lottery where the winner's purse was time in an imaginary world found in Elias's mind. Who was this boy I'd agreed to chauffeur?

CHAPTER 5

I peeked down at the bonnet of the lime-green beetle on which I sat. Guinevere's car, and the garage in which it rested, were both spotless. It was a quiet respite from what had been a loud day at the inn.

My laptop rested on wrinkled shorts. Napped and showered and alive again in fresh clothes, the temporary guardianship of Elias felt less the responsibility and more another twist in fate, and I sighed at yet another Plan B.

Bus brakes hissed on the road, and Elias hopped out and ran into the inn. Moments later, he quietly stepped into the garage. I slammed shut my laptop.

"Well, Ms. Neuro-typical. Let's get going." He tossed me the keys.

Neuro-typical? I slipped behind the wheel of the Beetle. "Is Guinevere going to give me final instructions?"

"No need. It's me." He climbed in the passenger side.

"Yes, I see that, but the where and the when and the programme ..."

Elias clicked his seat belt. "I know where to go." He glanced at me. "Honestly."

"Honestly," I muttered, and we slowly backed into the turn-around and eased up the drive.

"Now stop!"

I slammed the brakes and cursed as my heartbeat slowed. Elias calmly removed a handkerchief and wrapped it around his head, tying it in back. It completely covered his eyes. "A right at the top. Left at the lights, and then it's just a short drive."

His words. His cadence. They held feeling. He sounded comfortable and sure, which made me quite uncomfortable.

I drove out onto the main road.

"So just out with it. What's wrong with you?"

"That depends on who you ask. Mom, she calls me unique, her one of a kind. Teachers, they say I live on the spectrum, and they may be half right." Elias slowly folded his hands. "The kids at remedials—they call me no-brain. They'll say I'm an idiot. And most nineteen-year-olds can read, so who's to argue?" He held up his finger. "Okay. I'll tell you when to turn. Don't speak."

I drove, while my blind guide mumbled words beneath his breath. Five minutes. Ten minutes.

"Elias?"

"Left now!"

I screeched into a car park that fronted a windowless building. Elias removed his bandana, and gave me the thumbs up. "Seven hundred twenty-eight bumps in the road. Seven hundred twenty-eight from the inn to here." His triumphant smile melted, and he rubbed his eyes.

"Clara, I . . . I don't know why you're driving me and why Juan isn't." Elias swallowed, and his voice softened. "I do remember seeing you on the porch last night."

"What about on the plane? And our . . . talk at breakfast?"

He shook his head. "I don't remember. In fact, I don't remember half of my life."

"What's wrong?" I asked. "How do you live with that?"

"By holding on to the parts I do know. The good parts. Like whatever brought you here." He bowed his head. "I'm scared. Are you ever frightened?"

"No. Well, yes."

"Frightened that you'll be overcome by yourself? That a gentle monster inside of you might take over and never let go?"

Inside, I felt a twinge, and Elias must have noticed as he nodded.

"Well, what does that sign say?" he asked, pointing to the sign out front. "Mom never tells me."

"Moriah Academy," I read. "Bringing hope to the hopeless."

"Hopeless, huh?" Elias grabbed his bag from the back and pushed out of the car. "Not as bad as I thought. You know ..." He softly thumped the window. "I shouldn't have laid all that heavy stuff on you. After all, we've technically never met. It's a nice afternoon. I'm in there for hours. Feel free to walk around or whatever." He sighed. "Thanks for the ride."

I watched him slump toward the door. This was a different bloke than the one at breakfast. There were no secrets in him, and I jumped out of the car.

"Today, I watched fifteen sane-looking boarders hold a lottery for the chance to spend time with you in some make-believe world. Elias, please ... what's wrong with you? What do *you* say?"

He stopped but did not turn at first, and then he spun and walked quickly back toward me, stepping ten centimeters into my private space. "You're very pretty."

"That did ... that didn't answer the question."

"No, but I have to say stuff while I can." He let his head fall back to gaze at the sky. "What's wrong with me? I lose my footing, in here." He touched his head. "When a neuro-typical loses their footing, they yell or escape to the TV, or maybe the doctor throws them on depression meds. But when I slip, I fall all the way through. I feel the ground give way and I'm gone. It's a crack—a crack in what's real, and beneath there I'm stuck. Then, I guess I become someone else. Mom says I still know my name, but I walk a different world. The shrink calls it DID—Dissociative Identity Disorder—with a little added autism to spice up my other personality. I suppose he's right, but only I know how it feels to slip through the cracks. Then the monster shows up."

A bell gonged from inside and Elias glanced over his shoulder. "Not a scary monster, so don't leave. Just one that takes over." Again, he peeked up into the blue overhead. "Shoot, I did it again. You didn't ask for that, either." Elias repositioned his pack. "I'm sorry Mom forced you to drive me."

He turned again and walked away, made it all the way to the large metal door. He called back. "It just feels so strange. To be living my life, until suddenly someone else steals it, and about the only thing that joins us is my name. Names are important, you know."

He disappeared and I stood, arms weighty at my sides.

"I can't imagine."

Help Support Children of Incarcerated Parents
500 Days of Wandering, 500 Days of Hope
Day 241

    I woke this morning, my head spinning from the red-eye to ... Johannesburg. I wish I could portray for you the four creatures I saw as I cracked my eyelids. Huge, hulking, terrifying. A night in the bush changes your perspective. You find yourself doing without creature comforts such as bathrooms, and relying on a different portion of your brain. Choices here come from instinct, not experience, and I confess I am at a loss to explain what I am doing. I have been conscripted into leading this afternoon's safari. It is a job for which I am not trained ...

I finished my entry, posted, and waited. Five seconds. Ten seconds. "Come on. Where are you?" The screen flashed and my heart leaped.

My first comment, as always, was from my most ardent follower, the anonymous lad with whom I shared a bit more truth than the others thanks to private messaging. I hated lying to him at all, but with my travels going viral, I couldn't risk being exposed. He alone read my first post the day I left London, and at some point crossed the line from follower to friend. Though I'd never seen him, I imagined his POE somewhere near 20.

FFA: Are you afraid? Leading the safari.

Me: No ... That's not true. Yes. There's some ... unpredictability involved.

FFA: My folks took me on a safari. Thrilling, really. We saw not one animal.

Me: Thrilling.

FFA: Our Jeep ran out of gas, and we hiked six miles back to camp.

Me: Liar. (This I typed with a smile on my face.)

FFA: I'm just saying that vehicles can be unpredictable.

FFA: Still there?

Me: Have you ever heard of DID?

FFA: Did?

Me: No, idiot. It's an identity disorder.

FFA: I can't say I have.

Me: You are useless. Tell me this, then, do you believe in mentalism? That someone can know about you, can know about your past, before you tell them, or spend time with them or something of that sort? I mean, there's this bloke who drew some pictures of me and maybe some others I know, and if he knows about those things, then could he know about more secret things?

FFA: Most times those are mind tricks. Nobody can read your mind. But I do believe in gifts. BTW, what secret things?

Me: Very funny ...

Rap!

I started and looked up from my typing. Elias feverishly knocked on the glass as four boys quickly closed in. I searched for the auto-unlock latch.

"Open up!"

Too late; Elias's body collided with the outside of the car, and I jumped out.

"That moment just there would've been a really good time to open the door, Clara," Elias called over his shoulder.

"Clara? Not Juan, eh?" Four blokes again shoved Elias against the passenger side, shoved him out of the way, and leaned over the Beetle. "And how did you get roped into babysitting no-brain?"

"Free will." I peeked at Elias.

"Oh, you're his nanny. Kind of a Mary Poppins."

I walked around the bonnet. "Now I understand that you're emotional derelicts. You blokes have made that abundantly clear." I looked to the one on the far end. The follower. "How come you don't speak? How come this ugly beast does all the talking?"

The beast scoffed. "Ugly, huh—"

"Oh, sod off. Was I speaking to you? Was I looking at you? Do you have any sense of propriety?"

He frowned and mouthed my large word, and I continued with the one on the end.

"What's your name?"

"Brock."

"Brock, does this ugly one always speak for you? When you two are chatting with your mum—"

He looked nervously at his snickering friends. "We don't live together."

"But you'd like to!" Middle boy backhanded his chest.

Brock looked at me. "He doesn't always speak for me."

"Then let me ask you." I stepped nearer. "Do you enjoy torment-ing Elias?"

There was a pause. "No."

The other three stared at him, and Brock glanced their way and continued. "Knock it off! You two would've said the same. You told me today that Finch goes too far."

Finch slowly nodded. "So, you all talk. When I'm not around, you all talk. Not a problem. I'll just leave you and No-brain here. You can discuss whatever, you know?" Finch backed up. "One loser just turned into four." He sauntered away down the sidewalk.

"Hold on, Finch. That got all turned around." The middle two trotted after, leaving only Brock.

Brock walked up to Elias. "Well, that just ruined my life."

"Yeah," Elias said. "I'm sorry about that."

We stood in awkward silence, until Elias reached out his hand and they shook. Brock exhaled loudly. "Keep the nanny. She's a smart girl."

"You're tellin' me."

Soon Elias and I stood alone. "Maybe don't mention this to Mom. She has enough on her mind. They weren't really going to hurt me. I mean, not too much."

"That didn't appear to be the situation."

"Can't believe everything you see, right?" Elias glanced up, and then both to his left and right. He lowered his voice, and his eyes sparkled. "Say, come with me on a short trip."

I raised the keys and gave them a jingle. "That's my line."

"And you can use it in, in oh, half an hour. Don't worry about whatever Mom told you about the time. Juan is always late, so it'll be no problem for her. I, uh, I'd like to show you something."

Do not do this. Plan B be hanged. Stick to Plan A. Extract yourself now.

47

"How do I know you won't slip and become monstrous? I've met the monstrous you, and the monstrous you … No, I don't like the ring to that. How about I call him the Other One?"

Elias shrugged, and I continued. "Jolly good. The Other One doesn't exactly trust me."

"It's a fair question. You don't know when I'll slip away. I feel solid now, but …" He forced a grin. "But the way I see it, you're taking off. Someone like you has somewhere to go and someone waiting, right? So when I get into that car, I have you for about ten more minutes. I mean, if you were me, wouldn't you ask?"

His boyish smile. His eager grin. I had my own crack through which I could not again slip. I would not risk involvements, or get mucked up in responsibility. Both practices led to disaster; this much I had learned. There was safety in leading. Following … that always led to a mess.

I double-fisted his T-shirt and shoved his chest. For the second time in minutes, his body slammed against the car, but the backs of my fingers felt his warmth through the fabric, and I swallowed hard.

"Do not hurt me, or I will kill you!"

"Why would I—"

"Kill you!" I repeated.

"Okay." He raised both his hands. "I won't hurt you … Why would I hurt you?"

I released him and flattened his T-shirt. Once, and then again. "Well then?" I pocketed the keys and held out my hand. "Show me."

He stared, motionless. I watched him watch my fingers, and gently beckoned, helping him along.

"You took Brock's hand, but you won't take mine?"

Elias spoke to my hand. "I've shook, I mean shaken, er … shook … Holding is new."

"Oh, come on, you must have with some girl."

His face was terrified.

I took a half step nearer. "Okay, this *is* new." I slowly grasped his hand and fit his fingers into mine. I felt them stiffen, and then relax. "Are we okay?"

His eyes grew big.

"Good. Elias ..." The sentence stuck in my throat. "Lead on."

CHAPTER 6

Why had I offered Elias my hand?

While we trudged along the motorway, this question gripped me. I had provided many affections since leaving home—a few in London as well—that were far more excessive, more damaging. This was the rationale behind the POE scale.

But to my recollection, I had never once offered my hand.

Only one male could claim to have held it, and he spent my best years rotting in a prison.

The idea of his incarceration would have been unthinkable when I was a child. There was a time when Dad's firm hand held my small fingers and led me through the streets of London. I felt safe and I felt proud, and there was nowhere I wouldn't go as long as I held that hand.

I idolised him until the day he struck the copper, and, in truth, many days after. But soon my hands were required to clean the flat and care for Mum and the sibs. My hands were the first to forget what it meant to be led. My mind was second.

Lastly went my heart.

That's when I determined never again to offer my hand. Never to follow.

What am I doing?

"Ten minutes, Elias, and we need to turn around."

He picked up the pace, and we turned onto a gravel lane. A piece of country, so close to downtown. Around us, gentle hills swelled and fell, and we walked through patches of wood and field. Until we reached the sign.

Private. Trespassers will be shot.

I stopped, tugged at Elias, and then released his hand. I gestured at the sign and took a quick look around.

"The owner makes it quite clear that you, and I, are not supposed to continue."

"What does it say?" asked Elias.

"It says illiteracy is dangerous." I peeked toward his bag. "Dangerous like ... like your sketches. That sign says that if we continue, there is a dragon waiting to devour your drawings." My heartbeat quickened. "Specifically the ones you drew of the factory, of the prison. Of me."

I raised my eyebrows and waited. The time to settle the matter had come. Elias had been wrong about my departure. I would not leave until I knew how much he knew, and if his knowing—his "gift," as FFA would describe it—extended to the Great Undoing. If he knew about that ...

Well, he couldn't. No one could.

He dug in his bag and raised a sketchbook. "You mean these. Yeah, here's the thing: I didn't draw them. Any of them. I draw in stick figures." Again, he glanced toward the sky, a most confusing tic. "Art is all the Other One. He does that."

"Do you mean to tell me that when you're this you, those hands draw sticks, and when the mon—when the Other One shows up, those same hands suddenly are able to draw what's in those books? What does that mean?"

"I can show better than speak. Come on."

Elias dashed forward, and I rolled my eyes and jogged after. The road veered left and so did we, until we both froze.

"Solid," I said.

An amusement park spread out before us. A dead one, filled with unnatural silences. Dodgems and mini roller coaster cars clung precariously to rotted beams. A small Ferris wheel tilted, three capsules fallen and mangled beneath — a child's mouth missing his teeth.

But it was the silence that gripped me. An unholy, chilling silence. The squeals and shouts of little ones replaced by the whispers of wind whistling through vacant crevices and collapsed rides. I was in the cinema flick, one where the hero returns to New York City in the dystopian future and finds nobody. The world was empty, crumbling, and the sense of alone overwhelmed.

I was alone.

Well, alone, with both Eliases.

Into my loneliness fought a rogue memory, a pleasant one of the man I once called Dad. He had taken me to the circus, a temporary invasion of odd humans and colourful tents. And, of course, rides. Taken with horses at the time, I rode the merry-go-round thirty times consecutively. I even named my horse: Phantom. He was dark and fast, and though stuck on a pole, I could imagine him moving much faster than the others.

Dad never questioned my obsession. He stood at my side, one hand on the pole, the other around my back.

"You be my knight, okay?" I asked.

He smiled. "Yes, milady. Where shall we go?"

"Australia!"

We circled Down Under, my dad pointing out the Great Barrier Reef and each wayward kangaroo.

"Brazil! I want to see Brazil!" And so we explored. Don't tell me it wasn't real; my mind circled the globe that day, convinced my eyes had seen the world.

It never dawned on me that the whole time, I had been fixed to a pole.

Or that in a few years my knight would leave me to travel alone. "I don't want to see any more."

Elias glanced at me and back over what had once been. "This frightens you?"

"I didn't say frightened. I only said that I don't wish to see any more."

"No." Elias walked up to the fence that separated us from the spectacle. "You said that you don't *want* to see any more. Wanting and wishing are very different."

"Oh, blast—there's a whisker of a difference!" But inside, I softened. This boy heard. He listened, right down to the tiniest piece. It was a first for me, this being heard.

He waded into the field and approached the gate. "There's a hole here. We're almost there."

I stepped after. "I will not go inside. Not until you tell me what's in there."

He bowed his head, and when next he glanced back over his shoulder, his eyes were desperate. "Me."

How do you say no to that?

I nodded, and offered a quick shrug.

"Good. Then we need to hurry."

I stroked a shattered porcelain horse near the gate. "What happened to this place?"

Elias had reached the far fence, turned, and called back, "The owner was losing money, and he figured out that what lay underneath was more valuable."

"And that is . . ."

I crossed the grounds quickly and joined Elias. Poking my fingers between the links, I applied gentle pressure. The entire fence buckled out, ready to crumble.

"Dirt," he said.

I stared down into an enormous pit, filled with impressive mounds and conveyer belts that stretched to each peak.

"Most people are more interested in what's below the surface, you know?" Elias rubbed his face.

"So this is it? This is what you wanted to show—"

Elias grinned. "Nope." He backed away from the pit and walked to an old service garage, then pulled up the door. "This is."

He flung back a sheet, and beneath was, well . . .

"What exactly is it?"

He scrambled on top of the vehicle: part Jeep, part dodgem, part, part . . .

"I named her"—he swept his hand through the air—"the Elias." He stood on the front seat and smiled sheepishly. "I could think of a better name if you want me to."

I walked around both the machine and its maker. A little in awe. A lot confused.

"So, yeah," he continued. "The chassis is mostly from dropped thrill-ride cars, but I harvested the tires from a few service carts. The springs and bearings I found in the repair shed. It looks a little front heavy, but that's because I had to build the mount and wheel base around the engine from the tilt-o-whirl." He flopped down in a seat and lowered the lock bar over his head and into the proper position. "Safe though. This place was filled with lock bars and chest restraints."

"You made this. This you. The real, coherent you. The you who doesn't draw can build this kind of vehicle." I jumped in beside him. "You're a mechanical genius. You're . . ."

I swallowed, and tingled. I glanced at Elias. *You're a part-time mechanical genius and a part-time artistic, autistic bloke all balled up in a handsome package that seems to manage with the two personalities trading places inside.*

There was no bettering him. I could not predict him or understand him or ever know him. Elias was the ultimate variable, and my stomach turned.

"No, no. Not a genius. This is like what reading is for you. You look at the squiggles and the loops, and the puzzle opens until suddenly nothing means something, something more than the sum of the parts, right? I see one hunk of metal and then another, and the puzzle opens. They turn in my mind and just make sense. Together, they all mean something."

Blast. In an instant, I leaped the chasm from fear to affection. I wanted to kiss him. No, I wanted him to kiss me, and I didn't know why.

"Before I do something stupid, you can't tell me a thing about the pictures you drew, or part of you drew? You swear you don't know any more about me than what you showed me ..."

"I don't even know *what* sketches I, er ... he showed you." He held up his pointer finger. "I know your name." He raised a second. "I know you're smart and ... pretty." A third finger shot up. His voice trailed off, and he turned a fetching shade of pink before wincing and adding a fourth. "And I think I held your hand. Clara, the time has come to take her out." He reached down and tinkered with a metal switch.

"Wait a moment—you haven't tested it?"

"Nope. Juan only lets me sit in it. He watched me build the engine, but he wouldn't let me start it. Today's my day. Lower your bar."

"I'm not about to be involved in ..."

Elias punched a button, and his namesake roared to life, immersing us in a plume of bluish smoke. "It works. It so works!" He peeked over at me. "Now, those fumes? That's because I didn't have the right type of oil, but it'll do. It'll do."

I stood to get out, and felt a gentle grip on the arm.

"Please. I want you to come with me on the maiden voyage."

And the request felt like a kiss. An intimacy.

Another first.

"Fine, then. One short ride."

He lowered my lock bar, which snapped against my waist, and winked. "I don't know about short."

He fluttered the accelerator and we sprung forward. Elias shouted, and I screamed and fumbled for the shoulder harness. Wind and dust whipped across my face, and I don't know if it was the harness or the park or Elias's driving, but the contraption sure felt like a thrill ride.

Elias spun the wheel and we slid a neat circle and stopped, our nose facing the fence and the pit.

He looked at me, and I recognised the gleam.

He wanted permission.

"Right now," I yelled above the engine, "we should be in your mum's car, and I should be driving calmly back to your home and getting ready to ... leave." I paused.

"We should be, but we're in my car!"

He floored the pedal, and we lurched forward toward the fence. I tried to duck, but my restraints held me fast. I covered my face and waited for the clank of metal on metal. I never felt it. The next sensation was down, stomach-dropping down, the same down I experienced plummeting onto the Bamako airstrip in Mali.

We were airborne, and then came the bounce. Our front tires found earth first, sprung up toward heaven, and crashed down again. The Elias never faltered. All four wheels clawed forward through dirt, kicking up a spray of brown and finally slowing at the bottom of the pit.

"Ho!" Elias looked at me, joy and grime covering his face. "That was, that was—"

"The most idiotic ten seconds of my idiotic life!" I yanked at my restraints, but they wouldn't give. "Get me out of here. Get me out ..." I started to laugh. "... Out of here." My laugh gained force and volume and I screamed again. "I have never come so close to dying before! Insane. Bloomin' insane!"

He looked at me, wild eyed. "Thanks for going with me."

"Didn't know I had a choice."

He slowly shook his head, and we took off again, peeling around the mounds and tractors and small makeshift buildings that dotted the bottom of the pit.

"Just one last thing," he shouted.

Anything. Anything!

We flew toward a mound, up, up, up. The Elias churned and roared and slowed ... and pitched left.

"Uh, Elias? The tire that just fell off your vehicle, that's now bouncing down this heap ... would that be a problem?"

"I got this!" He winced. "I'll need to straighten her out and—"

Elias spun the wheel, but control was lost. We slid down and backward, and then sideways, and then the Elias flipped.

It was odd. We were sliding upside down, but the bar above our heads and the roller coaster harnesses kept us suspended from danger—at least I felt no danger. It felt the perfect ending to a perfect ride. I turned toward inverted Elias to tell him so. To let him know all was well.

One look from Elias, and I knew. The gentle browns of his eyes clouded over, and he looked lost.

He had fallen through.

We skidded onto hard pack, dust settling around us.

"Okay then," I coughed and fumbled for the bar release. "How do I get out?"

"You will not get anything from me. You can suspend me forever. I will not break."

You've got to be joking.

"Elias, it's me, Clara, and I need you to look up and find the

57

seam in whatever you've fallen through, because I don't know how to release these restraints."

He took a deep breath. "Ask the one who made this device."

"I am, Elias!" I lowered my voice and started to cry. "I am." I wasn't hurt. I wasn't scared. Tears made no sense. I only knew that I would likely spend the night upside down with a boy I knew everything and nothing about, and that soon I would pass out, and then blood would explode my brain.

But that wasn't why I cried.

"Elias!"

The voice was faint, but familiar.

Guinevere!

"Elias?"

"Here! We're here!" I reached my hand free of the frame and waved. "We're both . . . underneath."

It took ten minutes for Guinevere and Juan to reach us, ten more for them to free us from our cage.

It would take much longer to explain how we got there.

CHAPTER 7

"Has Ms. Phinn spoken to you?"

Juan eased down beside me on the bench. Directly in front of the inn, I had found this place ... a calm eye in the midst of the city.

This moment was not to be shared. It was for my diary and me, thoughts of Elias and a Loring Park pond that would not ripple. From the moment Elias stepped out of his remediation, I had felt at peace. The boy had that effect. Elias, too, seemed in that state — floating peacefully on the surface, his mind at rest — and then in an instant we plunged beneath. Violent, unexpected.

"Clara?"

I spoke but did not glance. "Guinevere. No, not since she drove Elias home from the pit. She probably wants me to go, but I can't leave." I massaged my tattoo. "Not until I know ... Not until I try to bring him back."

"That's not possible." Juan sighed. "Ms. Phinn's taken him to the best doctors in the country. His crazy is getting worse. It lasts longer, comes more often. He comes and goes on his own."

"He's not crazy," I hissed.

Juan flicked a pebble into the water, where it disappeared, leaving a tiny ring that spread and widened, touching and changing the surface until the rings vanished. My pond was no longer still.

"Okay, to you? Maybe he's just troubled. But, Ms. Clara, his

troubled part has created another world. He thinks we all live in it."
Juan chuckled. "That's what he's done. There are two of him. One
Elias lives in the USA, one in Salem, his country. He's named it.
He draws it. That's crazy to me, no? I mean, what do you call a guy
who's always searching in the clouds?"

He knows there's a crack. He's looking for the way out.

I faced Juan. "But even you don't bring him back from remedials
straight away. Sometimes you, too, went into that park. You've seen
what he's capable of building. Crazy can't do that. If he's so mad,
why chum with him, Mr. Five-hour-winner-of-the-lottery?"

Juan peeked at me, wondering, I think, what to share and what
to reveal. His voice dropped. "Because maybe, Ms. Clara, I'm crazy
too. Maybe when I talk to Elias while he's in his crazy world, I
feel I might someday belong. I don't fear. He requires no proof of
citizenship. Salem isn't real, but when I'm there I remember what it
feels like not to hide." He lowered his gaze. "In Salem, I have a real
family, a real place."

"And here you don't."

"Here I don't."

Juan stared out over the pond. "I think you'll find a lot of the
boarders want Elias to remain in his crazy place. Will they admit it?
Maybe not. But why else do they all keep returning to an inn in the
middle of downtown, with all its cars and crime?"

I frowned, and Juan stood. "It's not right, but Elias's Salem gives
people what they need. They can be whoever they want to be."

"That's horrible. Everyone using his delusions. You all want him
to stay sick in the head? Well, I had a brother—a younger, precious
brother—who also had a different type of mind, and we would've
done anything for him to heal."

Juan took three steps back toward the inn, and paused. "Is that
true, or was your brother somehow just right as he was? Clara, if the

world in Elias's mind is a kinder, safer one, why not enjoy it? I mean, we're all running from something."

I listened as his footsteps faded, and a distant door clacked shut. I flipped open my diary.

What has happened here? What is it about this place, this utterly ordinary place that acts like quicksand to my feet? The inn is beautiful, an oasis in a screaming city, but beautiful things never stopped me before. In Minneapolis, Kira was the draw, but she is not the hold. That, I fear, falls to a boy with two identities named Elias. The question is why, aside from his ridiculously elevated POE score.

I'm afraid. For the first time since I've left, I'm truly afraid. Worse than that, I'm not entirely certain that I'm afraid for myself.

Which means the unthinkable is happening. I'm becoming entangled with Elias.

And whomever I care about, I seem to lose.

I slowly closed my diary.

"FFA, I wish you were here. We were doing just fine, the two of us."

"Elias!" Guinevere hollered, and from deep inside the inn, a door slammed.

I rose. The time to own up had come.

I slipped through the back door and stilled. My confession was rehearsed, and I'd assumed I'd first need to calm Elias's mum to deliver it. But there were no sounds inside — not on the first floor or on any floor above. The air felt thick, filled with the residue of a thousand heavy words.

I'd missed the heated moment.

Now was the cooling.

A knock sounded at the front door. Nobody came out to answer it. Another knock. I glanced about, crept into the foyer, and slowly turned the latch. The door swung open.

"Steve Ringmann from EyeSky news, the local UBC affiliate. We'd like to speak to Elias Phinn."

I peeked beyond the reporter to the cameraman behind him. He was already hoisting the camera into position.

"I'd like to speak to him too," I said.

"We received a tip about a trespassing-related accident. Are you related to Mr. Phinn?"

"Related? Would you like me to be?"

A light from the camera shone in my face, and I shielded my eyes.

"Just look at me." Steve smiled. "I just have a few questions for you. Could you first say and spell your name, just so we get it right?"

Why was I answering? Maybe it was guilt, unused contrition. If I couldn't confess to Guinevere, why not tell the world?

"Clara Tomey. T-O-M-E-Y." It was a lie only by degrees. My mum's maiden name had often been my cover.

"Clara, can you describe your relationship with Mr. Phinn?" Steve thrust the mic in my face.

A quick glance back through the door. Nobody was coming to my aid.

"It's complicated. POE of twelve? Quite the mess."

Steve blinked. "But you are connected in some way ..."

I searched his face, looking for the answer to his question. Beyond the right fountain, just over the fence, a small crowd of neighbours gathered, likely curious about the news van. Yet they were all staring at me. Staring and waiting for me to answer this question, which suddenly felt heavy. Heavy like a wrecking ball.

Connected?

I needed to explain that I couldn't be. That connections and affection and death and pain were dominos, and that if I had reached the tipping point there was no purpose in continuing with this trip, and if that were true I should fly back to my hellish England where all of Marbury Street would scarcely recognise the return of their greatest failure. My hands shook.

"Your connection, Ms. Tomey?"

Heavy footsteps creaked the foyer floorboards, and I glanced over my shoulder. A gentleman lifted an umbrella and tossed it over my head and onto the porch, causing the cameraman to duck. "Get away from this inn." Strong hands squeezed my shoulders and gentled me aside. "Consider that my prepared statement."

An agile frame stepped in front of me, grabbed the microphone from Steve's hand, and launched it toward the crowd, where it bounced off the wooden fence.

"That, sir, can be considered assault." Steve turned to his cameraman and gestured to keep the film rolling. "I'm just doing my job."

My protector adjusted his cap and drew himself straight. "I fought in two wars, spent six months in a POW camp, and was married fifty-one years. Do not talk to me about responsibility ..." He stepped forward, grabbed the camera, and wrested it from a younger man's hands. After which he smashed it to the ground. "Or assault. You know nothing of either."

More loud, heated words were spoken, but they garbled in my ears. Soon the news van and the crowd dispersed.

My rescuer bent and lifted up a broken lens. He turned and handed it to me. "You might need this."

His face was old and leathery with wrinkles that deepened when he smiled. His eyebrows were bushy, and his stubble rough. I thought back to the lottery and recognised him right off.

"Walk with me," Jakob said.

His shoulders slumped, and he made his way slowly down the walkway.

"Thank you for coming to my—"

"But keep your mouth shut." He did not turn.

I sped up, but remained a few steps behind. He led me out of Loring Park, and before long we passed a tall steeple and crossed the motorway bridge. Ahead loomed a great rectangle, a giant, windowless mass marked the Walker Art Center. We veered right, through manicured hedges and into a deeper darkness.

"What is this place?"

He gestured about but did not speak. Foreboding images stood motionless; rooted mobiles creaked in the wind. Shapes surrounded, each twisted and cold.

A sculpture garden.

I took a deep breath and caught up. He peeked at me and slowed his gait. Together we wandered through the artwork: five-, ten-, twenty-foot creations growing up from the sod.

Finally, he stopped, staring at a man crafted of iron. The metal man was bent, worn.

"Do we look alike?" he asked.

I stepped back. "No. Now thank you, but why are we here?"

"What is the difference?"

Play along. You owe him that much. "Fine. You can still walk ..."

Jakob didn't smile. "Not a difference."

I winced, and rubbed the statue's face. "All right then, he has no heart. He is doing all he knows to do. Stand here in this garden. And ten years from now, he will still be standing. You, on the other hand, came to my rescue."

Yes, I owed him a debt, and I went about this stroll, but my patience was wearing thin. I had a purpose back at the inn, and who knew how long Jakob wanted to stand here.

He bowed his head. "I saved you from the horrors of a microphone. Years ago in a country I knew nothing about, I sent hundreds of souls to hell. I destroyed hundreds of families. Where was my heart then?"

"That was your job." I pressed into his shoulder. "Duty and all that."

"Yes. That's what they said. 'Jakob, this is your duty.'"

"And you had no choice."

He looked at me. "Do you believe that, Clara?" Jakob forced a smile. "Then I truly was this metal man. This may be true. I left my heart with my men and returned ..." He reached out and rapped the statue with his knuckles. "Clara, what are you doing here?"

"You asked me to come—"

"At the inn. With Elias. Why are you still here?"

I thought hard, and glanced down at the diary and the lens firmly in my hands. "I came to retrieve my bag. But that was last night. I suppose I could have been gone by now."

Jakob rubbed his stubble. "What are you trying to do to him?"

Lie. There had never been difficulty in doing so before, but here, now, with this old soldier, I stood disarmed.

"I stayed because he drew something, and I was afraid—I am afraid—he might just know the thing he can't know. A thing we will not be discussing. And then ..." I bit my lip. "Then I really met him and thought, maybe I could help. Maybe ... I could help him stay himself. Get the real Elias back, since nobody else wants to."

"You don't want him back either." Jakob's gaze hardened, and then softened again. "I saw him look at you. I'm afraid you will do more harm than good. Hollow. Have you ever felt hollow, Clara?"

"Yes."

"Then listen to an old fool. After my tour, I had *nothing* left to give my Anne. I loved her for thirty years, and gave her nothing but a good funeral."

I rocked. "People do what they think is right."

"That, Clara, is your problem." Jakob stared at the statue, shook his head, and walked back toward the bridge. I wanted to follow him, but my legs lingered. I reached out and stroked the metal face, and then my own.

They didn't feel all that different.

"Wait! So you're saying I can't help?"

Jakob turned. "I'm wagering that even though you weren't in the lottery, you're using him to reach Salem just like the rest of us, or you would be gone. You're too smart to believe that you have the answer to his condition. And until you accept that you're only here for yourself, you are of no use to him."

He pointed across Hennepin Avenue. The lights of the city shone. Minneapolis was no London, but all the players were there. The pub hoppers, night clubbers, and those who hung draped from balconies, yelling down to the street. But in the distance, Phinn's looked peaceful, with only one light still on.

"That beacon belongs to Bette. She returns here each autumn because she loves me." Jakob stared at the light. "She hopes that maybe, one day, we can be together."

A smile crossed my face; I felt it. "This would be the most wonderful thing for you. Your heart—"

"Will always be Anne's. But in Salem, you see, in Salem, Elias has decided that Bette and I are ..." His voice fell. "Married."

I frowned. "I don't ... I don't understand."

Jakob cleared his throat. "It is a foolish game played by old, desperate people." He walked toward the light.

And suddenly I did.

"That gives you both permission to dream. That gives her hope. That's why you both come," I said.

"So now you know my foolishness. Tell me yours. What brought you here?"

I closed my eyes and saw his face. There was no escaping.

"My dad. He ... he used to travel the world. A wandering do-gooder. He met my mum in London and stopped traveling. But one day, he said, one day he would take her anywhere, anywhere she wanted to go. The unspeakable happened, and Dad was taken from us all, and Mum died before one day came. But I have his map. I have his journal. I know where he's been. And I will take the trip he never gave my mum."

"He loves his wife and then he leaves? What are you not saying? What's your part?"

I said nothing.

"Does he know where you are?"

"He hates me."

"But you aren't running from him, are you?"

"I — I will not be speaking about this. You know nothing of what I did ..."

You sent hundreds of souls to hell? Maybe you do.

I lowered my head.

"Very well." Jakob sighed. "Clara, you are a beautiful young girl. Please, be kind to Elias." He gestured to his left and slowly drifted back toward the inn. "He's on the spoon."

On the spoon?

I walked beyond the wire art and the copper figurines, tarnished and corroded together, toward the massive grey silhouette at the far end of the sculpture garden. I paused at its base.

This piece formed a thirty-foot aluminum bridge in the shape of a spoon handle, the bowl raising into the sky. And fastened to the top of the bowl, twenty feet up, was a giant cherry, and standing on the cherry, grasping its stem, a figurine.

A figurine that looked remarkably like Elias.

"How did you get up there?" I called.

"Oh, it's you. Infiltrating my home ... following me around ... No matter. I imagined you would come sooner or later."

The Other One.

I walked across the bridge and stared up, stroking the smooth spoon with my palms. I could not join him.

"Why, precisely, are you standing on an oversized cherry?"

He glanced upward. "I'm closer to the stars. There aren't many here in the city. Cassiopeia, the Dipper, and of course Orion."

"And why do you want to get closer to the stars?"

He looked down at me. "They're the way."

I rubbed my forehead. "Right. Well then, I simply came to apologise for the earlier incident. I should have brought you home straight away."

"An apology? Don't think for an instant that I don't know what you're after. I would die to protect Salem. You weren't counting on that resolve."

I sighed. "No, I wasn't."

"Well, I'm done planning." He nimbly slid down the spoon, and stood before me. "Do you need to report in to whoever sent you? The spoon is free."

"No, I think I'll head back too."

Elias walked stiffly and purposely toward the inn. I followed close behind, catching up near the fountains.

We entered the front door, where Jakob waited.

"Hello, Jakob." Elias turned to me. "Perhaps you would like to interrogate Jakob. Good night. Oh, one last thing. Seeing as you've taken such a keen interest in my life, I've decided to take a keener interest in yours." Elias reached into his pocket, removed a folded paper, and handed it to me. "This is the first test. There will be more." He spun toward his bedroom door and soon disappeared into his room.

Straightening, I marched toward Elias's door and placed my ear against the wood.

"Are you sure you want to do that, young lady?" Jakob asked.

I spun around.

"I'm not sure."

He nodded, gazing longingly at the room. "I'd originally come down to talk to the boy myself. Thought we might sit back and reminisce … that's what we do. We talk about a simpler time when my wife and I, we—"

"Were you about to talk about me?" An old woman slowly descended and joined us in the foyer. "Is Elias in Salem?"

"Likely, but the entrance is shut." Jakob pointed at the closed door. "Bette, I'd like to formally introduce Ms. Clara."

Bette winked and hugged me deeply. "Oh, we met this morning! Are you waiting for him too? You didn't let this old sweet-talker take your place in line, I hope." She released me and scowled at Jakob. "I wanted to go dancing tonight, but I see that's not going to happen."

"You two can dance whether or not the boy is stuck in a fictional world." I glanced from Jakob to Bette and back again. "What's keeping you two? Go. Dance."

Bette softened and then frowned again. "What's keeping us? That man's stubbornness and that man's promise. Old mule!"

"It is not stubbornness to honour an oath. Clara, years ago I made a promise to dance with my wife, and my wife alone. It makes little sense, I admit. Why does an old man feel released to do in Salem what he can't do here? I have no explanation. But I will not break my oath." He turned back to Bette. "Though you, Ms. Drippy Faucet, do your best to wear me down."

Juan was right. These people wanted Elias bound.

Then again, Jakob might be right as well; to get an answer about those drawings, I needed him that way too.

What a twisted place this was.

Jakob yawned. "It's late. I'm old. I'm heading to bed. What is your plan, Ms. Clara?"

I exhaled hard.

"May I suggest letting Elias sleep and Guinevere marinate? I don't believe for an instant that she's still upset with you. These things happen too often for her to place blame."

I squeezed my forehead between thumb and fingers. "That's all fine, but maybe I should just be going."

"No." Guinevere eased down the steps. "The accident was not your fault, Clara, and I'd really appreciate it if you stayed one more night."

"I am so sorry. You gave me a schedule and I didn't follow it. I followed Elias, and—"

"And I am rather confident you gave him the time of his life." She sighed. "It came at the price of my heart, but such is the price of motherhood, especially to that one." She nodded toward Elias's door.

She placed her hand on my shoulder, gave me a squeeze, and disappeared down the hall.

Jakob slowly walked toward the stairs. "Looks like you're part of the family."

"One more night hardly constitutes adoption."

He forced a smile and ambled up the steps, an older version of the man who'd rescued me an hour before.

Bette and I stood in silence.

"A word of advice ..." I said. "You might have better luck with Jakob if you dropped the insults. Calling him stubborn and—"

"He loves it. He and his Elizabeth ... that was their style. He comes every summer because he misses her so. He comes to be insulted. To fall for her all over again."

"And why do you come?"

Bette lowered her gaze. "Oh, child. Didn't he tell you? I come because I love him. Always have. And you already know, this is the one place where Jakob and I can dance."

She moved toward the stairs. A little slower, a little more bent. I watched her go, a woman with a broken heart.

It's still not fair to use Elias.

Quiet again, I glanced down at the paper from Elias, and the dread from the plane returned. I slowly unfolded the sheet.

No.

It was unlike any of the drawings surrounding me in the foyer, or any I'd seen in his sketchbook. It was abstract, cloudy and hideous. But there it was. The storm.

The opening scene of my Great Undoing.

I felt a punch in my belly, and I gasped, peering deeper into the sketch. It wasn't clear. It could be another storm in another place on another day. The images visible through the maelstrom; they could be anyone, really. But that hope landed hollow.

He can't know what I've done. Nobody does. I pushed my hand through my hair.

The first test. There will be more.

I pounded on Elias's door.

Nothing.

"Elias!" I hissed. "You cannot go about showing me these and—"

The door swung open, and Elias slowly nodded and took a seat at the base of his bed. His gaze was upturned, toward a photo on the wall. I followed his line of sight, my breath caught, and I walked straight away toward the frame.

It was not a photo.

"Why is a sketch of *my* mum on *your* wall?"

Elias shook his head. "I have no idea. It's new. I hadn't seen it before today. I didn't put it ... well, I don't remember putting it there."

I glanced at the boy. His gentle voice left no doubt. Elias had returned. The Other One, the one who held my secret, had gone.

I sat down next to him, burying my face in the drawing I held. Minutes later, I glanced back up.

"Your—his—picture of Mum? It's a perfect sketch. It's her ... it's more than her. See her eyes? The weary in her eyes? That was Mum ... What's that flag hanging behind her?"

"Same as that." Elias pointed over his shoulder to a full-size canvas depicting a flag stiff in the breeze. "Doucette painted that. Have you met her yet? She and her sister share the second-floor loft room."

"Elias, I'm missing something—"

"Salem." He glanced at me and glanced away. "Everyone says the Other One calls it Salem."

"Juan tried to explain, but what is that, exactly?" I asked.

"Not a what. A where. An unreal country in an unreal world. My other world, I guess." He stood and walked to his desk and opened the drawers. "Now, when I'm right, I live here, but when I slip through, like I told you, like Mom says I did again today, the Other One takes over." He tapped the desk. "It's all in here. Look if you want."

I walked toward him and reached into the top drawer. Drawings and floor plans and maps. Three-dimensional renderings of sky-scrapers and people. Aerial photos of cities and islands: indeed, an entire world. Except there were no words. No descriptions.

I gently placed the pictures back. Except for one: My only photo of Mum, lifted from the pages of my diary. I glanced again at the picture on the wall. He could suck her image into his hallucination if he wanted to, but the original belonged with me.

"Maybe don't rearrange things. I guess he doesn't like that too much."

"Who does?" I slid Mum's photo into my back pocket.

Elias bowed his head. "You know, he wanders through Salem, always looking."

I gently closed each drawer. "For what?"

He pointed to a mini-recorder on top of the desk and shrugged. I picked it up and hit play. The Other One spoke in a tense whisper:

"I'm going through her things now. Stop. There is a strong pos-sibility that owner is important to my quest. Stop. Her instruction manual is unreadable, written in a foreign language ..."

My shoulders sagged. "My diary. That's probably my diary."

I continued to listen. "There is a photo of our newly crowned queen tucked inside. Stop. I am confiscating this evidence. Stop. Owner is devious, but I need her to translate the manual's words. Stop. Mom coming. Out."

I clicked off the recorder. "Those were my things. Elias, what quest? What are you looking for?"

"I don't know! I don't know, all right? All I have is guesses." He bowed his head. "But I can't help feeling that if my brain finds whatever it wants in the real world, the Other One won't need to create a new one to search in. At least we'll both live in reality. I've spent years looking through all this stuff, hoping and praying and trying to figure out what he's after, but now I'm worse. There seems to be more of him and less of me ..." Elias shook his head. "It isn't going to happen, is it?"

I paced back and forth, pausing in front of my mum. I tossed my hideous sketch into his lap. "Do you have any idea what this is?"

"Never seen it before," he said quietly.

Think, Clara. This one is safe to you, reasonably safe. The Other One? You need to figure out what he knows.

Elias flattened out the sketch. "What are *you* looking for?"

I peeked back at my mum, at the look in her eye, and down at the faces in the storm.

And then I caught it. On the floor. The ragged stuffed bear lying in the corner. Thoughts of Little T—my disabled brother who in my mind would always be a child—pushed to the fore, along with all the shame, shame so suffocating I'd do anything to escape its weight.

It was too late to help him, but just maybe ...

"If I take you on, do I have guarantees of a clean break at the end?"

"Take me on?" Elias blinked.

"When I am done assisting you, and we discover the purpose of the Other One's quest, and if in doing so that somehow reintegrates the two of you into one perfect bloke, will you, A, release me back to my travels without trying to make me stay or the like, and B, make sure he tells me how he knows about what I did?"

"No … I mean, of course I'd release you but … You don't just recover from two identities by figuring out what the paranoid side wants." Elias paused. "What travels … and what did you do?"

"Those are my affairs." I snatched the sketch back from Elias. Neither part of this boy could read. I only trusted half of him, and his other half hated me. Still, he was more than cute, and he reminded me of Little T. I had to help. I'd need assurances my efforts would come with no lingering obligations, but for the first time in months, I cared, and that made me vulnerable.

Quite compassionate, actually.

Then there was my own other half. I carried a lingering disdain for the boarders' enjoyment of Elias's illness. But Jakob was right: Lottery or not, I was no different. Details of what Elias knew about my past were apparently only available in Salem, and I needed to spend time with the Other One to get them. The drawings from the plane and the one tucked in my jeans had placed me among their manipulative number.

Quite a self-serving wench … actually.

I marched over and knelt down in front of him. "Your only job is to stay in the moment. Stay Elias. I need to have a chat with all the others who so very much want you to disappear into Salem, but for now, stay in this moment."

I reached my hand behind his neck and pulled his head near. I kissed him deeply. He did not kiss back.

"We'll work on it." I exhaled. "In the moment."

He swallowed hard. "In the moment."

CHAPTER 8

"Who moved my things? Who snuck into my room and moved my things?"

Elias's shout woke me with a start, and I threw on some clothes, scowled at the enormous faces, and burst into the hallway, where an interrogation was underway.

There was Guinevere, Jakob, and Juan, as well as seven or eight other guests. All were lined up in a row, while Elias strode back and forth, pausing to point his finger at each one.

"You. Mom, it was you."

"No, dear."

Elias squinted. "I see no lying in your eyes." He moved on to Jakob.

"This is mad!" I yelled, and walked determined toward Elias. His eyes grew large, and then softened, but it was Guinevere who spoke next.

"Go along with it, Clara. Doctor's directive."

"What a daft doctor." I turned to Elias and gave him a shove. "I did this. I searched through your drawers and listened to your tapes. I walked in and did it all. You gave me permission!"

Elias's mouth twitched, and he peeked at the ceiling. "I let you?" His voice was distant.

"You jolly well opened the door."

He faced the lineup. "You are all dismissed. Clara, I would like to speak with you."

"No."

"No?" Elias winced. "Do you know who I am?"

"Do you?"

He balled both his fists. "Manners. Think manners ... May I *please* have a word with you?"

"In time."

I marched passed Guinevere and whispered, "Don't worry. I've got this." I opened the front door, glanced back over my shoulder at Elias, and stepped into morning sunshine.

A minute later, Elias poked out his head. "Are you deaf? I said I want to talk to you!"

I felt a grin creep over my face—the joy of frustrating him was considerable—and I started walking north. Elias followed, his feet shuffling behind me. Now and then he asked to talk, but one scolding glance silenced him.

We walked for hours, skirting this unfamiliar city. I needed time to think. Finally, I was ready, and we plunged into the heart of downtown, making for the tallest building. After several near-death experiences involving road construction, we reached it.

"Why are we here?" Elias grabbed on to my shoulder and quickly released.

I froze. "You may do that again, if you like."

"No, that's okay."

"Very well, then follow."

We pushed through revolving doors and into a large, shop-filled courtyard. Offices surely filled the top levels, and hopefully, a quiet place to chat would be among them.

I led Elias Phinn to the lift, and we stepped on. I pressed the button labeled OD, and a minute later, we stepped out onto the observation deck. It offered a rather magnificent view.

I walked to the window, and pointed out over the city.

"This is much higher than your cherry perch. Even closer to your stars. You can see for miles."

Elias's jaw tightened.

"Listen, I brought you here because you pound about the inn as if you own the place, as if you own those people. You don't. You don't own anything you see out this window." I sighed. "You need to know that ... And I need to know what you're searching for."

Elias pressed his nose against the glass. "I know of more impressive cities."

"Hang the city. That is not why I brought you here!" I took a cleansing breath, slowly lowering my hands. "I'll start over. You're looking for something, and I'm going to help you find it."

He folded his arms. "How do you know I'm on a search?"

"I spoke to you about it, the you that right now is waiting beneath the surface, waiting to come up for air. I know that everyone says there are two Eliases, but I say it's the same you." I tapped the glass. "I heard your tapes. I heard you mention me. I heard you mention a quest." I rolled my eyes. *Here we go. I need him to trust me. Time to leave the truth behind.* "I'm willing to abandon all attempts to elicit information from you and simply be of assistance."

"Why?"

My mouth opened and shut. The lie was indefensible. Even to the imaginary part of Elias.

But what if *this* was the real him? Of course the kinder one talked a good talk, all boys did, but maybe this was the true Elias and I'd kissed the fake. No. I shook the idea from my mind. This one needed to disappear for good.

I fingered the sketch in my pocket.

But not yet.

"You can't help me find what Salem needs. It is my search. It's been given to me by our recently crowned queen, and I won't be sidetracked by your charms."

I let my arms flop at my sides. "Are you not listening? I'm offering you my help." I took a deep breath, stepped back and sat on the bench. "Odd. Someone once used that precise same line on me."

"Who?" Elias plunked down beside me.

I swept back my hair. "It's a tale. You sure you want to hear?"

His eyes grew wide and he folded his hands.

"Well, the heat in Mali had been overpowering that day. I was looking for shade, but I had no desire to slow. A deep voice trailing me kept asking, 'Are you not listening? I'm offering you my help.' "

Ninety percent of my blogged-about adventures had also been experienced by my Dad. But every so often I lost his scent — missed a train, took a wrong turn — and so it had been in Mali. Then my heart beat faster. There were no safe houses mentioned in his journal for those places, no friendly names. Panic normally ensued. Somehow following Dad's map settled me. As if he was still beside me.

A part of me.

I peeked toward Elias.

"I shouldn't have stopped, but I did, and trusted him right off. The young man had been following me throughout Bamako's openair bazaar carrying a silly guitar-shaped instrument fashioned from a gourd. The price had been a tenner, but was now down to a few pennies.

"I don't need your instrument," I told the lad.

"No, but you wander in circles, and maybe you have need of directions. I am the most reliable guide."

"The most reliable." I tried not to grin, but it was a challenge. "And you know your way around Mali?"

"I've lived here all my life. I speak English and French. I speak Bambara and Fulfulde. Nobody is as helpful as Cliq. I'll guide you.

For five pounds, of course. So come, come … where is it you want to go?"

"Timbuktu."

I had read about the place in Dad's journal, but that entry was made twenty years previous. Before the bloodshed.

Cliq grabbed my arm and pulled me between melon stands. "Fighting there. Nothing remains. It's a long road." He whistled. "So much fighting."

"Do you want my money or not?" I asked.

"You're traveling alone. I could have your money and more any time I wanted it." He was right. Strength marked his muscled arms — strength and scars. Pinkish-white gashes from recent altercations crisscrossed his forearms, rivaling the white gleam of his teeth. Tall, young, and handsome, I liked him at once — he didn't appear one to play it safe.

The bloke rolled his eyes. "Timbuktu …" He slipped into a language I'd not heard before. "Of all the places."

His wagon was waiting outside the bazaar. I climbed on, and he did too. Thirty minutes later, our path veered away from the Niger River, toward an expanse of nothing.

"So we begin. Tell me when you need to rest." Cliq lay down beside me in the back of the cart and immediately fell asleep.

The donkeys just kept plodding ahead along the road. One day, two days, three days.

That third afternoon, it burned especially hot. Beneath a cloudless sky, my neck blistered and my throat ached and my desire to reach Timbuktu vanished.

I thought about turning around. I could settle up and leave the country.

I didn't have the chance.

A Toyota truck squealed to a stop. Rushed words spoken in

Bambara passed between Cliq and the driver, and as the truck sped away he pulled his donkeys off the road.

"We'll stop here. Fresh fighting. Much blood. I won't take you farther."

I glanced around. "That village?"

"Sevare. Nothing there."

"Then that's where I wish to go."

Outside the wall sat a woman, her hands clenched. "Toward that woman," I said.

"No."

"To the woman. I demand it."

"No, she's outside the wall."

I leaped off the cart and ran to her, slowing as I approached. Her face was deformed, concealing her age. I greeted her in English and offered my hand. She stared at it, reached out and took it. I squeezed, and a little piece of her finger fell to the ground.

A leper.

Cliq would not let me back onto his cart.

"What happened?" Elias jumped in. "How did you get back?"

I blinked.

"I found three members of the Peace Corps in Sevare, one a trusting lad. I spent some time with him, and when night fell I continued, in his truck, to Timbuktu. The how of it is best not said. I continued on ... shamefully." I looked down over the city. "But the point of the story is that I'm not afraid of journeys; I know how to get where I'm going. I know how to locate what is very hard to find. Let me help you."

"I don't want shameful help."

I nodded. "I understand."

We sat quietly together, though I imagine our thoughts were quite far apart.

"Yes. I need a guide. An honest guide." Elias scrunched his face. "Can you be that?"

I took a deep breath. "I don't know."

"That's very honest," he said. "And you can translate the instruction manual? It leads us where we need to go."

"The instruction . . . you mean my diary? The one you were digging through? Of course I can read it. I mean, I wrote it. But they're just my thoughts. My private thoughts."

Elias glanced to the left and the right, and lowered his voice. "I have the map. The queen said someone would arrive with the manual that interprets it. It think we're supposed to go on this quest together."

I turned to Elias. His face was radiant and peaceful. Like Marna's, on a good day.

"But how much easier it would be if you told me what we're searching for. This would help me guide you."

Elias shook his head. "When I first met you, I had doubts. I may have been wrong, but when I'm sure I can trust you, after you pass the tests, I'll tell you."

The tests. The sketchings that revealed what he knew. Yes, this would be acceptable.

We rode the lift down and walked the long walk back to the inn. I didn't say much. Elias spoke nonstop. He spoke of Salem and its large cities, the people and their languages. He told of a small town that a group of the sick weren't allowed to enter, and he explained several local ordinances governing the usage of donkeys as transportation.

My world had become his, or his mine; it was hard to say.

How easy it was to slip through the cracks alongside him. To fall into the very same trap I had committed to free him from. As Elias droned on, my mind wandered to Jakob and Bette and Juan. Were they really using him, or simply enjoying him? What was I doing?

"... so I hung a picture of her in my room. I'll show it to you sometime. We have a very beautiful new queen, but she's tired. She's trying to do it all. Maybe that's why she asked me to help, to go on this quest ..."

My mum? Your queen?

An unknown boy thousands of miles from London was trying to assist my dead mum.

My mum's own daughter could have done so much more.

Though the dead spot in my heart did not feel it, there was no escape from the truth: I was beginning this search shamefully.

CHAPTER 9

After.

After our return and Elias's hasty retreat to his room.

After I found the biscuits Guinevere left out for us and after I washed up.

That's when I heard them. Giggles. Directly overhead.

I had not yet risked a peek into the upper studio, but I arose from my bed wide awake, the four faces in my room once again providing every reason to leave and explore.

I wandered upstairs and toward the noisy room with the door ajar. I strained my ears. My French was poor, but it took no understanding to hear the excitement in the women's voices. I knocked quietly, and they fell silent.

"We were carried away. I'm sorry that—" The door opened and two faces peered into the hall. "Oh, do come! Tell us about your travels in you-know-where."

"England?"

"Salem, of course!" They each grabbed an arm and pulled me into a room crammed with fifty easels. "Forgive the mess. No, don't forgive. You'll remember us from the lottery—I made quite the impression—my name is Doucette, and this is my sister, Roseau. We were hoping to speak with you soon."

"Artists."

"It is an effort," Roseau quietly said.

"It's more than that." I gazed across the canvases. "They're beautiful."

At the compliment, Doucette giggled again. "Please then, take a closer look. And this is only two month's work."

I wandered among their paintings, of rivers and mountains, faces and festivals. Vibrant, alive; I wanted to stand among them, live among them.

"Is this France?" I pointed to a landscape of rolling hills and poppies.

Doucette and Roseau peeked at each other, and Roseau sighed. "Actually no, that is—"

"Someday," interrupted Doucette, "we will have a show, and we will proudly name it 'Images of Salem.' Elias comes in here and sits in that rocker and speaks ..."

I walked over to the chair and rubbed the armrest with my hand, eased down into it.

"Perhaps it's not for you to sit in. He notices when it is off center." Doucette beckoned me to stand. "Sessions aren't so good when he is off center."

I rose. "So, you paint only his world?"

"There is no place on this earth where we could experience the beauty as he describes." Doucette sighed. "We are the artists, but I think we do not see as he does."

"No, I imagine you don't." I stepped up toward a painting, an aerial masterpiece. The perspective dwarfed that seen from the skyscraper's observation deck ... How absurd to think the view I provided would put Elias off balance.

"His words hold more information than we can obtain with our eyes. But we are the painters." Doucette gestured about the room.

"And the four monstrously sized men in my room ... did you paint them?"

"Non. That is Elias's work. Magnificent, aren't they?"

"But this ... We record all this for him," Roseau quickly added. "For him or for you?"

Doucette frowned. "It is all for him. Always, he comes in. Always, we listen and work. Always—"

"It is for us," Roseau said softly. "It was not meant to be so. We came to stay here three years ago quite by accident. We missed our plane home, to Paris, and stayed here. For one night, we thought. We were failed, defeated."

"You overstate our situation, sister."

"Non. And you know this to be true. Elias came up and paid us a visit, and we painted one mountain." Roseau closed her eyes. "And such a mountain. Had you seen anything like it?"

"Non," Doucette said quietly.

"And we discovered that our problem was not in the hand, but in the eye. We could not see."

"But Elias could," I said. "It's his gift."

Elias's gift. The thought of it chilled me.

Doucette plopped onto the couch. "So what do we do? Each summer we come back, and when we return with these paintings, our names begin to be spoken. I don't think we do him harm. We ask for nothing. He gives freely."

It is no longer a room for giggles.

"I don't know your plans, Clara, but ..." Roseau looked around the room. "Maybe wait to judge. If you stay long, you will see: It is frightfully easy to live in Elias's world. There is much less pain."

She was correct. It was easy. Addicting. Compelling.

But it wasn't right. Deep down I knew it, and I knew they did too. They were not artists. Elias was.

The real Elias knew nothing of my past. It was time to set him free, never to be used again.

Well, after I figured out from the Other One how much of me had been discovered.

My quest had begun.

"Do you see any themes?" I asked. "When Elias speaks, do you note any themes?"

"Stars," they said in unison. Doucette continued. "If it was up to Elias, every painting would be painted at night, which we, of course, cannot do. Always, there are stars and families of stars."

"Constellations," I said.

"Yes. He describes them in detail, and I admit, those descriptions we do not listen to."

"Nothing else?" I asked.

"Non. Only stars."

• • • • •

I entered my room and turned on the light.

Five faces stared at me.

"Blast! Elias." My heartbeat slowed. "A few things you may never do. Sneaking up on me is one of them."

"We need to leave. We need to leave now." He stood up from the chair in the corner.

"It's late. We'll start in the morning." I collapsed face first onto my bed. But Elias shook the frame.

"She said we need to go tonight."

"She?"

"I told you. The queen—"

"My mum said many things during her life, but I guarantee she did not tell you anything of the sort." I flipped over.

Elias backed up slowly. "Your mom, the queen?"

"Yes, my mum the queen, I mean yes to my mum, no to the queen ... at least not my queen. Maybe your queen."

He fell back into the chair. "Of course. How did I miss it?" He stood and paced the room. "It makes sense. Your sudden willingness to help me. Your possession of the instruction manual containing her picture—"

"You mean my diary."

"She would only entrust someone close to her with such a delicate set of documents. You would know what to do, where to go." He reached beneath my head and yanked out the pillow. "Come now."

I groaned and rubbed my neck. "Fine. We will walk around a tad and then come back, and tomorrow we will sort this all out."

"But Salem is a big place. You'll need to get us a car."

I sat up, a heavy feeling in my stomach.

"How far do you want to go?"

"I'm not sure. My map and your manual together will tell us. I know you like donkeys for long trips, but that's not an option in this part of the world."

"You can't just leave, Elias. You can't just leave your mum and take off who knows where without so much as a good-bye. You can't do ... that ..."

I lowered my gaze. *Nobody should put family through that.*

"It's unfortunate that it must be this way." Elias bit a nail and furrowed his brow. "She's kind." He seemed on the verge. The thought of Guinevere's worry looked to slow him, and he tightened both fists. Then his fingers extended, and his cadence quickened. "She would try to stop me. She is a good woman, but she doesn't understand all that is at stake. She sees a very small picture."

I nodded.

"If we don't find what we're after, all of Salem is in jeopardy. I see it now. I need your help."

"But the boarders. What about Juan and Jakob, Doucette ..."

"My teachers? I finished my lessons. History from Jakob. Art from Doucette. Government from Juan. My lessons are finished. My bag is packed. Now pack yours."

I slowly rose and gathered my things.

Guinevere would be devastated.

"Give me one day. Tomorrow night, we'll leave." I paused, jeans in hand. "I can do wonders as a guide, but some items take time to obtain. A car is no small feat."

"I believe you can do this." Elias handed me my diary off the bedside table. "We'll start at the bazaar."

"The bazaar?"

Elias folded his arms. "The one you told me about. We'll find someone there who can help us. Maybe Cliq."

What have I done?

"And how do you propose we reach the bazaar?" I asked.

"There's a new light rail in this city. I'm sure you can find it."

I finished packing.

We'll just ride the light rail system from Minnesota to West Africa. I'm certain we shall not have any difficulties.

"I'm stating, for the record, that this is not the best way to begin this quest." I grabbed my underwear from Elias's hands. "If you would condescend to tell me what we're looking for ... We might even find it nearby. Right here, at the inn."

Elias thought a moment. "Find us a car, and I will consider the next of your tests passed. Maybe at that point I can tell you more."

"Right." I snapped the clasp of my bag and slung it over my shoulder. "Well, then, let's get started."

Elias walked over to the disturbing face, the one on the east wall. He stared unblinking at the man for a long time, before reaching out and placing his hand over the picture's enormous mouth. "I can't hear you," he said, glancing over his shoulder at me. "I'm taking her away from you."

I buried my face in my hands. *I must be mad.*

We quietly left the room and the inn and wandered out beneath a full-moon sky. Elias's face brimmed with confidence, and I rubbed my eyes.

I was helping half of him.

I was using the other half.

What I was running from had found me.

CHAPTER 10

The light rail rocked and lurched over its tracks, and I gentled my head against the glass, dozing and then waking. Leaden eyelids raised and peeked across the aisle at Elias, sitting stiff and alert. That had been my posture as I left London, but thousands of miles soften the body to conform to its surroundings.

Again, I tried to find sleep.

"Where are we getting off?" Elias blurted.

I inhaled long and hard and forced myself to vertical.

"Right. Perhaps we could just ride the loop tonight and start off when I'm a bit more rested."

"That wasn't the plan."

"Really now? Because I don't recall there being a whole lot of planning inserted into this scheme. I don't recall minor things like ramifications and destinations being discussed, do you?"

Elias glanced at me and then let his gaze fall. "We discussed the bazaar. We discussed you finding a car for our journey." He reassumed his vigilance and folded his hands. "I will tell you what you need to know, when you need to know it."

"I'm a Sherpa without an Everest."

"Yes."

"Wait. How do you know that mountain?"

"Everyone knows that mountain."

"Do you know the Amazon River?"

"Of course."

"Canada?"

"I know my geography."

"The United States?"

Elias paused. "Of what? The states of what?"

"The fifty United States of America."

"I've not heard of it."

I folded my arms, and whispered, "Fascinating."

Elias shifted in his seat. "Are you guiding me or not?"

I turned to face him. "Apparently I'm not as of yet." Above his head, a route map presented our options, and I squinted through bleary eyes. "Right. Now I am. The university. We will be getting off at the university exchange."

"What's there?"

I hoped Kira had only partially disowned me. Either way, she was the only other soul I knew in this town and so would have to do. Knowing her, she would still be awake. Alone was an entirely different matter.

We exited the train and walked toward the shifting shadows.

I had experienced enough universities to know there was little difference between them. Nightcrawlers came out with the moon in groups of three or ten. They took over the streets and the car parks and the lawns, moving loudly between parties, both drawn to and creating mayhem.

Which gave fraternities, locked in unspoken competition, their most noticeable function: to become the beacon of urban wild; to throw the most damaging parties.

Yes, finding fraternity row, and by extension Kira, involved simply following the noise. For Kira, second wildest would never do.

"That's it."

I pointed ahead to the three-story mansion. "That is the bazaar."

Bodies draped over the balcony, and from their cups beer showered down, shimmering in the beam of the searchlight set in the front yard. Shrieks punctuated the steady beat of club music that shook the ground on which we stood.

As we walked across the lawn, Elias spun a slow, complete circle. "It isn't how you described it."

"No, it has changed. But that would be it. The only sorority hosting a party. That little bit of rebellion will be where we find Kira."

A girl staggered into Elias, stumbled to her knees, and pulled herself to her feet using Elias's jeans and shoulders as a ladder.

"Thanks." She smiled and kissed Elias firmly on the lips. His eyes opened wide, and he stood, frozen, throughout his ordeal.

It was hard to say if he enjoyed it.

Deep inside, I burned. Why, I did not know. I had no claim over either the desirable half of him or the paranoid half I'd helped run away. Was it a buried mother instinct? It didn't feel that way. This feeling was darker and heavier, and I stepped forward and broke her lips from his.

"On you go."

She disappeared into the night.

Elias cleared his throat. "This is definitely not how you described it." His eyes twinkled.

"So it's better, or worse?"

"So far, better."

"Come on then." I grabbed his arm and pulled him toward the front door. "Pay close attention to your bag, as it will be crowded inside. And whatever happens . . ." I clutched his hand, and though he recoiled I squeezed all the tighter. "Do not lose this hand."

"It's not mine to lose."

I shook my head and we pushed inside.

Eyes. Everywhere, eyes. Pulsating white in the light of a giant strobe. They flickered our way, but cared nothing for us, and I took a deep breath and pressed through the bodies. They gave easily, swaying as if barely upright, which was likely the case. The music pounded, and I headed for the stairs.

Elias's hand tried to escape mine, but I would not release him. Losing him in here would be a disaster.

We reached the first step, and I checked on Elias. His free hand covered his eyes. "I can't deal with this kind of light!"

"Okay!" I pressed my lips to his ear, but yelled anyway. "Let's get you upstairs!"

I stepped behind him and pushed him upward. He stumbled and straightened, and we emerged on the second floor, in a central hall surrounded by six doors. Three girls lay unconscious on the floor.

Elias knelt at their side. "Were they attacked?"

"Yes, I suppose. A self-induced alcohol attack."

Elias shot me a look I remembered. One first given me by my mum when I came home with a lowly set of marks. Disappointment. That's what it was. I hadn't felt the emotion directed toward me for months.

With Elias, I felt it again.

"They could have been warned. You knew about this place and didn't tell me? I should have warned them."

"About drinking?" I squeezed my forehead between thumb and forefinger. "They wouldn't have listened ... She didn't."

Elias slipped his bag off his back and dug, eventually pulling up a sock. He wiped the spittle off a girl's face, and gently placed the sock on her lap. "So that's how you travel. You ignore pain so you don't have to get involved." He stood and shouldered his belongings. "These are your people. Or have you taken us out of Salem?"

I rolled my eyes. "These are not my people. These are idiots acting like idiots."

Again, the look.

I wished I could reel back my words, reign in my tongue. I wished many things. I closed my eyes and remembered: Mum had returned from the factory blitzed.

Early on, it was not a common thing. Most days, her pay ended up where it should, in the hands of our landlord or converted to something for Teeter's and Marna's stomachs.

But when the day was hard and her boss unyielding and her depression as thick as fog; on those days, the few pounds she made ended up at the pub. She drank herself into oblivion.

I never blamed her. My father received my guilt-born hatred. And as I evolved into Mum and my mum reverted to a child, I thought of ways to exact revenge. To my young mind, the fact that Dad sat well fed without work or responsibility in a clean, dry room while the rest of us died a slow death seemed quite unjust.

He committed the crime and we paid the punishment.

Mum stumbled in late one night and I jumped to my feet. I caught her thin frame as she collapsed in the doorway, and together we reached her bed. I removed her shoes, her glasses.

"I'm sick," she moaned, turned her head, and churled over her bed, a combination of beer and blood. I grabbed a towel and sopped it dry as best as I could. Then I went to the drawer and removed a dishtowel. I wiped her mouth and placed the towel gently over her midsection.

I sat down beside her, surrounded by stench and sadness, and I never loved my mum as much as I did that night.

"I know you've been traveling, and I'm sure your diplomatic trips are important." Elias straightened. "But now that you're home, you need to spend more time with your people. Look at them. After all, the queen won't live forever, and then it all passes to you."

I opened my mouth to speak, and let it fall shut.

"No answer?" Elias asked.

"We need to find Kira." I stepped forward and pounded the first door. A girl peeked out.

"Kira Haley?"

"Third floor, end room. Doubt she's there now. If she is, she won't want to be interrupted."

The door closed, and we traipsed up the stairs and down the hall.

"Stand behind me, Elias." I knocked hard.

Her door flew open. "Now is not the time ... Clara?" Her face brightened, and then darkened. "You finally decided to visit. Well, I'm a little busy right now."

"Who is it, K?" A male voice from inside the room.

Kira stared at me. "Nobody."

I stuck my foot in the doorframe just in time.

"What do you want from me?" She slowly widened the crack.

"I need the bloke gone, and I need your time. I've been crap for a friend, but I need you now."

Kira tightened her lips and flattened her T-shirt. "Out, Drew."

"Are you kidding?"

"Out, Drew."

Drew cursed and pushed Kira aside. He glanced at me and winked before storming into the hall.

"I think you might just have saved me. Let's lock the door and catch up." Kira threw her arms around my neck, hugged me deeply, and then stiffened.

"You brought him."

I said nothing.

"You didn't really come to see me," she continued.

More silence.

She licked her lips. "I suppose it's too late to get Drew back, so you might as well come in." She exhaled. "Both of you."

"Thanks." I followed her in. Elias did not.

"Come on in, Elias."

He gestured to me and I walked toward him. "How well do you know this girl?"

"Well enough," I answered with an exaggerated whisper.

"Where did you meet her?"

"London."

"You are kidding me." Kira laughed. "What's wrong with the guy?"

"No, he's . . ." I turned back toward Elias. "If you trust me, please, trust Kira."

Elias looked up and down the hall and slowly entered the room. "Have a seat." Kira pointed at a chair, and grabbed some gum from her desk. She started an obnoxious chew, and plopped onto her bed. Elias still stood.

"Or, you know, keep standing." Her voice raised. "Like a freaking statue."

"Shut it." I plopped down beside her, stared about the room. Rather tidy as universities went. My gaze fixed on the painting of Jesus hanging on the wall.

I pointed at the frame. "Why is he here?"

"My roommate's. She says it keeps her from doing something stupid."

"Don't believe her. It's a non-god."

I hadn't always believed that. My early years were filled with simple prayers and church steeples and real belief. Dad said God was real, so it had to be so. Mum tried to keep up the act after Dad was gone, but I was a good guesser and she was rotten at charades. Besides, a fiction only willing to bring his own son back to life did little good for me, little good for Little T.

No, this picture could not be counted on. Dad once said that since Little Thomas was born different, he'd have a special place in non-god's heart. But Jesus, Dad, and Little T all disappeared on the same day.

I hadn't seen any of them since.

I wrapped my arm around Kira's shoulder. "There are things I need to say and explain. There are reasons I haven't texted and . . . I don't understand all of them myself. But I need you. I don't have any right to ask your help after these last days, but there it is."

She whispered into my ear, "He is kind of a nut, you know."

"At first glance."

"And second and third and—"

"Kira."

"Well, look at him."

Elias stood, his hands folded, and his eyes sad.

"Yes." I smiled. "Look at him."

Kira sighed. "Okay, out with it. What can little old me possibly provide for you?"

"My money and your car."

CHAPTER 11

Kira wandered to her desk and extracted a biology text from the bottom of a textbook stack. As she raised the book, an oversized envelope fell to the floor.

"You kept that much money in a biology text?" I swiped the envelope off the carpet and lifted the flap.

Kira glanced from me to Elias and cocked her head. "Safest place to store any valuable. Nobody here opens that book." She reached out and messed up Elias's hair. He immediately tried to flatten it down. "Something about him though ... When I cashed out your account, it was at fifteen thousand dollars. What are you writing on that site, anyway? And stop counting—it's all there."

I stood and approached her. "Now, a question about your car—"

"No," said Kira.

"I would take fine care of it."

"No."

I glanced at the money in my hands. "Fine then, what's it worth?"

Kira peeked at my money as well. "It's a nice car."

I peeled off seven thousand dollars in crisp one hundreds, and shook the bills in her face. "Seven thousand, cash. Would you sell it to me?"

"A classic, really."

"It's rubbish, but I won't argue. Nine thousand."

"How would I get around without it?"

"Ten."

"Seriously?" Kira snapped. "Done. I would've sold it for seven, but after the last few days ..." She stretched out her hand and I filled it with dollars. Her eyes widened and she pointed over her shoulder at the key hanging on the wall. "She is all yours, honey. Steering is a little splashy, but she'll get you where you need to go, which is ..."

Kira glanced at me. I glanced at Elias.

Elias glanced at the key.

"You did it," he said, a look of awe on his face.

"Yes. I purchased you a getaway vehicle. Against all better judgment."

But judgment no longer mattered. To the Other One, the answer would always be yes. Yes to an insane journey. Yes to ten thousand for a car. I'd spent my years, and the past handful of months, running from what I'd done, only to discover pieces of my greatest shame leaking out of Elias's mind and onto the page for the world to see. To find out how much he knew, to regain my sense of privacy? No price was too high.

Kira blinked and stashed her money inside a physiology text. "May I have a word with you?"

I pushed Elias down onto the bed. "Stay right here. In this room. I need to go speak to my friend."

We left Elias and slipped out into craziness. The hall was filled with students performing some strange chant. Kira pointed down and I nodded. We didn't find peace until we were on the front lawn. There, I explained the mission I had been conscripted into.

"He's cute. The curly blond hair, those eyes, the rest of him." Kira shook her head. "No doubt about that, but you're the smart one. You're brighter than this. You don't know him. It doesn't sound like you know where you're going. I mean, who just up and takes off?" She rolled her eyes. "Besides you, but that was months ago. You don't kidnap a guy who's not all there."

"Actually, there's twice as much to him as there is to the rest of us. Do you remember the address you took me to from the airport?"

"The Loring Park joint."

"Tomorrow, I need this hand delivered to Guinevere." I handed her a letter. "Tell her I'll bring Elias back as soon as I can. Tell her that he was determined to leave, that he was going and I was worried, so I went with him and I'll do everything I can."

"I have no car to deliver this with."

"Find Drew ... just find a vehicle. But I want it done in person. Tell Guinevere how Elias looked. That we're just fine and he's not kidnapped or gone missing. Well, he is missing, but tell her he's with me, and I'll sort it all out and get him back."

"Yeah, okay." Kira took hold of both my hands. "Will we get time? Just you and me?"

"When I get back. Yes."

The pounding music suddenly cut, and for an instant the entire house fell silent. Then angry shouts rang out from inside.

"Elias." I ran toward the door with Kira close behind. I sprinted up the steps, and gasped.

There he stood, perched on top of the six-foot speaker, its frayed cord in his left hand while he gestured with his right.

"Look around you! You're making a mess of the place!"

A plastic beer cup bounced off his face, and the party cheered. Elias wiped his eyes with his sleeves and continued. "Citizens of Salem! Your queen has sent me to you, and your smiles don't fool me. You're not happy living like this!"

The moment was surreal. A sometimes-autistic young man with two identities lecturing a room full of zombies on feelings and reality. I pushed through the crowd. "Elias, get down."

Too late. In the dark of the room, large shapes grabbed Elias and hauled him from his perch. They hoisted him and his bag above their heads and passed him toward the door. Voices raised, but none belonged to Elias. He alone seemed a calm center of this storm.

I jostled to my left and clutched Elias's leg as he passed overhead.

"Enough, you bloomin' idiots!" I screamed, shoving and clearing space with my free hand. "Set him down. Set him—"

A large body collided with mine and I fell backward.

I felt my head strike the floor, but remembered nothing after.

• • • • •

"Hey, Clara."

My eyelids fluttered open. Kira and Elias sat one on either side, and above me shone the stars, unusually bright for the city. My body ached and my head throbbed. My mind searched for the last time I'd received such a smearin', and I thought of Dad.

Had I actually attempted to break him out of jail? Ironically, I could not recall. But it didn't matter; I spent hours each night planning the deed. I was ten and I was convinced it could be done. I had seen it on the telly. An accomplice on the outside needed only to sneak in a tool, hidden in a book or a piece of fruit.

I selected a banana.

The most useful tool found in our flat was the flathead screwdriver, and while I was not sure what Dad would do with it, I knew he could poke and dig and tap Morse code, and I was certain that with enough time, Dad would be free.

I rose early and slipped out the door, heading for the Underground. I joined the thousands on the subway, and then boarded a small train. Finally, I walked two hours and stood in front of the jail, loaded banana in hand.

I approached the entry, and the man in the uniform smiled, and came out of his booth to greet me.

"Are you lost, missy?"

I shook my head. "My dad is in there, and I wanted to give him this banana."

"Must be a very special banana. May I see it, miss?"

In my small fist was the handle of the protruding tool. I dared not give it to him. I held it up. "I've come a long way. Can I give it to him myself?"

Amazingly, I was let through the gate, though now I see my plan was doomed from the start. I was buzzed into the facility, then buzzed into the main building, where I was asked to leave all my belongings, including the secret-filled fruit.

The man behind the window slowly extracted the screwdriver. "Blimey, there's a screwdriver in this banana. Good thing I noticed it; that would hurt his teeth. Let's just leave that here."

"I needed to plan this better," I said.

The insult was that I never was allowed to see Dad. Mum was called, and I was held in the lobby until she arrived.

The injury came later.

The first and last time Mum ever gave me a wallop. She beat me badly, until my head ached and my body throbbed; she beat me for loving Dad.

"Clara?" Again, Elias spoke.

His face was bloody and puffy, and Kira had crimson splotches on her jeans. I pushed myself up to my elbows.

I lay in an alley on a discarded mattress too big for the dumpster.

"You missed quite an event." Kira smirked. "How's that head?"

Elias helped me to a sit.

"Hard to say," I said, and winced. "Where are we?"

"My house—what's left of it—is a block away." Kira pointed, and then rubbed my forehead. "Elias carried you here. Do you remember that?"

I shook my head.

Elias slowly reached out and took my hand. Our fingers clasped and I blinked.

"Are you back?"

His eyes were soft, soft and sad. "Kira filled me in on a lot of it, but I'm really sorry, Clara. I'm so sorry for getting you into this."

I hugged him, and he squeezed back. How strange, to find myself drawn to half a boy. I don't know if I hugged him from my heart or if I hugged him because Elias had returned to the surface. Maybe the embrace found its origin in gratitude. It didn't matter.

His arms reassured. His arms protected.

His arms felt safe.

"You know, Clara, I thought you were insane running off with this guy."

I released Elias and glanced at Kira, and she continued, "But I kind of get it. Not totally, but I get it."

"Running off hardly explains our relationship . . ." Elias shifted, and I sighed. "What happened, then?"

"You were on the ground," Elias said.

"Yes, and you were in the air."

"And I suddenly saw you, I mean *I* saw you—me, not the Other One—and I needed to get you out."

Kira's eyes sparkled. "This guy absolutely destroyed about ten seniors to reach you. Then everyone began to destroy each other, and soon the dance floor was chaos. But Elias scooped you up, and we slipped out before the cops arrived." She shook her head. "I have never seen such a wild night, and I don't know that I have much of a house to return to . . . Isn't that awesome?"

"Awesome." I reached for my head. "There are other words."

Kira swallowed and lowered her head. "So what are you two going to do now? Now that your leader is . . . sort of missing."

I glanced at Elias.

He stood and paced. "I hear we're leaving. I hear you bought me a car, and Mom doesn't know we're gone. And I know nobody here, including me, knows what we're looking for."

"This diminishes our chance of finding it, yes."

He froze. "Except, I think I might know. I think I know where I, where we were going. And I'd need a car to get there." Elias pushed his hand through his hair. "I think the Other One wants to go east. I think he's looking for a Lightkeeper."

PART 2

CLARITA

CHAPTER 12

East.
It feels different than west. It doesn't matter the country, there's an urgency to east. Life accelerates.

However, our journey started quietly. We drove through the night sharing few words. I didn't want it this way. I wanted to speak to Elias, to hear his gentle voice as long as it remained. I wanted to know why he hadn't shared this hunch about the search before. But Elias was lost in a different place, racking his brain, I think, for pieces of memory, anything connected to a Lightkeeper.

We soon crossed over the St. Croix River into Wisconsin.

"Rest area, please," Elias said, and I eased off the road at the next stop. I pulled into a parking stall, and he exited without a word, slowly walking into the visitor's building.

He was troubled, and I couldn't imagine living his life. How could anyone bear the weight of not knowing when or where their mind, their entire existence, would suddenly vanish?

Through the glass walls, I saw him staring at the map. A long stare. Long enough for me to extract my laptop and pound out an entry.

A different type of entry:

Help Support Children of Incarcerated Parents
500 Days of Wandering, 500 Days of Hope

Day 244

America. Wisconsin. I had not planned on this as an excursion. I confess that until yesterday, I had not heard of Wisconsin, but now I find myself passing through. I am not alone. For the first time in many months, I have a travel companion, and for the first time since my tour began, my destination is not my own.

I am driving to the East Coast, I think. Likely to another state of which I have not heard. I am looking for a Lightkeeper. Here I will attempt to explain the unexplainable. My companion, a big-hearted bloke, lives with a phrase imprinted on his heart. He does not remember where he heard it. He does not recall what it means. He only knows the words, and impressions tethered to them. The phrase? 'And now it's time to find the Lightkeeper.' The impressions? A lighthouse. The salty air. The starry sky. That's all he has. But those fragments poke him like slivers in his mind. He wakes with them and sleeps with them, and pictures of a lighthouse, of the stars, they fill his room, though he doesn't know why. To his recollection, I am the first person with which he has shared them.

And so we go searching for his impressions. Faint and buried. I have gone many places during these days. But if I could help free him, if I could give him the gift of clarity ... If we could find this Lightkeeper, I would consider my trip a success.

Send.

I peeked up at Elias, now tracing the map with his finger. It was entirely possible that the object of this search had no basis in reality. But even if the quest was for a myth, it had already taken effect, pulling from me my first heartfelt post.

FFA: You didn't ask for money.

Me: Huh? Oh, I didn't ...

FFA: Wisconsin is very beautiful.

Me: How would you know?

FFA: I've been there a couple times.

Me: With your parents ...

FFA: Sure.

Me: I don't believe you. I'll wager you're an average bloke who's never left London and never will leave London, and soon you'll be riding the Underground to your dead-end job, and one day you will look at your life and wonder why you wasted it all.

FFA: And I'll wager this entire site is a sham.

I slammed shut my laptop. Nobody had ever questioned me before. FFA had to believe me. Of all people, he had to believe me. I couldn't lose my confidant and the only decent boy I knew, other than Elias, of course. I slowly peeked at the screen.

FFA: I'm sorry, Clara. I didn't mean that. Tell me about this companion.

FFA: Clara?

FFA: Clara????

Me: Here.

FFA: I apologize. Please. Tell me about your companion.

Me: Just a bloke.

FFA: Anything more?

I relaxed.

Me: Would that bother you?

FFA: It might.

Elias climbed into the car.

Me: Gotta go.

For the second time, I shut my computer. Even though Elias couldn't read a word on the screen, I needed FFA safely on the other side of the pond.

It felt an unusual variety of cheating, in which my steady consisted of an anonymous avatar, and the other guy was, well, half of Elias.

"Who was that?"

I stroked the top of my computer. "A mate."

"Does he think you're crazy?"

I slipped the computer back into my backseat bag. "You were staring at that map a long time. Did you find what you were looking for?"

Elias shrugged.

I exhaled long and slow. "I was beginning to wonder if you would ever come out."

Still, silence.

"Fine. I don't know what he thinks. He's a boy from London. I've never met him. Yes, he probably thinks I'm crazy." I lay my head on Elias's shoulder. "Am I?"

He lay his head against mine. "I better get some sleep."

We threw back our seats and soon drifted away.

CHAPTER 13

I traveled long distances in that dream. London was as I remembered, dreary and grey. Teeter and Marna were decorating their walls with marker and crayon. This act, above all others, turned Mum's remaining strength to wrath.

"Stop it," I said, and they both spun. I expected them to rush into my arms. After all, it was nearly a year since I'd been home.

They did not move.

"You're back," said Teeter. "Did you enjoy your trip?"

"I-I don't know that I would use the word 'enjoy'."

Marna stood. "You were gone a long time."

"Yes. I'm sorry."

"Are you?" asked Teeter. "You left us alone."

At this point, I felt the terror of loose footing. That maybe this wasn't the real world. Maybe I also had slipped through.

I peeked up at my flat's ceiling, but could see no light.

"You were hardly alone," I said. "I waited until the day Dad was returning. Children left with a parent are not alone."

Marna and Teeter both frowned and looked at each other. Teeter marched toward me. "What Dad?"

And a ball, not a golf ball but a wrecking ball, shifted in my belly. I ran out of their bedroom and through the flat. "I'm back. Where is everyone?"

I found Mum in the kitchen, slumped over in a chair. Her head rested on the table. Her arms hung down at her sides.

"Blasted again."

I found the exit to the dream and slowly floated away from the scene, feeling very alone and wondering if my mum had been blasted after all.

My eyes opened.

My body was stiff. I rubbed the back of my neck and peered toward the east, where the sun hinted its arrival. Dawn had come to Wisconsin, and FFA was right: with colourful trees and rolling hills, it was beautiful.

"We should get go—"

He already had.

I jumped out of the car and ran through the rest area. I circled the building and dashed back, searching the back of the car. His bag was gone. The feeling of the dream returned, and I panicked. I would like to say my mind's concern was fixed on Elias, but if FFA were here, I would admit to a different truth.

I was nervous for myself. Floating around this world was a boy who might know my most terrible secret. What could he see? Did he hear the scream? Did he see my Dad's shouts? Perhaps non-god was getting even.

A gnawing loneliness worked through me, and I needed to find Elias. Guinevere had certainly discovered our departure. This responsibility was not lost on me.

I turned the key and squealed backward. East. He would head east, perhaps waiting for dawn to guide his way.

I accelerated onto the motorway. With every mile covered, there was less chance of finding him, and five miles down the road there was still no sign.

And then there was.

Elias walked on the side of the road, his pace brisk and his thumb extended. I slowed to a stop and lowered the passenger window.

"Just where did you think you were off to? I thought we had a deal. I thought we were in this together!" I pushed out of the car and rounded the bonnet, carrying equally the urges to smack and hug him. I stopped well into his personal space. "Have you nothing to say for yourself?" I jabbed him in the chest with my pointer. "How could you just leave me alone?"

"Leave you? I thought you left me."

I stepped back. "I was right there in the car. What notion filled your brain ... Ah. I see, left you for FFA," I said, and the thought made me smile. "Oh, Elias, I've never seen him. We aren't together, so no worries."

"You've never seen who?"

"FFA. The one who you ... you thought I was with." I paused. "He is what this drama was all about, isn't he?"

"Listen. I don't know who you're talking about. I went for a walk and you disappeared. How can I trust you if you aren't reliable? This quest is no small matter."

The Other One.

"I didn't disappear. You started walking. It was you." I slumped back against the car. How short my moments with the coherent Elias were becoming. Six hours. That's as long as I had him, and I slept away the time.

"But you're right. It is no small matter." I opened the passenger door. "Please, get in the car. We have some distance to travel, correct?"

He ducked his head inside and pulled it back out. "What do you know about the destination?"

Lighthouse. Salt air.

Lightkeeper.

"Nothing, but I am sure you will tell me, test me at the appropriate time."

Elias rolled his bag over the seat and climbed in. I slowly walked around the back. According to my mobile, we were thirty-four hours from the coast. We could be there and back in three days. A frightening three for Guinevere, but perhaps forgivable under the circumstances.

With the sun in my face, and the feeling of loneliness fading to memory, I pulled back onto the road.

"As you surely know, Salem is a very strangely shaped country. One moment you're in it, the next you are not," Elias said.

"Yes. I've noticed that. One moment in, next moment out."

"Your importance as my guide cannot be overstated. As we search for ... as we journey, we must remain in Salem. The country is surrounded by enemies, as dangerous as the one we've been sent to find ..." He paused. "Only in Salem will we be safe."

So we're looking for an enemy.

Elias dug in his back pocket and removed a folded wad. "It's time you saw the map. This will keep us on track." He unfolded it and spread it over his lap. I glanced over and cleared my throat.

"That ... is an autumn constellation map."

"That is correct."

"Which, if we were looking for Andromeda, may serve a useful purpose, but we're not looking for small points of light, are we?"

At this, Elias hinted a grin. A rarity. "Not points of light."

"A Lightkeeper." I shook my finger toward the sky.

Elias quickly folded the star finder. "What do you know about that? Where did you hear that name?"

How firmly I had judged those at the inn. How cruel, I thought, to gamble for Elias's delusions. But as I listened to him, I could not escape it. This is who he was right now: the Other Elias. This was him. The real world had gone, and Salem was all that remained.

"My position as ... as your queen's—"

"Daughter, certainly. She would have mentioned the Lightkeeper to her own daughter. Do you have any ideas where we need to go?"

"The East Coast, perhaps? With lighthouses and salty air? She said nothing concrete."

"My sense exactly. So we will use this map and your manual and piece together the precise location. See ..." He swept his hands over the map. "As long as these stars show in the sky, we can be certain we are in Salem. I suggest especially watching for Orion. Based on its position, we can remain in Salem while we journey east."

"Is that so?"

Elias nodded. "So during the day, we cannot travel or we may end up entering another country entirely. We will stop each morning in Salem and wait for night to fall. If it's clear, and we see Orion in the correct position, we'll know we're still on track."

I frowned. "Or we could just drive to the coast."

Elias's voice turned hard. "You are my guide, and my queen's daughter, so I trust you with my life. But *I* was placed in charge of this quest. You need to trust me with yours. Trust me with how we should proceed: Only at night. Only beneath Orion. Always east. Oh, and one last item. As we pass through Salem, it would be best if we were not known. Our high profiles make us desirable targets. I think we should change our names."

A burn ignited deep within me. My name. Was it beautiful? Was it homely? It didn't matter. It was mine. Untouched by anyone since my birth.

"I would very much like to keep my name."

"Then at least *use* another. For our protection." He thought. "Clarita. How does that sound?"

"Awful," I said.

"Good, and what would you like to call me?"

This is a very bad time to ask me this question.

"Clarita?" he asked.

Words forced out from between gritted teeth. "Jason Bourne."

"Jason. That will work fine. Now, daylight is almost here. We'll need to stop shortly. Clarita, will you kindly guide this vehicle to the center of Salem? And we will wait for evening to head further east."

"Sure, *Jason.*" I removed my mobile, my voice a mutter. "The center of Salem. There is no Salem. You need proof? Here, watch me enter the term Salem, Wisconsin. Watch absolutely nothing ... pop ... up."

I stared at the screen.

"What does your machine read?" So confident, I wanted to smack him.

"There is one. Salem, Wisconsin, located in Kenosha County, between Milwaukee and Chicago ..."

"Of course there is. How long until our arrival?" asked the new Jason.

"A couple hours."

"That's more daylight driving than I'd like, but it'll need to do. Wake me when we arrive."

Minutes later, Jason slept deep and content.

I drove agitated and confused. In the recent past, I had forfeited my name, feigned citizenship in Salem, and now was driving toward the center of my new homeland.

"London is home. London is home." My breathed mantra confused me still more. Not since Dad was whisked away had home carried a positive charge. I gladly allowed England's memories to fade. But now they were an anchor.

Home was falling through the cracks.

I blinked hard and focused on the road, allowing my thoughts to travel on paths that led back to Marbury Street.

Clarita. How does that sound?

Clarita. Clara.

Home.

CHAPTER 14

One half hour.

In one half hour, we would reach the town of Salem, and the lunacy would reignite. My mother would be hailed as queen, and I would slip back into character.

I drove through morning waiting for my cue.

Elias slept, and I took my gaze off the road to stare at his face. It was perfect.

"Which one will wake?" I wondered, and pushed my hand through his hair. He shifted and slowly opened his eyes. I smiled, and he smiled back.

"Where are we?"

"Miles from Salem."

He straightened, and pressed his nose against the window, at an encroaching tree line that advanced right up to the road. And what trees they were! Like arthritic hands thrust out of the ground, they twisted toward the sky. But unable to reach it, they gnarled in on themselves. Most disconcerting.

Behind them, stalks of corn stretched to the horizon. We were on a road seldom traveled, and Elias glanced over at me.

"Tell me a story, Clara."

"You called me Clara?" I asked.

"Is there another name I should know?"

I breathed deep. "No. Clara is the proper name. A story. Well, let's see. Have I told you about my family? My sibs or my 'rents?"

"No. I thought maybe you hatched."

I slapped his shoulder. "I have them. I have a father—at least I did. Let's see, a story … He came home and announced that he and I were going on a date. This wasn't unusual. Dad often took me to Pasqualy for ice cream. But this time he added, 'We won't return home until next week, so pack extra clothes.' I remember squealing with joy. I don't remember why."

"Attention maybe? You were probably getting everything you wanted from him. Your dad and you, alone," Elias said quietly.

"I was young. Eight. Maybe nine. We ferried our auto across the Channel to France, and began to drive. I don't think he had a route in mind. We just drove and sang his stupid songs at the top of our lungs. We sang until I laughed, and then I laughed so hard I cried, and then we sang some more. We sang our way through Europe, south, south, always south toward the sea."

I paused. "It's been a long time since I've sung."

And in each town, it was the same routine. Dad would pull up to the pub or the church, it didn't matter which. "Stay in the car, my Clara." He'd disappear for a moment and return, and then we did have a route. We drove to the shabbiest home in town—old ones, leaning ones—and pulled up the drive. "Knock and hand them this. Tell them it's from a friend, a friend from afar." He would hand me fifty pounds, and I would run to the door and hand them money, and together my dad and I crossed the continent, giving away all our savings.

We reached Italy and sat staring out at the sea. His arm was around me and we had no money, but I never wanted to leave. And he sang, gently. I just listened to his voice and the waves and watched the sun set over the Mediterranean.

We slept in the car on the way back; he had only enough money for food and ferry. I couldn't wait to tell Mum about our trip.

So I did.

Dad slept in the car again that night. Mum was so irate, she would not let him in the house. I climbed out of bed and snuck out to where he was and crawled beside him. And he sang me a lullaby."

I shook my head. "I have no idea what the fool was thinking. All the money he gave away could have saved us when he chose the slammer over his family."

"Sounds like you gave it away too."

"Weren't you listening? I was nine."

"He sounds like a good man."

"You know nothing—"

"Stop!"

Elias reached for the wheel and gave it a tug. We swerved into the ditch, narrowly missing two gnarled trees before I regained control and weaved back onto the road.

I slammed on the brakes and yanked the key from the ignition.

"Rule number one. Never! Never touch this wheel. Rule number two ..."

He didn't hear rule number two.

Elias pushed out of the Fiat and rounded the auto, knocking feverishly on my window.

I tried to join him outside, but the door bounced against his knee and slammed shut. I fought to lower the window. "As I was saying, rule number two—"

"Give me fifty pounds." He thrust his hand into the car. I slapped it and pushed it back outside. "You are not giving—" I peeked over his shoulder. "The Antique Barn does not need my fifty pound ... dollars. I have dollars. You are not giving them fifty dollars."

"How many dollars is fifty pounds?"

"Seventy-five, maybe eighty, but it doesn't matter! You're not giving it to them. Yes, it looks dilapidated, and I'm certain they could use it."

Elias placed his hand on my shoulder. "It's not a gift; I'm buying something from them." He stretched his hand toward the front lawn. "Look at that beauty."

It took a bit of time to narrow down his interest. The Antique Barn's property was littered with junk. Signs and tools and rusted motors, all meters from the road. But when I followed his gaze, there was no missing it.

"You want to buy an aeroplane."

Elias's face lit.

"But the fuselage is riddled with holes. There's no propeller. There's one wing."

"These hands can rebuild it." He lifted both paws to show me.

I slumped down in my seat and slapped my own over my face. "And it's bloomin' big. It's a plane! There's no room in the trunk of a Fiat."

Seconds went by, no answer, and I peeked up. No Elias.

And then he reappeared, giddy.

"This car has a hitch." He placed his hand on my shoulder. "Clara, let me do this. This would be ... real."

I straightened. "Is anything about you real?"

He quickly glanced over his shoulder, an eager puppy.

"And you can what, make this auto pull that? And you can fix it? For what? You aren't flying it. The last time I let you into one of your contraptions ..."

Elias slowly, with a shaking hand, swept the hair off my face. I could think of no more objections.

"You're going to need more than eighty dollars. I'll meet you there." I restarted the car, performed a neat u-turn, and pulled into the driveway of the shop.

Together, we surveyed the junk, and I slapped my hand over his mouth. "Let me do the talking. All of it."

He nodded, and I lowered my palm. We entered the two-story building. "Horrors." I sighed.

There were no words for the interior. Every meter was home to mounds of rubbish, none of which seemed worthy to sell. But Elias poked about with interest. I wandered to the counter, and read aloud the large sign hand painted in crimson:

Welcome to The Antique Barn, where a handshake seals the deal.

"Elias? I have another rule. Do not shake anyone's hand. Do we understand each other?"

"Who do we have here, poking around my treasures?"

An older man, greying and paunchy, stood on the bottom step, leaning heavily against the railing.

"I need to have that plane," Elias blurted.

"Elias!" I turned back toward the gentleman. "We're just browsing about your shop."

"Hmm." The owner grinned. "So you don't really need the plane."

"Yes, we do!" Elias pounded the counter. I eased him back.

"No, we don't."

"Seems to be dissention in the ranks." He winked at me. "Name's Kirby. Any interest in taking a closer look?"

Elias pumped his fist. "Absolutely!"

"Come around the counter, son. We'll take the side door, leave Miss Negativity to continue her browsing."

They both exited. "Absolutely no negotiating prowess whatsoever." I puffed the hair off my face, and followed.

Elias was already circling the plane. "So what do you want for her?"

"Getting right to it, huh?" Kirby removed a tin of Copenhagen and offered some to Elias. "It'll give you hair on your chest."

"Don't need hair. Just the plane."

He slipped the tobacco back into his flannel coat pocket and stroked the piece of junk. "I'm conflicted, son. Really, I am. I'd love to let you experience the roar of flight, the wind in your hair. But it ain't just a matter of what I got into her, not with Bessy here. She done become a symbol of my store, which is my life. Lettin' her go would be like lettin' go the heart of the place, lettin' go my name."

Elias has no problem asking for that.

Elias doubled over and felt under the plane, and soon stood holding a chunk of rusted metal from its underside. "How much, Mr. Kirby?"

"Then there's the sentimental piece. I flew her myself, when I was not much older than yourself. I flew her north in the Canadian lands. Rugged, lonely places. Me and Bessy, well, we come through a lot of weather together. And don't think you're the first to try and separate the two of us."

"Price?" Elias pressed.

"Got all her parts in back. Every one. Just need a few days a' peace to set her to rights and we'll be sailing the blue skies again." Kirby spit a grotesque wad onto the ground.

Elias stood, waiting.

"Son, I can't see letting a functioning piece of aeronautical machinery go for less than fifty."

"Fifty thousand?" Elias asked.

"It's just a thing, ain't it?"

"Deal."

"Deal?" Kirby stepped back.

"Deal?" I ran toward Elias.

"Deal." Elias slapped the side and reached out his hand. Kirby quickly grasped it, and I groaned.

"Clara, I just sealed the deal. I just purchased a functioning aircraft!"

"With whose money?" I asked, offering him my most horrid gaze.

"Well now, functioning is in the eye of the beholder," Kirby fisted the nose of the plane.

"Not true," said Elias. "You told me you could fix her up in a few days. We'll be back through to pick up my functioning piece of aeronautical machinery, isn't that right, Clara?"

I lifted up my palms. "For fifty thousand?"

"Now, hold on." Kirby pointed at the plane. "I never agreed to fix nothin'."

"But you did say you could. We agreed on a price for a working aircraft. So let's see those parts you are going to put on her."

Kirby removed his baseball cap and scratched his head. "Thinkin' more on it now, time gone by and all, I can't quite recall their *exact* location."

"So the plane doesn't work ..."

Kirby furrowed his brows. "Well, maybe we can come down a bit on that price."

I sighed. "Jolly well time—"

"No, sir." Elias interrupted. "I took you as a man of your word. I want my functioning aircraft."

"Persistent kid, aren't ya? You remind me of my own. Listen, son. Maybe I let my enthusiasm tilt the truth a little. Here's the honest of it. The vert stabilizer and the rudder are smashed to bits. There, I done said it."

Elias folded his arms. "I needed those. I trusted you. It'll cost me tens of thousands for those parts alone. We shook on it ..."

And in that moment, Elias's insanity turned to brilliance.

"And a handshake seals the deal," I added.

Elias nodded. "It should, so I don't feel right going back on you. I tell you what, I will let you sell it to me, with all the parts but those two, for forty thousand."

I dashed inside the shop, grabbed Kirby's handshake sign, and returned to Elias's side. Kirby read his own undoing, glared at me, and faced Elias with a sigh.

"And as long I'm bein' completely above board, I haven't seen the other wing or its flaps for some time. Not the propeller either."

"Hmm. Well, I wish I knew that earlier." Elias winced and shook his head. "That wing plus flaps? Even used, an easy twenty grand. Five grand for the propeller. Five more to patch the fuselage. I really shouldn't be so generous, but if I subtract those items?"

"Elias, you did shake on it," I said.

"You're right. It wouldn't be right to go back on a deal." He turned to Kirby. "Okay, I'll do it. You may sell it to me for ten thousand."

My, but Kirby was red-faced. "Nose wheel! Top of the engine cowl! Both elevators! But that's all that's gone. The engine is solid, all there."

"Great." Elias turned to me. "Clara, allowing for those pieces, it looks like we owe Mr. Kirby one thousand dollars for this function-ing piece of aeronautical machinery. But I was also looking at that steel-framed trailer out back. What do you want for it?"

Kirby's foot began a furious tap, and his jaw muscles bulged and loosed.

"Oh, shoot. A hundred bucks for the trailer and get yourself gone. And don't think me or mine'll help you move either piece of trash."

Kirby spun, paused, and looked back over his shoulder. He offered me a quick nod, his eyes twinkling.

I walked up to Elias. "Impressive."

"Yeah, only if we can get this secured on the trailer. I need you to go into the next town and find some help. Big guys. I'll need a bunch of them."

"You're asking me to leave you. What if . . ."

He gently took my face in his hands, held it softly. "I'm solid."

"Solid. Right. I'll be back soon."

• • • • •

SALEM

Unincorporated town

I sped into town, swung a sharp right on Antioch Road, and came to a complete stop. A Citgo, two vacant buildings, a row of homes, and that was it.

"Hardly the metropolis."

I eased forward, looking for where blokes might congregate. Finding boys had not been a problem this last year. Extracting myself had. But now the fluttering feeling I had for Elias made my concerns irrelevant. I needed lads. Lots of them.

Elias could already have slipped back beyond my reach, and if he did, he would not hesitate to set out alone.

I pulled into the Thrift Trip car park and hurried to the door. I shoved, but it wouldn't give. Three shoves later, the neon *open* sign still mocked me, and I pounded on the window.

"Push a little!" a voice muffled out from inside.

I'm trying, you daft idiot!

The door flew open and a man stood in my path. Thin, gaunt— not the type I was seeking.

"I need to find some men."

His eyes roamed me uncomfortably up and down. "Don't think that'll be too hard."

"Can you tell me where I should look?"

"Pretty much."

"I don't know what that means."

He pointed toward the door, and gestured beyond and to the left. "Siebert's Pub. I'm thinking you'll find what you're lookin' for."

"Guys?"

"Pretty much."

I forced my way out the door and drove across the street. He was right.

Blasted boys spilled out of the pub, a beautiful cream-coloured two-story with white fencing and a large porch fronting Antioch. They joked and jostled, beer in one hand, trouble in the other, and I felt a pang of worry.

These were the scenes to avoid, the places to turn and flee. I knew this. I'd experienced it. But there was no choice. Elias gave me no choice.

I zipped into the park and exited the car. A group of twenty blokes gathered on the porch.

"Hey!" I yelled. "I need a favour."

It took five seconds for the porch to empty and the circle to re-form around my Fiat.

"Favours." A voice cawed, dark and ugly. "I'm good at favours."

"Why you?" Another laughed.

"I'm just sayin', the girl needs something, and I'm the one to give it to her."

And just like that, I was in the middle of a small riot. Normally, I'd have watched it play out, but I hadn't the time.

"Don't you want to hear what I need?" I asked.

Silence.

"I need the strongest of you. I bought an aeroplane, and I need it hoisted onto a trailer of sorts."

"A plane?" The loudest of the lot stepped forward, held out his beer, and when I shook my head, took another swig. "You bought that old pile a junk plane near Emerald Grove? Where you gonna fly to, girl? Why leave so soon?"

"Is there anybody else other than this inebriated cabbage who might feel inclined to do a kind thing?"

The majority fell into a confused silence, but not the blowhard. "What was those words you said? Was that some type of insult?"

I pushed by him and out of the ring, and marched straight into the pub. The age of those collapsed over the bar put me at ease.

"Excuse me!" I raised a chair and let it thud to the floor. "I need a hand moving an aeroplane, and those boys outside don't seem too interested in helping."

"Yeah, well, they don't mean much harm. This town doesn't give 'em much to do. Exceptin' the obvious." The voice came from above, and I walked to the stairs and climbed.

I stopped on the second floor, face to face with normal. A normal man, wearing a sensible shirt, sensible jeans, and sporting a sensible attitude.

He glanced at me with a safe glance. "Now that I look at you, I see the problem. I'm Haller, by the way, proud owner of the quieter establishment next store."

I peeked out the window. "Chubby's Pizza?"

"No, no." He smiled. "Look past that. The Ranch Sweet Shop and U-Haul."

I wandered by him. "And this place up here?"

"The old boarder house. Back in the day, the train depot was below and folks'd stay the night up here. Still can." He smiled. "If you can get by the wanderers below. There's nothing else in Salem left of what was. An abandoned jail. An old silo. But the rest is gone."

"Haller, I really do need moving help."

"Probably won't find it in this town. Not now."

"Then I need to get back." I hurried down the stairs, and out into the thick of competition. The lot of them had set up picnic tables, with the loud mouth locked in an arm wrestling battle with a larger lad.

"Hey! England girl!" The cabbage winced and grunted. "You want to know who's the strongest?"

I didn't slow. I hopped into my car and gunned the engine. The crowd parted, and I squealed back down the road, saw the Sweet Shop, and screeched into the turnaround. I had to reach Elias quickly, but my nerves placed me in no condition to help, I was starving for moments with a rational mate.

I grabbed my computer and my uplink. I needed FFA.

Help Support Children of Incarcerated Parents
500 Days of Wandering, 500 Days of Hope
Day 246

Still in Wisconsin. Somewhat desperate. I need to find help rather quickly. Keep me in your thoughts. I'm losing time, and I never know how much time he has. He fades in and out, and when I last saw him, he was solid, but that could change in an instant. Last time I slept through him. We passed in my dreams, and when I woke, he was gone. Now, I'm in another town, and I don't know what to do. It's just a stupid aeroplane. This makes no sense. I know. But nothing does anymore.

Send.

FFA: Marna is ill.

Me: She often is. Fevers and the sort. Wait, how do you know the state of my sibs?

Me: Hello? I demand an answer!

FFA: Very ill.

I took a deep breath.

Me: Go on ...

FFA: I stopped in yesterday.

Me: You have just crossed a line about which we have never
    spoken!! You know where I live? How long have you known??

FFA: I'm on Upper Marbury. You're on Lower. But that doesn't
    matter. Marna is ill.

Me: Never write me again!!!!

I'd never raged at FFA before—he alone had been my constant
friend across five continents. Try as I might, I couldn't hate him now,
even after his intrusion. Somehow, he had become ... necessary.

I stared at my blinking cursor. He wasn't writing. I couldn't bear it.

Me: Listen, she just needs rest. She'll scam out of a school for a
    few weeks, and then she'll look almost human. She'll return
    to classes and her teachers will rip into her. Everything will
    be set to rights. She doesn't need you. Dad can handle it.

FFA: Marna won't stop crying, at least yesterday. Is it always like
    that?

Me: I said she doesn't need you! Stay away from my family.
    And if you tell my dad where I am, I will fly home and
    strangle you.

FFA: I just thought you might want to know ... If I'm honest, it's
    not the first time I've stopped in. Your dad, your sibs—Clara,
    it's a mess. You might want to come ...

I slammed shut my computer and stepped out of the car. Upper
Marbury? So he was wealthy. Sure, he lived in London, just not *my*
London. Upper Marbury was home to spacious gardens and fancy
boutiques, and at least one do-gooder. FFA probably was assigned

charity work in school, and Lower Marbury was a great place to find the desperate.

Marna's ill. I need to be there. I could be in twelve hours. I could be wiping her brow with a damp face towel the way I had for Mum. All I'd have to do is leave Elias.

"England girl!" A cabbagy voice, ugly and familiar from down the street.

"Everyone, just sod off and leave me alone!"

There had to be somewhere in this town to think.

I strode fast and strong and angry through the streets of Salem, my new country. Thoughts entered, slipped free, and new thoughts took their place: thoughts of a lurking lad who looked after my family and a sister lying in a bed and never getting up.

Ahead was the silo and the prison, and my legs carried me to the latter. A one-room cinder-block building with curved roof and wooden doors. Bars still filled the two small windows, and I peeked into the blackness and ducked inside.

It, too, was filled with junk, and so seemed a suitable spot for me. I stepped over a wheelbarrow and crawled to the back of the dank and dark and spidery room, where I plunked in the corner, drawing my knees up to my face.

What was Dad doing? He certainly wouldn't know how to care for Marna. I alone had seen her through her illnesses. Now that Dad and FFA were besties, they probably played cards while Marna coughed up a lung.

And I rocked, and swore, and rocked until no more words came.

Afternoon turned to evening and then to night.

Through the small window, stars came out, maybe the same ones Mum watched from the other side and Dad saw from London.

Marna or Elias. What do I do?

I hummed the lullaby Dad used to hum, and felt my mobile vibrate.

Clara, I need u. Been using Drew's car a lot for lots of things, u know? He always put on the brakes, until last night. Nobody here to talk to. I need you. Come back. K.

I stared at Kira's text. Flippin' everybody needed me, and no matter who I helped, I would be letting others down. Marna. FFA. Now Kira.

Real people with real problems.

I was still stuck in Wonderland.

CHAPTER 15

have just spent an entire night in prison! On purpose ... I have decisions to make ..."

I slammed shut the door to the sweet shop and stared at Haller. He took off his glasses and set them on the counter.

"So that's where you went. It's a rough old jailhouse." He shook his head. "Your crime must have been heinous."

I squinted, shielding the sunlight with my hand. "Which crime? The long-ago one? The best friend one? The sister one? What if she doesn't recover? How could I lose another? Then there's the Elias issue."

"I'm not sure of all your offenses, but I do know even prisoners get hungry and thirsty. I can take care of that." He straightened. "Besides, sure sounds like your thoughts have been punishment enough."

I'd actually done precious little thinking over the past day. I was too busy feeling, feeling as I hadn't allowed myself to for months. Most criminals leave prison harder, tougher, but this abandoned jail had the opposite effect on me.

Haller gathered an assortment of chocolates and boiled sweets while I looked around the place.

It was cluttered inside, but cluttered in a manicured fashion. A red-and-white tablecloth hung smartly over a small table; behind it, plants and shelving and stuffed animals lined the walls. The Abominable Bumble from *Rudolph the Red-nosed Reindeer* guarded the calendar, and straight ahead was the most charming little ice cream shop/soda fountain I had seen.

"All hand-dipped in the back, mind you. You'll not find a better chocolate, and you look like you could use a few."

I stared at myself in the mirror. In the days since my arrival in Minnesota, I had narrowed, stretched.

I looked like Mum.

"Here you are." He rounded the corner of the counter and lay out a row of candies. "An assortment of ten, no cost to you." We sat at the table and I devoured the chocolates. "Where you from?"

"London."

"Can't say as I remember a Londoner in these parts."

I continued stuffing. "It's a peculiar story. This is Salem, right?"

"Technically. But like I said, this is only a remnant of Salem. The heart of it has died. The bustle. The railroad. Gone. Not many who remember what was." Haller rubbed the stubble on his face. "So what's this about an airplane?"

Elias.

"Blast, I should probably check on the lad ... I need to go." I pushed back from the table.

"You're sure free to leave. I just can't help wondering what's gotten a girl like you in such a confusion."

I pause. "Have you ever run from reality? Have you ever run because reality was too much, too suffocating, too ... just too? And then you find a fiction. And the fiction feels more real than the real ever did. Have you ever felt like that?"

Haller took a deep breath. "No. No, I can't say as I have. I do know that fiction ...." He picked up an empty chocolate wrapper and tossed it into the trash. "It eventually becomes a mighty poor substitute for what's real." He popped the last chocolate into his mouth.

"I really can't stay any longer," I said.

"Off to it. Find your fiction." Haller pointed to a picture on the wall, his eyes wistful. A woman. His love, I was sure of it. "Sometimes fiction is all you've got, and however long they stay, well, who am I to provide counsel on reality. Does this fiction warm your heart? Does he make you feel alive?"

I paused. "Half the time."

"And the other half?"

"I'm using him to try and get information I want."

He sighed. "Not so foreign after all. Young lady, as we say 'round here, looks like you're in a heap a mud."

"A heap of mud," I repeated, pushing back from the table. "My heap is waiting."

Twenty minutes later, I pulled up in front of the Antique Barn. The plane was gone, the property silent.

"Elias!"

I burst through the door, noted the "handshake" sign glued and returned to its original place. "Elias!"

I ran around back. "Mr. Kirby? Elias?"

It's been too many hours.

"Follow the path, young lady!" A husky voice came from the woods.

I veered down the dirt road and into a shack, and there stood Elias and Kirby, with the aeroplane resting on the trailer; Elias's face one big grin.

"I was hoping you'd come back soon. I've done all I can with parts from the shop." Elias hopped down off a wing. "We owe Mr. Kirby another two hundred. Sorry, we shook on it, so it's a done deal."

I stared at the plane, patched and fixed to the trailer. It had a fresh coat of paint, and for a one-winged craft, it was actually rather beautiful.

"But how did you ..."

"Turns out Mr. Kirby is quite a guy. Comes from a family of ten."

"A mighty strong ten." Kirby straightened. "Ah, shoot, your boy won me over. Nobody can call me unreasonable, and watchin' him slave alone? Well, the whole brood pitched in to move the thing."

"Clara, there's something you need to see."

Elias took my hand and led me toward the back of the fuselage. "I told Mr. Kirby that Bessy sounded too bovine. I needed something wild and free. He hand-painted it."

I quietly mouthed the words:

Clara

A Light in the Sky

"She's not quite as pretty as you, but maybe when I'm done with her ..."

I walked over to Elias and hugged him. It was true; I was stuck in some deep mud. But this mud did feel soft and warm.

Marna will pull out of it, whatever it is.

The thought did not soothe.

Elias stepped out of my arms and frowned. "What happened? You look so tired."

"I'll just leave you two alone." Kirby stepped out of the shack.

I gently took hold of Elias's head, squeezing it between my palms.

"We're chasing wind. We're going to a place you can't name in search of something you can't find. It's not real. None of this is real. A Lightkeeper? What is that? You don't know. Either of you. Especially the Other One, the you who calls me Clarita and wants me to read the stars. That's crazy. This is crazy. And at home, things are happening. Real things. Real ... things."

Elias swallowed and stroked the plane, his fingers pausing on my name. "You should leave. You're right. Everything you say is right." He took hold of my forearms and pulled free, his strong hands clutching mine. "I'm presently of sound mind, and I release you from any promise you ever made to me or Mom or ... the Other One." He forced a smile, and sighed. "You should go."

I lifted up my arms, and let them flop at my sides. "That's not what I'm asking for! Can you give me anything more? A purpose for this trip. A reason."

Elias climbed slowly back inside the plane. "Have you ever felt safe? Completely and utterly? That's what I feel when I think of the Lightkeeper. I have no fears. I just know everything's all right. I don't feel that at any other time, except maybe a little with you." He glanced around at his creation and hopped down. "I don't know the reason the Other One is looking for this Keeper."

I stepped nearer. "The Other One thinks it's your enemy."

"No. Not true. Can't be." Elias shook his head. "I would like to find out."

I stood for a moment. "When did you get sick?"

Elias folded his arms. "Guess I won't be needing the trailer."

I shoved his chest, but it had no effect, and I tapped my finger on his skull. "Stay with my question up here. When?"

"I can get myself home. It's 20,005 bumps in the road until we're through Wisconsin."

"Answer my question!"

"When." Elias sighed. "Eight. It's what Mom says."

I started to pace. "Think about that. Both you and the Other One share a memory. A word. A phrase. Some impressions. It's the same memory, before the one of you became two. Good for you, horrifying for him, but the same memory. If anyone knows how to set your mind to rights, it would be this Lightkeeper. Maybe this Lightkeeper can ... reconnect you, and you'll be just, shall we say, you. That's a reason not to quit."

"I don't think it works that way."

"But maybe?"

Elias grinned. "It would be medically impossible, miraculous maybe."

"Yes." I nodded. "An unheard of; miraculous maybe. That's hope enough. Let me get the car."

I walked away from the shack swelling with optimism. Why hadn't I seen it before? The existence of a unifier before Elias's split meant that unifier was more than a key to his recovery ... On it rested the hope of his entire quest. Stars and Salem—all that talk was foolishness. But this memory was real, and worth the search. Medically sound reasoning? No. But at least logical to me. Whatever I had to do to discover the memory's origin, I would do.

To heal a boy with a sick mind. To bring him back to life.

It couldn't take away my shame, but if Little Thomas were here, he would have approved.

CHAPTER 16

My second trip into Salem was less frantic than the first, though it carried as much purpose. Somewhere ahead lay the key, the connecting memory in Elias's mind. And although it seemed a miracle that it should be found, it also seemed the only thing worth searching for.

I was rather certain that I was the first Fiat to pull a plane sided by a boy with two identities through Salem, Wisconsin. That thought was fleeting. As I drove by the chocolate shop, the weight of my surroundings overpowered.

"It's empty. There's nothing here," said Elias.

"An old prison and a combination sweet shop and U-Haul rental, but otherwise you're right."

"And this is where the Other One wanted to visit?"

"Salem is on the street sign, and that's enough for him." I slowed on Antioch Road, watching residents pause and stare in front of tiny houses. They were guarded, but I was too, and even through the glass our tension fed off each other.

"So, where do we go now?" Elias asked.

My stomach fell. Sanity provided me no answers.

"We need the Other One, the paranoid one. If I'm going to help keep you real, I need to step into his hallucination, and I need you to let me."

"You *want* me to disappear?"

I looked off. No. The part of me who saw in Elias the same trusting eyes of Little T? No, that part wanted him to stay, and stay forever. But the Other Me ... the me desperate to discover what he knew about my great shame? That me needed the Other One. For direction. For more sketches. For the truth.

Oh, what a lying mess I was.

"Clara? I mean, do we really need the Other One to keep going?"

"Still figuring out the process." I turned back toward Elias. "I think the Other One gives me the narrative, speaks of the stars, and I am to interpret the signs."

"Can you interpret?"

"Well, I can tell stories."

"My mom tells stories." Elias's fingers tapped nervously. "But you have no clue what you're doing."

"That's true. I enter Salem into my GPS and perhaps off we'll go, but ..." I pulled into Cliff's Shooting Range and stopped the car. "He does seem to have ideas. They're cracked, but they're ideas. Maybe for the first time, we really do need him?"

Elias pushed out of the Fiat and slammed the door. I joined him and we leaned over the top of the car, staring at each other.

"I don't want to slip. I mean, it's frightening. I might never come back."

"He might be our only way to get you out permanently. It's a lot to ask, I know ... Are you willing?"

Elias pushed both hands through his hair. "But I can't just make him come. There's nothing I can do to control that."

Shots in the distance. I rounded the car. "Are you still taking medicine?"

He answered slowly. "Maybe."

"Elias. I want you to hear this. I am not leaving you. I will not leave you. I will stay with you until we figure this out."

He stared back, unblinking. "You want me to stop taking the stuff and see what happens. I already know. I get anxious. And my hands they, they start to lose their grip, and my feet go next, and then the floor opens and I'm gone. I'm down there. I see something like light, but the Other One, he doesn't let me up. Without meds, he probably won't need to."

"And he'll think he's in charge." I grabbed his hand and walked toward the aeroplane. I climbed in and gestured for Elias to do the same. The sun was going down. It seemed a nice place to spend the evening. "But he won't be in charge. We'll be using him to find this Lightkeeper and get you out, and hopefully it will be permanent."

My heart ached. I'd used many people on my trip, but never someone I cared for. My victims had faces. They never had names.

Elias's shoulders drooped, and his voice lowered. "Truth is, the stuff I take isn't working anyway. Doc was going to make a change, and I was going to go off my meds completely before starting the new one. I suppose I could . . . I mean, I could do it now. It's just that the pills, they're like security—bad security, but security."

"If you don't want to, I totally understand." I lay down on my back, looking up at Elias. "Come here."

He bent over halfway, and I reached my hand behind his neck. "We don't know how it works. But wouldn't it be worth it if there was no more fear . . ." I pulled him closer. "No more slipping." I pulled him nearer still, his face six inches from mine. "No more apart."

He tensed. "I'm scared."

"It is scary, leaving the familiar. Leaving the medication. Leaving—"

"No," Elias whispered, his breath quick and warm. "I'm scared of you."

I released his neck. "I am not exactly in a dominant position here."

"You'll leave. I mean, after a while of hanging around him, why would you stay? I'll be gone and I'll be a freak and then I'll be all alone."

I took a deep breath. "I will not go. I have only made one other vow in my life."

Elias twisted around and lay beside me, shoulder to shoulder. We stared in silence at the deepening stars.

"Your vow." Elias nudged me. "Did you keep it?"

I feigned sleep.

"Clara, I need to know if you kept it."

Another deep breath.

Some questions are best left unanswered.

• • • • •

I woke with the barrel of a gun inches from my nose.

My breath caught, and I slowly reached over to pinch Elias.

"Let 'im sleep." The gun tapped my fingers and I drew them back. "Ever killed anybody, Clara?"

Against the moonlit stars, the frame and voice hinted girl, but the gun and the question didn't fit.

I shook my head.

She gazed at me. "But you're running, right? You and him. You're running from something big, maybe something you did? Something he did?"

"Do I know you?" I whispered. "Is it money you're after? Perhaps I can help —"

"Get out." She cleared her throat and glanced about. "We need to walk."

A minute later, I was trudging through thick undergrowth, a girl with a gun stepping at my side.

"You knew my name," I said.

"You left your car door open. That's stupid number one around here. Stupid number two was not readin' the signs. *Range closes eight pm.* Still here after that? Cliff authorizes me to plug you with a bullet. It's been some time since I've pulled a trigger, but don't think I'm rusty."

She nudged me on with the barrel. Deeper we crunched, until there was no sign of sky and the path disappeared beneath our feet. Thick silence surrounded. Breath and the crack of branches — that's all there was. And then, as we broke into a clearing, sound returned. The licking tongues of a flickering fire, fronting the silhouette of a small cabin standing just beyond. Crickets chirped and water bubbled, and my captor motioned me toward a log beside the blaze.

Think, Clara. You've been in strange scrapes before . . .

My mind woke up.

"What's your name, then?"

She swept back her hair. My, she was beautiful, but in a different way than I'd known before. This girl was wild and fierce — traits I'd experienced in Kira — but more than that, she seemed noble. Dressed in army fatigues, she was an original, definitely one for my diary.

"Izzy, short for Lizzie, short for Isabelle, short for Isabelle Iv—, though if you call me anything but Izzy—"

"Yes, you'll shoot me. So, Izzy, you brought me here for what end?"

Izzy gently set her gun in a guitar case, and plopped down on the other side of the fire. "He as good looking in the daylight?"

I offered a Kira smirk. "He is more than adequate on the eyes."

"Thought so." She reached into a box and pulled out an apple. Juice flowed down her chin as she ate. "So, you're from Minnesota by the plates, but not by the accent."

"Australia, actually."

Izzy tossed the core into the air, grabbed the gun and fired. Bits of apple rained down on me. "Best not lie." She set her gun back down. "Don't think that because I like you, I won't kill you."

The breeze shifted, and the fire's smoke blanketed me, stung my eyes. I squinted and shielded my eyes, my throat thick and sore. When next I risked a peek, Izzy had moved nearer.

"Let me tell you about killing. It hurts," she continued, though her words didn't seem meant for me. "For a long time, it hurts. And you'll do anything to wipe the red off your hands ..." She turned abruptly. "But you wouldn't know about that, would you, Clara? Sophisticated Clara with the good-looking guy. Life has handed you roses. It hasn't given all of us roses."

I had no idea what to say, and I forced a smile.

"I've been stuck here a long time. I've been waiting for someone to show up and take the two of us away." Izzy patted her guitar case. "The guy looks tame, but you have the eyes. You're going to take me out of here."

I closed my eyelids. "Why are you doing this?"

"Because, Clara from across the pond, after slinking around this town for years, it's time for me to move on. This place has kept my gun loaded and kept me hidden, but it's hard living alone, and on the run. I'm betting you know that. Minnesota plates this far into Wisconsin? You're clearly heading east." She leaned forward. "You're going to take me with you. I've put in two long winters here. The real cold is coming. I don't take up much room."

"Izzy, this is complicated. It's not a normal jaunt."

"Okay." She moved over and plunked down next to me. "Let's simplify. I'm coming or I'll kill you."

No. Izzy was a big no. Three times she had mentioned killing in the span of five minutes. She was wild, or mad. Either way, she was unpredictable. Izzy couldn't threaten her way onto this journey. One crazy was enough to look after.

"Then you'll have to shoot me." I stood, turned my back on the fire ... and fled. Running, stumbling, toward the edge of the clearing in the direction I'd arrived. Remarkably, after fifteen minutes of searching, my feet found the trail, and I huffed back toward the plane.

I burst free of the woods. Ahead, a streetlight illuminated the aeroplane.

"Wake up, Elias! Wake up!"

I jumped onto the wing. The plane was empty. I peeked at the car, and my shoulders slumped. There he sat, passenger-side ready.

Izzy lounged in the back.

I slowly opened the driver's door.

"Clarita! I don't know how you do it. You found us a guard. She might come in handy."

"Elias, may we talk a moment?"

"No need." He nestled into his seat. "I agree with your assessment of the quest. She will be useful as we face the dangers ahead."

More lunacy.

I climbed inside. "Hello, Izzy, short for Lizzie, short for Isabelle, short—"

"You might wanna drive. The night is partly gone." She stroked her guitar case.

"Right." I started the ignition and paused. There, resting on the console, was a second sketch, a second hazy, shaded, unclear sketch. I slowly reached down and took hold of it.

A slipping figure, all hands and mouth, with a face twisted in horror. All around the face was motion and emotion, like a tortured Van Gogh. It alone was the focal point of the terror.

Like Mum had been that night.

I lowered the sketch onto my lap.

"Does that interest you, Clarita?"

"It disturbs me."

"And why would that be?" asked Elias. "You passed another test by providing a guard to secure our trip."

Gift. Mentalism. How he knew the opening moments of the Great Undoing no longer mattered. I just needed to see the credits; that is, if my heart could endure the show.

CHAPTER 17

Our search for the next Salem took us through Chicago. I knew it by the signs. I felt it by the tolls.

But I would not hurry. The best way to eliminate the limpet wedged in the backseat would be to make our travel so intolerably slow that she could bear it no longer.

I set the cruise control at forty and relished every honk.

"Clarita, why is everyone passing us?" Elias looked around. The disappointment in his voice was palpable, and tragic. I had gained a suspicious Izzy and I was losing a trusting Elias. The medicines' effects were quickly passing, and the boy who placed his faith in me was long gone, but I told myself he was still there, somewhere beneath, looking up, trying to escape.

Meanwhile, my transformation was complete. I had forced Elias into this state, yes, for him but also secretly for me. For what I stood to discover from the Other One. I wasn't like the boarders at Guinevere's inn; I was far more hideous. I didn't just wait for the Other One; I set him free.

My motives were as distinct as Elias's personalities, selfishness and selflessness alternately driving my actions.

And at the root of it all was Little T.

That one epic failure drove everything.

"I don't want to get pulled over," I said.

"Speed up."

The first two words from Izzy since we left.

"No."

"Speed up."

"No."

Elias, now Jason, was clearly uncomfortable with feminine conflict. He fidgeted and crossed and uncrossed his legs. "Maybe we should go Clarita's speed for an hour and then Izzy's speed for an hour."

"Speed up." Izzy's voice was soft and certain.

"No." Again, I matched her resolve.

"I can't have my guide and my guard arguing. How are we going to quietly find the Lightkeeper with all this bickering?"

"Toll ahead. Izzy, your turn to pay."

Her face bunched in the rearview. "I will pay if you speed up."

"No."

We came to a halt. A Fiat pulling an aeroplane. I smiled at the tollbooth operator, a thin man with a pleasant face.

"Dollar ninety, please."

I held my hand back over the seat. "You heard the gentleman. I need the toll."

Fifteen seconds later, my palm was still empty.

"I apologise. My companion must have misplaced the toll." I glanced back at the tollbooth. The man's eyes were wide; his hands and the gate slowly raised and he nodded me through.

I frowned. "No toll?"

"No toll."

I pulled forward and glanced in the rearview in time to see Izzy place her rifle back in the guitar case.

"Did you just hold up a tollbooth?"

She shrugged and yawned. "Or you did."

"We are going to be apprehended in minutes!"

"Then I suggest you speed up."

I could wait. This seemed the logical move. I could wait and tell the copper about this strange girl who threatened me and the toll boy. I exhaled hard. And then I would need to explain why I was kidnapping Elias. Why I couldn't turn around. Why he was off his meds. Where I was born. Why I ran away.

"Blast!" I floored the accelerator. "I should think we will blend right in pulling a plane on the motorway. How many cars have you ever seen pulling a plane?"

"We need to get off the road, Clarita." Elias rummaged for his star chart. "There! Orion is the only constellation visible in the sky. What does that mean? Get out your manual—we need an interpretation. Quick! Recalibration!"

We hit eighty miles an hour. I was rummaging in my bag, Izzy whistled in the backseat, and I was now an accessory to a new crime. "Izzy, hand me my diary. In the left bag. By all means, I'm certain the manual will solve the dilemma."

She acquiesced, and I fought with the dome light and the diary pages and swerved about the road.

"I don't know what Orion means! I need time to look, and I can't do that at these speeds—"

"I know what it means." Izzy placed a hand on my shoulder.

I glanced at her hand, so gentle, reassuring. Hours ago holding a gun to my head, now treating me as her best mate. I rolled my eyes. *Perhaps a second individual with an identity disorder.*

"Tell us, Izzy! Don't you think, Clarita? We should listen."

I rolled my eyes. "By all means ..." I shrugged my shoulder and wriggled free of Izzy's hand. "Let's sink deeper into this nightmare."

I peeked over my shoulder. Izzy slowly sat back, the wild pride gone from her face. In its place was a sadness, and she dropped her gaze. It felt good to see her weak, whatever the reason.

"Well then? Speak, mighty Izzy."

She took a deep breath. "My dad was a great fan of Greek mythology and drilled it into me. I know all about Orion. In mythology, the guy was something. The son of Poseidon, the sea god. He could walk on water, and that's where his problems started. He wandered across the sea to a small island of Chios. He ran into trouble, got drunk, as those Greek gods often did. He went after Merope. Bad idea, 'cause she was the daughter of Oenopion, who was no small guy. Anyway, Oenopion got pissed and blinded Orion, who took off, stumbling ... Are you following?"

"No," I said.

"Yes, she is." Elias sighed. "Go on, Izzy."

"No!" I conked the wheel. "I'm not! I don't see how a blind, drunk, and likely upset Greek god from a Greek myth has any import on this ... thing we're doing."

Izzy cleared her throat. "I will continue. Orion bumped, literally, into Hephaestus. That god was lame. Physically lame. But he ran a big forge, with Cedalion helping as his apprentice. Cedalion guided the blind Orion to the east. Way east. To where the sun lived. The sun, Helios, healed Orion. Orion was so thankful that he carried Cedalion around on his shoulders. That's basically what happened."

"Anything else?" Elias's eyes were big.

"Oh, Orion did some other stuff. He went back to revenge his sight. No luck. And that's when the story turns. He went hunting with Artemis, but he was still so filled with bitterness that he decided to kill every animal on earth. Earth found out, sent a scorpion after him, killed Orion, and Zeus stuck Orion in the constellations. That's it, more or less."

"And from this emotionally edifying myth, we're supposed to gather what exactly?" I asked, checking in the mirror for flashing lights.

Elias grabbed his sketchbook and a pencil from the glove compartment and began a furious sketch. "I don't understand the mystery. It's all so clear now. Izzy has made it so clear."

Five minutes later, he stuck his drawing in front of my face. A beautiful portrait of Izzy and Elias and me, racing through a field, the moonlight on our faces. We were chasing Orion. Izzy and Elias wore faces aglow, while I looked back, frightened. I grabbed the picture and ripped it from his book, crumpled it in my hand, and tossed it out the window.

"Why did you—"

"I don't know!"

Elias crossed his arms. "We left on a quest. So did Orion. But we're wandering; we don't know exactly where to go. Just like Orion. Then we meet Izzy, our Cedalion. And she leaves her home and we all go east. We're practically carrying her around on our shoulders. Oh, don't you see it?"

"I see a remarkable set of coincidences."

"Orion searched for Helios, sunlight. We search for the Light-keeper. When we find him, we'll end the threat, and Salem will heal. But there's danger. We are being pursued now even as we pursue. We just need to keep following the stars." He shook his map in my face. "We're so lucky to have a wise guard who can also interpret my map."

There was nothing to say. Luck. Fate. Happenstance. A girl with a gun set our course, and I was to follow as if her story held biblical weight.

"So, Ms. Wisdom, where would you like me to drive?"

"Salem!" Elias raised his pointer. "We must to stay in Salem."

Izzy stretched her head forward into the front seat. "Salem. That's the word for peace. Peace, huh? Yeah, I'm all for peace."

I coughed loudly.

"Then let's stay in Salem." Izzy turned from Elias to me. "I know there's one in Ohio. It will ... It will be our Chios, our island of danger. Then, we'll head for Salem, New York. There's a Salem there too. That's where we'll find our Hephaestus. That's where we'll find our forge. From there, we'll head east. East to the sun."

"And you know of all these places?" I asked.

"Intimately."

"Well, then." I slowed and eased off the road. "It doesn't seem as though there is a need for me on this trip. It appears you have found not only an able guard, but a suitable guide. She is delusional. She is accommodating. She is . . . attractive. What more could you want?"

I stepped out of the car and opened the rear door, dropping the keys into Izzy's hands. "This trip is yours. You win."

"Win what?"

"Oh, shut it! It has been quite clear since you stuck your weapon in my face that the only thing you wanted was him." I pointed into the front seat. "Well, here he is! Why you want him, I don't know!" I reached over her lap and grabbed my bag. I yanked and walked away from the car, before plunking down on the shoulder and burying my head.

The car revved and pulled out. I listened as it disappeared into the distance and a strange weight of emptiness settled over me. I had nowhere to go. For the first time since I left home, there was no next step. No Plan B. There was only me.

"You abandoned us!"

I whipped around, and Elias huffed toward me with his bag, collapsing beside me.

"Why are you here?" I buried my head again.

"I can't abandon my guide. I love her."

There was no way I heard correctly. "You love me."

"Yes."

I took a deep breath, threw back my hair, warmed inside and slapped him across the cheek. "Then what was all that Izzy affection?"

"What Izzy affection? Clarita, we needed information. We got it. We got rid of her."

Two cars rushed by, slowed, and continued on. "Probably this isn't the best place to sit," I said.

"You chose it." Elias took a deep breath. "You know, it will now be a much slower quest, but the good news is we know the next steps."

I stood and raised my hands to my hips. "So we're following her path."

"Do you have a better interpretation? Look. See how bright Orion is tonight. Doesn't it feel right? The story? The everything?"

And it was at this moment that everything I learned in school, every lesson in logic, every concrete decision I'd ever made seemed baseless. Yes. It made sense. It made sense that I was nearly shot and that I was sitting on the side of the road. It made sense that the most important task in life was to follow a Greek myth.

And as in the myth, someone had to die, and I realised that someone was me. The me of London. The me of the past eight months. Both lay dead on the side of the road, but perhaps there was something on the other side of death. Something lighter and brighter.

I had been bent both on helping Elias become whole, and discovering the final piece to my puzzle. I still was. But if neither occurred—if I passed no more tests and received no more sketchings, if I never held the true Elias again—it would not destroy my world. This Elias loved me. The Other One. The one I once thought monstrous.

This was my journey.

I would not break my word again.

"Come on, then. We've a bit of a jam here, and transportation will be needed."

We started to walk.

"Can I hold your hand?" Elias asked.

"Can I stop calling you Jason?"

"Deal."

And we strolled along the motorway, likely going nowhere, but for the first time going everywhere.

"Clarita?"

"How about we use Clara?"

"Clarita?"

"Yes, Elias?"

He stopped. "Why was there an aeroplane attached to the car?"

CHAPTER 18

I need to rest."

I was grateful for the farmer who had offered us a lift, as well as the bumpy hours spent in the bed of his pick-up. But now, once again trudging along, this time up the off-ramp leading toward Fremont, Ohio, my bag weighed heavy. Yet, I was certain that if Elias drew a sketch of me again, I would no longer be looking backward. I would be face forward, my face shimmering in a bright future glow.

We turned into a field and sat. "I need to write something."

"Some calculations in the map manual?"

"No." I grinned, it dawning on me that I hadn't posted a new entry in some time. There hadn't been time to recollect, only to feel. "I need to post on my blog."

I removed the laptop and clicked to my page, watching my fingers work from memory:

Help Support Children of Incarcerated Parents
500 Days of Wander ...

I couldn't finish it. I watched Elias, at peace, on his back in the field, his right arm propping up his head. No more lies. I deleted the heading.

This is somewhat of a deviation for me. And as I find myself far from home, I also find that somehow I have found it. Yes, I've found home.

Does that sound odd? Can you rediscover a place you've always been? Or at least you've always wished you'd been? Does any of this make any sense? Likely not. No requests. I'm in ... I'm in ... Salem.

FFA: You sound happy. Blissfully happy.

ME: I think I am. Is that normal?

FFA: Not of late. You always seem ... discontent.

ME: You know me too well. LOL

FFA: Salem? Salem, Massachusetts?

ME: No, just Salem. Salem everywhere. Though I believe I am in Ohio.

ME: FFA? Is it ... is it okay with you that I'm happy?

FFA: Clara, I need to tell you.

ME: No news. Not today. Yes, Marna is not well. Yes, you have seen my dad and he is likely an imbecile, but nothing today. Tomorrow you may strike me with a new calamity, such as an explosion on Lower Marbury, but not today. Can you do that, mate?

FFA: Hmm. Mate. Marna looks better. But, Clara ... I'm the imbecile. This is your dad. I've been following your travels, which, BTW, track a lot like my travels. The journal, the map I gave you. Do you still have them? I really miss you.

FFA: Clara, it's Dad, Sean.

FFA: Clara, are you still there? Clara, please. Teeter doesn't speak to me, and they both ask for you, Marna through tears.

FFA: CLARA!

FFA: Clara, I need you here. I don't know how to care for them alone. We're losing the family.

FFA: Clara.

"Clarita? Are you okay? You're rocking. Are you cold?"

Mum only a memory. Dad and my confidant one in the same. It made no sense. My life made no sense.

But if FFA was ... Dad, and he said it was, there was no escaping it. Dad abandoned us, yes, perhaps shared a hand in destroying us, but he never lied.

He left that for me to do.

My body numb, I gently set the laptop into the dirt, stood, and zombied onto the road, where I lay face down on the center line. The tar was cool against my skin. A feeling I knew; one I could trust.

It didn't matter from which direction a truck came, as long as it came soon.

All I could think of was FFA. My best friend had died, and in his place arose a deceiver. Which meant Dad had lied after all. For eight months, he pretended.

"Liar, liar," I muttered, saw Izzy's concerned face, and stood. I climbed into the rear of a vehicle. Maybe an ambulance. Maybe a nuthouse wagon. Which one no longer mattered.

Liar.

Or maybe a truck came and flattened me after all.

I bounced around in the darkness. My soul must now be heading to its final destination, and judging from the lack of light, the outcome appeared evident.

My life provided little wiggle room with God; surely I was getting what I deserved.

Dad? I vomited in the blackness. Likely the first churling soul to make the downward trip. My mum. Gone. My dad ...

Everywhere.

Would I see Mum in short order? No. Despite her shortcomings, surely she would make the upward journey and trade factory cement for streets of gold. At least I hoped she would. Though it would again leave me completely alone.

But Dad, his life a vapor, floating in, floating out of mine; we would meet again soon. FFA? Dad?

Deceiver. Like me.

"Clarita?"

Elias spoke quietly, and his hand found my ankle. "Are you awake?"

"I am," I said quietly. "So we're not in hell."

"No. I didn't know what happened to you." His grip strengthened around my calf. "You were lying in the road. Breathing, but not there. You just disappeared."

"I wish I could disappear." I sat up, wiped the spit from my face, and scooted away from the little pool at my side. "Am I in the plane?"

"It's a strange turn of events. Yeah, you are."

I nodded, though I knew he would not see the gesture through the dim.

"But now the three of us are back together, and we should be safe in this thing. As far as I can tell, we can't be too far from the next stop. It's all coming together. We will remain in Salem and finally rid the Lightkeeper of power, and our queen will be pleased."

"Your queen won't know. Your queen passed on months ago."

There probably was a better way to say it, but I didn't care.

"No, you're wrong." Elias's voice shook.

His hand left my leg, and I stood, groped in the dark. "Where are you? Where are we? I need light. Elias?"

A skylight opened, two side windows slid back, and sunlight poured in. A U-Haul. The plane and the two of us were in the back of a modified U-Haul truck, with the plane and a sawed-off wing resting on the deck.

"Who is driving this contraption?"

"Izzy," he said quietly.

Elias sat in the corner and shivered. It was cold, but not that cold. His face twitched, and I climbed out of the plane and went to him. I realized I stunk, retreated, and dug for a fresh shirt, ducking behind the plane and quickly returning. I knelt at his side.

"I should have told you about Mum earlier. I'm so sorry."

Elias's lip turned stiff. "What killed her?"

I blinked. What killed her?

"A drink."

He pushed his hand through his hair. "Poisoned?"

"I suppose."

Elias shook his head. "She wanted this trip for you."

This was not true. But I had no strength to argue. I sat beside Elias, and he began to cry. I gathered him near, and he shook in my arms, and with every shake the sting in my own eyes sharpened until I could hold the tears back no more.

I cried. It had been months since I cried for her. Together, we bumped over the road and held each other and sobbed.

Was it ten minutes? No matter. It felt healing and tragic, and I pounded the metal wall with my fist. I tried to feel, feel for my mum, but I still couldn't. My mind was filled with Dad, the man I destroyed, the man I loathed, slumped at the table with Teeter and Marna and an empty chair. My empty chair.

I couldn't rid my thoughts of the man.

"My dad—"

"The king?" Elias sniffed. "I haven't heard about him for years."

"He's asked me to return home."

Elias fell silent.

"He's my family."

Again, he said nothing.

"He needs me."

"I could never ask you to stay after you've been ordered to leave. But ... I need you, too."

"Right. Well, then I have another decision to make."

I glanced out the window. Rolling hills in the flame of color. Reds and yellows and greens, splashed with orange, surrounded us in the most beautiful of scenes. Each farm, each home we passed, was painted immaculate white. It was a postcard. A beautiful postcard. I'd blog it, but Dad would likely be waiting.

"How do we make Izzy stop?"

Moments later, the U-Haul slowed, turned left, and left again, finally resting in a car park.

Outside, I heard footsteps, and then the back door raised, and the full force of the sun lit up the inside of the hold.

"You reek," Izzy said.

"I was ill."

"Yeah, no kidding. Let's clean that up and air it out."

Elias climbed down. "Clarita has been called home."

"To London?"

"My dad says he needs me, which wouldn't matter but for my sibs."

Izzy started pacing. "So your dad, a grown man, asks you to come home, and this adventure ends. And you ..." She stuck her finger in my stomach. "How many times are you going to bail on this guy?"

I glanced at Elias. He lowered his head. "She can go. I understand. I'll find my way."

"I'm not bailing on anyone! I'm just doing what needs to be done!"

"And when did you develop a responsible attitude?" Izzy asked.

Shambles. My life was in shambles. My family was in need. Elias—the real one—was trapped inside this boy's shell. But this boy loved me, and was as close to family as I'd had in years. I promised to see this through, to unite him if I could. I think if I did, I could love him.

I threw up my hands. "I shall continue on until we locate this threat. Then, I'll need to travel home, but I'll return. I promise."

The words came with little thought, but now, with them ringing in the air, they seemed right and true, and the issue was settled. There was no bringing Mum back. Dad was an adult, by degrees. He would survive another week. Marna and Teeter would survive as well . . . they always had.

"Where are we?" I continued.

"Salem, Ohio, as promised." Izzy stretched. "And you're welcome for ditching your ride for something more secretive, though it took driving back to Wisconsin to do it. See, there's a chocolate man in town who owns a U-Haul rental."

"I've met him. Kind of him to trade vehicles."

Izzy winced. "Not so much a trade. But, anyway, I returned for the two of you, and there you were. Face down beside each other. I was sure you were gone."

I pictured the scene. Elias, lying at my side in the middle of the road. In my greatest distress, the Other One did not leave.

"Well, if this is Salem, we're safe, right?" I said, forcing a smile toward Elias.

"Remember Orion's story." Izzy marched toward the cab and pulled out her guitar case. "Not safe here."

"Of course you're safe here." A woman's voice rang out from the other side of the truck, and we walked around the vehicle. She was dressed pleasant and casual in her sandals and oversized shirt. "You've chosen one of the safest towns in the country. Now, I see you're in a U-Haul. Moving to Salem?"

"Moving?" I asked, and Izzy whacked me on the shin with her guitar case. Quite by mistake, I'm sure.

"Yeah," Izzy said. "We were so eager to ... you know ... to—"

"Move into the old Yarrow house? It's the only property up right now. Right next door to mine," filled in the woman. "What was the likelihood of running into each other?"

"Yes." I frowned at Elias. "What are the odds?"

But I had long ago abandoned the concept of chance. That existed in the real world, where it was a constant throughout my eight months of travel. However, in Salem, the laws of probability were suspended, and bumping into help seemed the norm. First Izzy, then Haller once more, and now a woman who took us for neighbours ... something beyond luck propelled us toward a Lightkeeper. Each step seemed guided by stars and stories, fantasies and fictions.

Given past sins, the alternative—that non-god had me by the neck—was too terrible to consider.

"Correct." Izzy flashed me a terrible glance. "Move into the old Yarrow house. Mom and Dad decided to send us out ahead with the first load while they finish up back home."

The woman folded her arms. She was still, a calm pool. At peace. There was no hurry in her.

Izzy stepped between Elias and me, resting her hands on our shoulders. "I'd like to introduce my brother and sister. I'm sorry I didn't catch your name."

"It's Claudia Vanderpool. But for a soon-to-be neighbour, just Laudia."

Izzy was quick. I had thought my reasonable intellect plus eight months of traveling certainly produced a gold-medal liar, but years of homelessness certainly gave Izzy first place. I smiled a silver-medal smile.

"This beautiful but vomit-scented girl is Clarita, my twin."

You idiot!

"The ride didn't suit." I clenched my teeth. "And Izzy, I know it's painful, but this is our new neighbor and she needs to know. There's no Mum anymore. You need to sort that out." I turned to Laudia. "Mum has passed."

"Passed? Your mom died? Oh, my dears, I'm so sorry. I had no idea. We spoke on the phone a week ago, and there was no mention of illness or ... or children ..." She slowly folded her arms. "Your accent. It's not like your mother's ... was, or your sister's."

Izzy stepped in front of me. "Two years studying abroad, and she comes back thinking she's a Londoner." She slapped me hard on the back. "I'm still working on getting the old Clarita back."

No, Laudia wasn't buying it. But she wasn't rejecting it either. She looked too relaxed for that. She was waiting for one of us to dig the hole too deep, and seemed to be enjoying the burial.

There was a pause, and all eyes turned to Elias, clearly lost in feverish thought, trying to make sense of this narrative. It was flawed, twisted by Izzy and I, but it might still work, and if it did, it would provide us a place to stay for a day or two. All Elias had to do was lie. Or not say anything. A mute was a perfectly acceptable inclusion at this stage.

"My name is Elias, and I'm in search of the Lightkeeper. We consulted the star map and took into account Orion's story, which led us here. The Lightkeeper spreads pain throughout Salem, and needs to be stopped. We are aware that danger awaits in this town, but I have brought Clarita as a guide and Izzy as a guard to help me on this quest. I see the truth in your eyes, and so have decided to bring you into our confidence. Can you help us?"

Oh dear Lord!

Izzy bit her lip before joining me in glancing back to Laudia. Her face gave away nothing for far too long. But finally she cocked her head and broke into a broad smile.

"My son, Kenton, is absolutely going to love you. He spends hours lost in those video games he creates. I swear sometimes I don't

know what world he's in. Feels at times as if I've ... I've lost him."
She paused. "Perhaps you will be able to help me find him?"

"I hope so, Laudia. I will do anything to undo the Lightkeeper's treachery while I'm here."

Izzy and I exchanged glances once again.

"Well, you likely want to get settled ... somewhere. Why don't you walk with me? You can come back for the truck." She hinted a smile. "Now, I assume you have a house key."

Elias started to answer, and I cleared my throat. "Another issue. With so much occurring in the last week, we forgot to grab one."

We strolled through rows of mature trees and cared-for lawns. "Then you will be our guests for a few days. I insist. It will give you a chance to meet Kenton and get to know Peter, my husband. He will be very pleased to meet you, as it really was him who convinced David to move out here."

"David?" Izzy asked.

"Your father David, yes. I'll be sure to call him and let him know you arrived safely."

"Right. Father David." Izzy gazed left and then right. "You know, this generosity is too much. We really had planned on staying with the truck."

"And we would hate to intrude," I blurted.

"We accept your invitation." Elias sped up. "Don't listen to my overprotective company. I can't wait to meet your man."

It came in waves, the hurting. The whispered memory of Mum and the thunderous thought of Dad back home. His cadence now occupied FFA's words on the screen, and gave them voice. "Come home." The waves chose this moment to drench me, and my legs weakened. What did it matter if our lies were discovered? I lagged behind the others, my second "family" walking briskly in front of me, and my first family consuming me. Would Mum have approved of Izzy, the girl with whom I was spending time? She never had trusted Kira. Kira! I'd completely forgotten about her. Would Dad approve of Elias? Either one of him?

Auntie Joan, Gerald and Charles, cousins both; they would ask if there had been word from me, if Dad knew where I was. Uncle Robert would inquire too, and maybe now Dad would tell them. Maybe he would say, "She's in America, in Salem, Ohio. She's blissfully happy. At least she was for one day, until I asked her to return and ruined her life."

"I'm sorry, Clarita, did you say something?" Elias spun and stopped, waiting for me to catch up.

I shook my head, reached out and stroked his. Somewhere inside, he was counting on me; he had listened to me and ditched his medicine. I blinked London away. "Let's catch up. No telling what Izzy might say next."

CHAPTER 19

It turned out that my new family was wealthy. Quite wealthy.

Then again, everyone on South Lincoln Avenue appeared to be. Wealthy and owning a taste for the old.

We wandered by their homes, mansions all.

"I suppose you've seen pictures of the place." Laudia gestured around the historical district. "Does it compare?"

She paused in the middle of the road and turned a slow circle. From that vantage point, we were equidistant from four mansions.

It was a test.

"Of course, Dad's shown us a bunch." Izzy bit her lip and winced, offering me a quick shrug.

It would have helped matters had the homes been somewhat similar, but they weren't. There were two with porches, two without. One brick, one stone, and two clapboard. Two white, one with a turret. And my favourite, one with towers rising on both ends.

"Of course, they were rather blurry images, Dad's pictures being what they are," I jumped in. "Most of the photos we've seen were taken on the inside."

"Hmm." Laudia was not smiling, and doubt filled her eyes. "We should get off the road."

"Right." I never was good at multiple-choice exams. "Well then, let's get home." I took a step toward the two-towered home, and Elias grabbed my arm.

"None of these. These don't feel right. Is there a safer place to stay?"

Izzy rubbed her face. "Our home is fine, I'm sure. Dad wouldn't purchase a home that's not safe."

Elias scratched his head. "I don't even know your dad!"

Through it all, Laudia watched my face. I was her tell, my reaction the true or the false of it. Show panic, and our story would crumble beyond repair. I pasted on a broad smile.

"There is a time to work out our personal issues, but standing in front of our future neighbour, this is not it. Elias, you probably do have a better recollection of the place. Lead on."

He nodded sharply and turned to Laudia. "Lead on."

Laudia relaxed and laughed, and set off marching down the street. "It's just another block."

Izzy stepped nearer to me. "He's going to blow this, you know."

"Maybe, but he just saved us from intense embarrassment, and he's the reason you're not stuck in Wisconsin, so go with it. Nothing makes sense, and then it will, and when it does, nothing you knew before will make sense." I threw my arm around her shoulder. "Welcome to the world of Elias."

"I'll be back in a moment." Laudia returned from her home with a spare key, and soon we all stood inside. "I'm wondering if perhaps you should stay at our home, just until your parents arrive. Don't get me wrong, it's not a trust issue ..." She peeked at me. "Not completely. But until I can contact your father ..."

Izzy eyed the key. "I know it's a lot to ask, but we've been driving so long. We just need to rest, and I think we might best do that here." She stretched out her hand.

Laudia exhaled. "Yes. I can understand that." She dropped the key into Izzy's hand, and again I thought our guard a genius.

Our new mansion had nine bedrooms, four baths, and numerous other sitting rooms and lounging areas. Slightly larger than the Phinn's B&B, it nevertheless felt much smaller, with tinier spaces inside. Still, the porch was beautiful, the clapboard siding a brilliant restored white, and the eight columns majestic.

And it had a tower.

I dropped my bag on the foyer rug and breathed deeply.

It had been so long since I was home. Since I felt at home. And as I watched Izzy and Elias roam the bottom floor, I held no fanciful notions that I actually belonged here. Yet, in a strange way, I did. For this night, I belonged. I belonged here, with Elias. I looked up at the rising staircase.

Sure, there was reality. That was in England. London and the events that took place there, festering remembrances of Dad's request, both felt like an anchor. Elias peeked behind an ornate mirror. He was not the only one to have slipped. I, too, had fallen through the cracks, as surely a resident of Salem as Elias was himself, and I didn't want to return.

Maybe this was home.

Maybe Elias was happier in Salem as well.

I shook free.

"Thanks, Laudia."

"I'll leave the three of you to your explorations. There are … many things to discover in this home." She gazed around the room and folded her arms, giving herself a squeeze. "Many things." She turned to me. "You can see it's been vacant for quite a few years. There are reasons for that, depending on what you believe about this town."

A proper chill took me. "If there is something we should know, I would appreciate you telling us so we can sort it out."

Laudia thought a moment. "What's true, what's rumour, it's all hard to say after one hundred fifty years. Just perhaps stay above ground. And ... if there's something you wish to tell me, I'm right next door. I promise the result will be better for you than if you tell my husband."

Izzy shifted, and I said nothing.

"You're sticking with your tale? Very well." Laudia licked her lips. "Peter will be so pleased to see you in person."

Izzy yawned. "You know, we're tired. I'll just have the strength to move the truck and then I'll crash. I have a feeling my brother and sister also need—"

"Food," Elias said. "I really need food, and we accept your kind hospitality. You've shown yourself to be a kind and generous citizen of Salem, even in these hard times."

"Hard times?"

"In these days following the death of the queen."

Izzy slapped her forehead.

"The Queen of England?" Laudia glanced at me.

I stepped forward. "Well, you could say that. She was in England when she died."

"You never mentioned that detail!" Elias glared. "Don't you think I might be a bit interested in the location of her passing?"

"It slipped my mind. She was my mum, you know!"

"Wait." Laudia held up a hand. "Who are the twins here?"

The next minutes saw our flimsy story crumble, followed by a long silence.

"We should, uh, all enjoy the pleasure of your company this evening," I said. "What time should our family come over?"

"Six o'clock will do. The next brick house down." Laudia looked each of us over and shook her head. "Welcome to Salem." She slipped out the front door.

"Well, I think that went quite nicely, don't you?" I stretched and rolled my eyes. "You know, she doesn't believe a word we said. Izzy, will you go get the truck?"

She stomped toward the door, turned, and stomped back toward Elias. "One lie. That's all I needed you to tell. One little lie. But no, you don't do that for us. Instead, you develop a Winnie-the-Pooh-type fantasy world to live in, and you expect us to lie and live there, but if we make up our own Hundred Acre Woods, you won't even visit." Izzy shoved Elias in the chest. "You're going to get us caught." She spun around, pausing at the front door.

"I'm sorry about your mom. Whatever part of that is real, I'm sorry, Clarita."

She too quickly disappeared out the front door.

"It's just you and me. Just like when we left." Elias climbed the stairs and out of sight.

Just like when we left.

CHAPTER 20

"Clara!"

I raced up the stairs toward my name, my real name. "Where are you?"

"Higher! Keep going up!"

That doesn't help.

I threw open a door and entered the tower, reversed tracks and re-entered it on the next level.

There he was. Elias. His eyes clear and face sad.

"Where am I?"

He ran into my arms and embraced me. I pressed my cheek against his chest. This was all I could hope for. Yes, I was home. He and I or the Other One and I or the searching me and him or the helping me and him ... All of him with all of me. It felt right, and he buried his face in my hair and breathed heavy against my neck, and a tingle worked its way down my spine, among other places.

I slowly eased him back.

"We're in Salem, Ohio."

"Ohio?"

I balled my fists, breathed deeply, and opened my hands. "Okay. Some other details you should know. You hired—rather, picked up—a guard. Her name is Izzy. She carries a shotgun in her guitar case."

"Ohio. Izzy. Shotgun. Got it." He paused. "Is my guard pretty?"

I kicked him in the shin. It was involuntary. Honest.

He reached down and rubbed his leg. "Be calm." He hinted a grin. "I was just curious if the Other One has good taste, like I do."

"Well then, perhaps she is a tad . . . Oh, blast, you'll find out soon enough. She is lovely."

Elias ran his hand through his hair and gently tapped his head. "I don't remember anything since the medicine talk when we were in the plane." He ran to the window. "Where is that, by the way?"

"In the U-Haul."

"What U-Haul?"

"The one that belongs to the chocolate maker."

He slowly turned. "Which you rented for me?" His face lit up.

"Which Izzy stole for you . . . Listen," I said. "This is taking too long. The short of it. We picked up lovely Izzy, the stray, who threatened her way onto this quest . . . Just nod if you follow."

Nod.

"The Other One fancies our quest as a re-creation of the story of Orion, and in a strange twist, that has brought us here, where we met Laudia, who lives next door. She might still think we are moving into this home, but this narrative is so sufficiently messed up that you can't make an error. All you need to know is that now Izzy and you and I are siblings moving in to this mansion. Our dad is to arrive next week; Mum is dead."

Nod.

"David is the name of your dad. We are meeting the neighbours in an hour. Peter, the man of that house, knows David, so we will be discovered . . ." I paused. "Finally, my actual dad wants me to come home. I guess things are falling apart, and I couldn't live with myself if more tragedy happened."

Elias squinted and took a deep breath. "Is that part true?"

My turn to nod.

Elias walked over to me. "You, you need to go home. Right? I mean, that's your dad."

I took his hand and led him to the top of the tower. The floor was splintered hardboard, and there was not a scrap of furniture. I sat down in the middle of the room, pulling him toward me.

His face was so unsure. He lay down beside me, and I turned toward him, pressed into him. "I made a contract with myself. We are going to see you through to the end. We are going to find this Keeper and scrape together your shared memories, and then you will be you and never leave me again."

"I told you, that isn't how it—"

I kissed his neck, once, and felt his heart beat faster.

"It is. It has to be. And in the meantime, do not ever suggest that I leave you again."

I kissed him again, and he squirmed. I drew him near and kissed him long and full and deep. His mouth tensed, and I pulled back, placed my fingers on his lips. "Relax here. Let me lead. After all, I am your guide."

Five minutes later, I was lost in this boy. My mind had been given over.

He opened his eyes wide. "Clara, where are we going?"

"I think you'll enjoy it when we arrive."

"I don't ... I don't doubt that, it's just there's so little of me." He rolled over and sat up, turning from me. "It's like I'm never home. I'm a sailor, and I come home after long trips but the rest of the time ..."

"The rest of the time I get to look for you, and look at you." I wrapped my arms around him from behind and rested my chin on his shoulder. "I know who you are. I know who I am."

I kissed his ear and sat back. "Help me, Elias." I lifted my shirt and raised my arms. "Elias?"

"Yeah?" He turned and froze. He reached for my shirt and quickly pulled it back into place.

"This isn't what you want?" I asked.

"I'm not sure what's safe to have."

I threw back my hair. "You know, the Other One told me he loved me."

"He did?"

"He did." I crept nearer and pushed Elias onto his back, laying on top of him. "What does this one say?"

His movements became more fluid, patterned. "This one. This one ..."

"Yes?" My lips moved gently over his face, his neck, his upper chest.

The door flew open, and a man strode in. "Hello, neigh—" He walked straight up to me, still perched over Elias, and stretched out his hand. The most awkward handshake I'd ever given. "Thought I'd come get you. Izzy's already at our table. Food's nearly cold. I told Laudia I'd come and get David's kids, but I see now food really wasn't on your mind."

I turned and flattened my top.

"Is this typical sibling behavior in your household?"

"No, sir." Elias swallowed hard.

He took a deep breath. "I know David and his wife were not able to have children—it's been a source of some pain for him over the years, and one that we have discussed at length. But I also don't believe in throwing strangers out on the street, however deserving. The history of this house, especially, would not stand for that. But know this: I will not accept lying. Or using this space for this type of ... recreation."

"It was my doing," I said.

"No. It was both of your doing, and for what it's worth, I place the lion's share of responsibility on you." His finger met Elias on the nose.

I stood. "But you don't understand. He doesn't even know what's going on half the time. If he was normal, maybe, fine, make your judgments, but he's not. He's no protector. He's vulnerable."

"So that's it." Elias also rose. "A charity case. Maybe it would be best if you went home. Your work here is done."

"But that's not what I meant."

"Sir, if you would take me to Izzy, I would appreciate it. I can straighten this out," Elias said.

Peter Vanderpool nodded. "You are welcome to come." He turned to me. "As are you."

They left me standing alone in the top of the tower.

Idiot, Clara. What were you thinking?

I trudged down, and paused at my bag. I lifted my laptop and logged on to my blog.

I stared at the blinking cursor. Dad waited on the other end, blinking back.

My hands started over the keyboard, paused, and started again.

What do you do when you've destroyed someone you love? Again.

Send.

I slammed shut the top and stuffed the laptop into my bag. I didn't want to hear his answer.

It just really mattered that he heard my question.

CHAPTER 21

I called this meeting to give you one last chance to come clean."
Peter positioned us on the couch, with Elias in the middle. Laudia
sat in a Lazy-Boy, engaged in a furious knit.

My stomach growled. I'd missed dinner. My hosts didn't seem
to show much sympathy.

"So, let's start at the beginning." Peter pulled a chair directly in
front of Elias. "Are you connected in any way to these young ladies?"

"Yes."

It was in the way he said it. My Elias was gone, and I slumped
into the couch.

"And would you be willing to describe that connection?"

"Guard and guide. Beyond that, everything is privileged
information."

"But clearly not sisters and brother?"

"What really makes a family these days?" Izzy forced a smile,
and quickly fell silent.

"Guard and guide," Elias repeated. "That's all you need to know
about Clarita and Izzy. And don't assume those are their real names.
Don't think I'm that foolish."

Elias sounded smug. He also seemed to be digging a deeper hole
with every word.

Peter winced. "Were you not just ... in a compromised position with Clarita?"

"Oh, you've got to be kidding." Izzy glared at me, and I shrugged.

"I was not, and I never have been in any compromising position with Clarita. That would be disrespectful."

Peter sat back and scratched his head, peeking toward Laudia. "I just saw those two all pressed together."

Laudia gasped, and Elias shot to his feet.

"Apologise to Clarita immediately! Do you know who she is?"

Peter said nothing.

"Do you not see the resemblance between her and your queen?"

"My queen?" Peter rubbed his eyes. "I tell you, I know what I saw."

"Very well." Elias folded his arms. "Then we need to leave. We will move on. If lies are going to be told in this place ... Izzy? Clarita? Let's go."

"But what about your ... parents?" Peter asked.

"Clarita has none, I don't either. Elias has half a pair." Izzy smiled. "We are family. I don't care what you saw or thought you saw. We're family. They're all I have. Thanks for the meal."

"Wait!" Laudia exhaled. "Just wait. Please. We have a son. I told you about him. Kenton, he's ... he's lost. He rarely answers us anymore. Would you, could you talk to him, Elias?"

"It would be my pleasure, but I need to take Clarita."

Peter took hold of his wife's arm. "I don't trust that girl with our son."

Laudia broke free. "With Kenton? Don't be ridiculous."

She led the two of us toward the back room on the main level. "He's in there. Don't bother knocking. He won't respond. I miss him so much."

Laudia opened the door to a darkened room. "Thanks for this. If you get through to him, I don't care what Peter saw. I want my son back more than you know." She gestured us in and closed the door behind us.

The room was bathed in the eerie glow of several computer screens. Electronic gadgets and caving gear littered the floor, and beneath the covers of the bed, a young-man-sized lump.

"Kenton. My name is Elias." The Other One approached. "I'm here with Clarita. I want to talk to you."

No movement.

"He's dead," I hissed.

"No." Elias bent down, picked a brick off the floor, and hurled it at the head end of the lump. Still, Kenton didn't move.

"He's not there. See the shape? Asymmetrically impossible for a human." He strode forward and pulled off the comforter. Several pillows, but no boy.

"So now what?" I asked.

"Now, we wait."

Elias pulled a chair to one of the computer screens. A battle raged. Bloody awful.

"It's running by itself, looping over and over." I plunked down on the bed. "So we are going to wait for what, exactly?"

"We'll wait for Kenton. This family needs our help. This is the Lightkeeper's doing."

I lay down, suddenly knackered. "All the evils in the world cannot be the result of one person's life."

Elias breathed deeply. "Tell me more about your dad, my king."

He had me.

"My dad, the king, is unique in his ability to destroy things."

"Is he? Or did some of that get passed down to you?"

"I've never destroyed any ... I've never ..." I started to hyperventilate, and the room spun. "Maybe I could tell you a story from my travels. From the manual."

Elias shook his head. "No, I want to hear about this hideous man."

The hideous man ... right.

He loved to fly. Planes, balloons, helicopters. I, on the other hand, possessed a childhood fear of any place too high or buried too deep. The surface seemed a perfectly respectable place to live.

But his laugh, it was—it probably still is—infectious. It used to wash away all fear. When he laughed, I was safe, and willing to try anything, including helicopter travel. I may have been five, perhaps six. And he took me to the fair. "Helicopter rides, ten pounds!" the man cried out. It did not appear much of a helicopter. It was small—not the large transport helicopters of today, but the small, zippy ones. The glass ones.

The ones with no doors.

It was meant for two. Two seats. Two seat belts. The pilot climbed in. My father climbed in.

"Have a nice trip, Daddy."

He laughed, and soon I was caught up in his arms. The helicopter lifted up, and the pilot was manic—first angry, then joyful, and then angry again. The helicopter was manic as well. Flying, soaring, dipping, stalling ... only to regain momentum.

The whole time I looked out into the blue of the sky. There was no door. There was no belt. There was only my dad's arms. His strong arms, and his laugh.

I was so afraid, but all I could do was laugh, and press back into Dad's chest, and when all was done, ask for another.

I peeked at Elias.

"He doesn't sound like a rotten man," Elias said.

"No," I whispered. "He doesn't."

He isn't.

From inside the closet, a crumbling, and then a grunting and a scratching. I jumped to my feet, but Elias sat as stone, calm and fixed, and slowly I lowered myself down.

A muffled voice forced itself from behind the door.

"So it's the seventeenth left and then a right. Seventeenth left and then a right." The closet door flew open and a boy tumbled out, the light from his miner's hat temporarily blinding me.

I blinked away the light spot. The boy was short and stocky and filthy, his cheeks covered with either soot or dirt. He seemed unaffected by the presence of two strangers.

"Two people in my room. Two people I don't know in my room." He paused. "But the seventeenth left and then the right." He ran to his desk, reached over Elias, and grabbed a piece of paper and began a frantic scribble. "Done." He slowly turned.

"I have some questions for the two of you." He took off his helmet, and his gaze fell on me. Stuck on me. Traveled me. I had felt those eyes wandering many times before, and I quickly rose from his bed.

"I'm Kenton," he said.

"Yes, I shall say you are. That is Elias, and I am Clara—Clarita. My name is Clarita."

"Nice name. You are in my personal, private, very unvisited bedroom, where I keep my personal, private, very unvisited things. Did Mom let you in here?"

"We're temporary neighbours. We moved in next door for a few days."

A huge smile crossed Kenton's face. "Down and the first left and up."

"It was not intentional," Elias said. "We had planned on staying in town, but your mom was kind."

"Downtown. That's the challenge, but very possible." Kenton turned to a computer, clicked a key, and typed furiously. "Now if you'll excuse me, I have some work to do."

Elias wandered the room, staring at *Star Wars* posters on the wall. "You're in trouble, Kenton. I see it. And I'm here to help."

"Trouble?" He scoffed and glanced at me. "Who is this guy?"

A wonderful question.

Elias flipped on the light, and we all squinted. "We aren't here by chance, or simply your mother's request. We followed my star map, as well as Clarita's interpretation manual. And Izzy's with us too."

"Star map?" Kenton slowed on the computer and glanced over his shoulder.

I rolled my eyes. "I know it's a little strange. It must seem a little strange, unbelievable, really. Ridiculous. Bizarre. Ludicrous—"

"Clarita . . ." interrupted Elias.

"Right. Well, Izzy and some mythical story about a constellation brought us to this town. You must think us completely blasted or crazed or—"

"Brilliant. Not brilliant like me, but . . ." Kenton rummaged for his miner's helmet and carbide lamp. He held them up. "Find one of these, and one of these in your size. There are plenty around. You are not going to believe what the stars can do." He did a little jig, which for this chunky lad proved quite the sight.

We strapped on helmets and followed him into his closet, the door of which he shut behind me. "Okay, now where is it?" His meaty hand grabbed my ankle, and remained.

"That is not what you are looking for."

"No, that's right." He released me. "Here, it's here. Now scoot back against the door. It's a drop."

The floor creaked, and the closet filled with dank and cool. I looked down, and my light illumined not carpet but dirt ten feet down.

"Tunnel," Elias said.

"Railroad." Kenton slapped him on the shoulder and descended thin brick stairs. "Someone to show. Finally, someone to show!" His voice sing-songed into darkness.

"Go ahead, Elias." I slapped his shoulder as Kenton had done.

"No, you're my guide."

Your guide to unreachable places.

I carefully descended a rough-hewn ladder until I stood on the earth.

The air in the underground cavern was still, and an unnatural heaviness pressed in around me. Up. Out. I wanted out. I looked up, but my beam illuminated little beyond the hole. The real world was hidden from view.

Panic took hold, and I reached for the ladder.

"No, wait!" Kenton said.

I scampered back up until my head poked back into the closet. I took a deep breath and my stomach sank.

Because I had just climbed out. I was afraid and it was dark so I just climbed the ladder. I turned my beam toward Elias, watched as he looked about. My Elias, the half who trusted me; I broke his ladder. His medicine, imperfect as it was, likely provided him an occasional escape from his darkness. But I would not let him have it. I tried to keep him in his panic so I could rid myself of my own.

Shame swept over, and hideous me descended the steps once again, to be with the Other One. To know what my lost Elias was feeling trapped beneath his brain's surface. Though I hated it below, I owed him that much.

Kenton stretched out his arms. "Are you okay?" He didn't wait for my answer. "Good. Now behold the Underground Railroad!"

Elias turned toward me, and blinded my eyes.

Kenton clicked his tongue. "You aren't responding with the right amount of awe. In school, weren't we taught that the railroad was underground in name only? That it meant 'secret'? And that's mostly true. Slaves moved from the south to the north, stopping at 'safe stations,' which were really homes or farms of sympathetic people along the way. Mostly under cover of darkness. But here in Salem, one of the northernmost stops on the railroad, the town took the underground part seriously."

"We're *in* the underground railroad?" I asked.

"Slave families hurried through right where you're standing. Some of the unfortunate ones are still down here, but those were the ones who got lost."

Kenton turned and walked, soon coming to a fork, and another fork.

I quickened my steps and glanced back. "If it's such a labyrinth..."

"Don't worry. I practically live down here," Kenton said. "Let me continue the story. See, everyone in Salem knows of a few stations in town. Six or seven entry points to underground passages are marked. The Quakers who once lived in these 'stations' hid hundreds of slaves, but they're all private homes now and people don't realise what's beneath." He stopped walking. "Nobody knows that the entire town is connected by a crazy tunnel system, and not just the homes. This maze stretches the length of Salem. That offshoot there ends up beneath the present-day school."

Unbelievable. The air was thick, but the spirit was thicker. Hope and fear rolled into one. Voices. You could hear them.

"Are we alone down here, Kenton?" I asked.

"You feel them too? Sometimes I swear I do." Kenton glanced about. "Sometimes. Sometimes they're weeping. Sometimes they're humming. Always there's a hushing. Dads and moms telling their children to hush." He lowered his head. "Once I heard a dog too. Plain as plain."

"But you keep coming down."

"Yeah." His voice gained strength. "And here is the awesome part. How do you think they navigated this tunnel?"

"Luck?" I asked.

"No. Not luck. Look up."

I did. The spot from my beam shone on a brick ceiling.

"What do you see?" Kenton jumped like a puppy.

"Light."

"Exactly. Now, a lot of those escaping couldn't read, but thanks to all those miles traveled at night, they could read the sky. Every exit point from down here corresponds to a star in a major constellation. That's what I'm doing right now. I'm plotting all the exits. Gemini there. Two lefts and you reach the Leo exit. How cool is this?"

"It's fascinating but ... So we came because of this story about Orion. Izzy or Elias said there would be trouble waiting in this town, but that we needed to follow Orion. Where's that exit?"

Kenton wiped his forehead. "Well, that's the thing. If you're really my neighbour, Orion's belt exits up into your place."

I whipped around. No Elias.

"Elias!"

A hand slapped over my mouth. "The distance between here" — Kenton pointed up — "and the floors above is sometimes paper thin. No sounds. Besides, for a lot of reasons, we should backtrack to the Orion exit."

I ripped his hand off my mouth. "I need to find him. He'll be fine, right? I mean, he can't get in too much trouble down here."

"If his light goes out and he gets cold ... Well, that won't happen. Follow me."

We weaved back the way we came. At least it felt a tad like the way we came. "Slow here. Look straight ahead," he said firmly.

Wrong thing to tell me, and I glanced to the right. Large skeleton, small skeleton. I screamed, and again received a taste of Kenton's smothering fingers. "Straight ahead. That's not going to happen to Elias. Our station is just ahead. By that ... light."

Elias. He sat cross-legged on the ground, staring at the brick wall, and the scratchings etched into the brick.

"One. Two. Three. Three days or three weeks." His voice was distant. "How long were they hiding down here?"

I slapped his helmet hard, but he did not turn. "So much sadness in the past. Who knew this cancer was growing in the heart of Salem? The queen didn't. The king doesn't. We need to set this right. We need to find it and stop it ..."

The urge to shake him overpowered. If there was an evil Keeper, he had no power over the slave trade. Elias should know. But the Keeper was still the touchstone, the point where both of him came together. Even after my great embarrassment in the tower, I was more determined than ever to reconnect his dots. This Keeper; I wanted to see him as badly as I wanted my dad ... I rubbed my face. The words, like a distant echo, sounded again. *I want Dad.* Hundreds of children sitting in the dark, hushed by their mums while their fathers checked out the next passage.

I want my dad.

I heard it stronger.

I want my dad.

It reverberated in my head.

Dad, I love ...

No! I would not give him that prise. Never again.

Pounding shook from above, and Kenton doused his light, gesturing for us to do the same. He quietly climbed the ladder, and I sat down next to Elias.

"We need to help these people," he said.

"Elias, I don't pretend to know my American history, but this happened over a hundred years ago. They're all gone."

"Are they?"

Kenton descended and whispered, "Police. Did you do something? Are you hiding something? Cops are searching your house. They'll search down here. We need to move."

"Not without my guard," Elias said.

I stroked Elias's head. "Think, Elias. Izzy's not there. She's smart. Why would they be looking if they found her?" I turned. "Kenton, help me. We need to find Izzy. If you were brave and arrogant, like

Bonnie or Clyde, and mighty good with a shotgun, where would you make your last stand?"

He relit his beam. "Follow me to Arcterus. You'll see!"

Twenty curved minutes later, we reached another set of stairs. "This is tricky. You'll come out beneath a bright-red trolley set in the middle of town. Glass on all sides. She could see everyone coming from every angle." Kenton swallowed. "But it would be a death trap. Wait. This is crazy. This isn't some Wild West shootout. Nobody does that anymore."

Elias and I exchanged glances.

"I'm not going up there with you," Kenton said. "I can't."

I nodded and kissed him quickly. "Your mum, she worries. She worries you've gone where she can't go, and I see why now. I see it. But don't leave her," I said. "Please, don't leave her. She just might need you someday."

"Maybe for another kiss I'll consider letting her in on—"

I granted his wish.

He wiped his brow. "Yeah, I mean, what could be the harm in telling her, you know?"

Elias nudged me. "Maybe for a kiss I would consider—"

I slapped his helmet. "Not before we discuss the business that occurred in the tower."

He cocked his head, and I climbed the stairs. The rock above my head crumbled, but there was no opening. "Ever been out this way, Kenton?"

"No. Just an educated guess. Here, use my hand pick." Kenton removed the tool from his pack. "I knew it would come in handy one day. I'll seal up the hole tomorrow." He handed me the pick, and ten minutes later I stared up at the bottom of what must be a trolley. I pounded on the metal underside, and a shotgun blast sent a shell not one foot from my head.

"Hold on! It's Clarita! Come out! Come down. We came to get you out."

Distant sirens grew nearer.

Izzy's eye appeared through the hole made by her shell. "I can hold them off. I have great sight lines all around. You two go. It's been a pleasure."

"If you think I put up with you this long just to watch you perish in a gun fight …" I crawled onto my belly, jumped up and ran around to the trolley door, and climbed in.

I grabbed my bag and Elias's pack and leaped back out, pitching them toward Elias's waiting arms. Back into the trolley, I took hold of Izzy's neckline and yanked. She broke free and shoved me onto the floor.

"I swear, Clarita, I will shoot you myself."

"Oh, shut it! Go ahead."

Flashing lights screamed nearer, and Izzy lowered her gun, stared at the hole her shot had made, and grabbed her guitar case. "Okay, London. Lead me to the promised land." She followed me out, and ten seconds later we were safely into the tunnel.

"This is absolutely my most awesome escape ever!" Izzy pumped her fist. "I am definitely coming back—"

I shook Izzy hard. "Are you raving mad? Is everybody here mad? Do you have some sort of death wish, or is this journey all a game, because I really need to know who I'm traveling with. That was all for show. I mean, you wouldn't hurt a copper … would you?" No answer. "Or would you …"

"We can discuss this later, Clarita," Elias said. "Where's the truck, Izzy?"

"An abandoned farm outside of town," she said cheerfully.

Kenton exhaled. "Okay, well, that could be a problem."

Elias dug in his pack and brought out his star map. Kenton stared for a moment and swept his hand over the constellations. "So we're here, Arcterus. We've come from Orion. We need to get you out of here, out of Salem."

"No," Elias said.

"Yes, says the guide." I smiled. "We need the easternmost station."

Kenton shrugged and pointed to a small constellation on the eastern horizon. "That should be here. I've not mapped it this far, but there should be a way up."

I grabbed the map from Elias's hands and handed it to Kenton. "Carry on."

As we trundled forward, the lunacy of this whole experience struck. For days, I had silently mocked the craziness of following a star map, and yet here I was, following an eastern star. I placed all my hope in it.

Reality did me no good. Not on this journey.

The tunnel narrowed from five meters in diameter to four meters to three.

Behind us, voices.

"Police," Izzy said.

"I don't think so," Elias said. "Those voices have been here a long time."

Two meters.

I removed my bag and dropped to my knees, shoving it in front of me. "Kenton? We can't go on." My voice muffled, even as those behind me grew louder.

One.

I pushed ahead, the faint grunting of Elias and the sound of men's voices now all I heard. That and my breath. Loud. Forced. Desperate.

Then, stars. Brilliant and bright. The world opened and the grass waved and the trees rustled in the blackness of night. I turned. The lights of Salem were bright behind us, but before us there was nothing.

"Wow." Kenton stood and brushed himself off. "So this is how they got out. Right out of town. You'll be following a slave route for a while, I figure." He handed the star map back to Elias. Izzy finally emerged, her guitar case scraping out of the cave-like opening.

"Terrible."

"What? The crawl?"

She shook her head and muttered. "Terrible. Terrible."

I rounded her shoulder. "Maybe we weren't the only ones traveling through."

"I don't believe in that stuff."

"You might soon," Kenton said. "Over that ridge is the only abandoned place I know. Abandoned for good reason. And after I tell you the story, I need to leave. I forgot to reshape the pillows beneath my blanket."

Kenton pointed. "If you follow Salem Road east, soon—"

"You arrive at a T, and the right turn looks like it's headed back into Salem," Izzy said.

"So you went left, and it turned into gravel, and then there it was, a big, old vacant Civil War place. An entire family died in that house. It was brutal and sad. This was back in, like, 1940, but five of them lived there. Mom, dad, three kids." Kenton breathed deeply. "Everything was going fine, right? But then this traveling shoe salesman blows in. He sets up a shop in town. Soon he's having an affair with the wife. She says she's gonna leave her husband, but then, suddenly, she changes her mind. A few days later, the whole family is found dead, and the drifter has moved on. But every once in a while people still see his car. Driving back and forth in front of the house. Maybe from remorse. Maybe from anger. Freaky stuff."

"And you hid our truck at that house?" I asked.

Izzy's hands raised to her hips. "I was not given the haunted history of Salem, Ohio, before I arrived."

"It's all right." Elias nodded. "We're all here. We're close to the truck, and we met Kenton, a fine citizen of Salem. We rescued Izzy and found our way through a very sad darkness, dangers that we knew from Izzy's Orion interpretation would be waiting for us. We're definitely on the right track."

I exhaled loud and slow. Maybe Elias found comfort and certainty from the events of this place. Not me. I didn't discover anything. I lost what I had. In my lack of control in the tower; in the below-the-surface panic I so lightly put Elias through ... I lost what little self-respect I owned.

The Other One didn't know about my failures, but what would my Elias think?

"We should go," Elias said.

Kenton swallowed. "You really need to? I mean, you probably do, but it'd be cool to have you stay. I don't care what you all did." He scratched the side of his neck, lowering his voice. "It's just me here. Me and these tunnels. My parents, they think I'm crazy... they're perfect, you know? And I'm this freak."

The night fell silent, and Kenton continued. "Just nice to have a couple other freaks like me nearby, you know?"

Izzy strode up to Kenton, reached up and gently held his face in her hands. "I get it."

The longer they stood, the smaller my earlier kiss became. Twice now, both in the tower and in the tunnel, I had given boys exactly what they'd always requested. But Izzy's words were going somewhere my affections couldn't reach. I felt such the fool.

We all stood as statues, until Elias reached into his pack and removed a pencil and sketchbook. He looked at Kenton, and five minutes later gently tore the drawing from the pad. He handed it to Kenton, whose eyes grew wide.

"Seriously?"

Elias smiled. Kenton pressed it into his chest. "Okay, yeah, okay." He started to cry, dirt on his cheeks smearing to mud. "I need to get back." He carefully folded the gift and raised it in the air. "Thanks, Elias."

It was the time for my gentle gesture. Izzy and Elias had both extended a farewell moment to Kenton. But standing there, I suddenly felt the needy one. The empty-handed outsider. The shared freak who threw around kisses like currency.

Kenton disappeared back into the hole.

"May I ask what you drew for him?" I asked.

"No."

I wanted badly to know. I wanted him to draw something happy for me. I wanted to cry again.

CHAPTER 22

Haunted things. I never gave them much thought. Not because I had any strong beliefs either way, but because my life was filled with enough haunted places; I didn't need more to consider. But Kenton's story stuck with me—it seemed to weigh on us all—and we wandered slowly toward our truck, parked in the drive.

With a Camry next to it.

"I thought you said it was deserted." I squinted toward the windows of the house. There were no signs of life.

"The car wasn't there," Izzy said. "You think . . . I mean, it sort of sounded like Kenton knew what he was talking about. What kind of car would a deranged shoe salesman drive?"

"Definitely a late-model silver Camry." I slapped her arm. "But it doesn't matter. We aren't here to stay."

It was a quick load. The plane was intact, and our packs joined it in the back. The three of us squeezed in the front, with Elias in the middle, his star map open on his lap.

Izzy again took the wheel. "So, you two still up for east?"

"Stay in Salem," Elias said.

I punched in the word. "Salem. Salem, New York." I leaned over the dash and peered up. Orion shone bright above us. "Still on Orion's path." I chuckled. And froze.

From outside the truck, a scream. A child's scream. From inside the house, candlelight.

"Go. Go!" I shouted, and Izzy revved the engine and threw the U-Haul in reverse. Tires gnawed at gravel, and a cloud of dust surrounded us as we hurdled backward. She executed a tight turn in the road, and we accelerated.

"We will return to Minnesota by a different route." My heart pounded.

"I should have helped the girl." Elias sighed. "Whoever it was."

"And if it wasn't a who?" Izzy asked.

Elias slumped down. "Then I would have nothing to worry about."

I gently squeezed his shoulder. "Not everyone can be helped by a picture."

He silently reached back and handed me a new sketchbook. "Page one."

I slowly flipped open the cover, and my stomach sank.

It was the third.

Twice before, I had received sketches, dark and foreboding. Following the touch of Elias while in the tower, I had almost forgotten to be selfish. Now with the appearance of my next sketching, my other motive resurfaced.

The picture was the most grotesque of the three. Indeed, it was almost pure emotion, the subject recognizable only by its eyes. Horrified eyes affixed to a child's body. He knew. Now, there was no doubt. First the storm. Then a figure slipping to the ground. Finally, the horror in my eyes as I stared down. Elias hadn't been there. Just like the voices in the tunnel; they hadn't been there either. Not really.

But somehow Elias saw what he could not. He knew too much.

"Does that sketching help?" Elias asked quietly.

"Yes."

Salem, Ohio, reminded me of many things. How much I missed the real Elias. How strangely fond I felt toward my dad. But perhaps most of all, the tunnels, and Kenyon's story, reminded me that the past never stays hidden. The closet never remains shut. The truth always leaks out.

And that alone filled me with more fear than I'd felt in years.

Elias alone saw my Great Undoing, London's secret until now. He knew I was running. He had to. Why I ran, why I came, why, just why. Yes, it filled his sketches of me. But maybe he didn't know it all. If not, and I told him, could he ever trust me? Would Dad have begged me to return if *he* knew?

I glanced at Elias, who stared back at me.

I would tell him all I knew. The next time the Elias from the tower returned, I would tell him.

Though it might spell our Great Undoing.

"Get some rest, Clarita." Elias nestled stiffly into me. "We'll need to sleep while we can and find a place to hide during the light."

"I got this," Izzy said. "I know just the place, and we can spend the day."

I stared out the window, whispering to nobody in particular, *I'm so sorry.*

Do you know how many late-model silver Camrys are on the American road?

It turns out that there are quite a few, and as we chugged through the night, I spotted several.

At the Shell station.

At the rest stop.

But I experienced them as shadows, fading in and out of dreams, dreams that filled with Elias and London in equal measure. Yet Mum I did not see, and I awoke wondering if I would ever see her face again, or if she had died to my dreams as well.

• • • • •

"Well, we're here." Izzy stretched. "Niagara Falls. So much traffic in and out, it's a very public place to hide. Does that suit you, Elias?"

He craned his neck to see out my passenger window. "I've heard of this place. Let's check it out."

We eased out of the truck and wandered along the rapids, a river growing wilder and wilder until it vanished, plunging into mist and foam. I knew people had risked the drop. Elias plunked a quarter into the observation telescope, and Izzy walked along the shoddy rail. She kept glancing over the edge, I knew, to find a way down.

"You'll die."

"Maybe," she answered quietly.

I squeezed her forearm. "And that doesn't cause you to think twice?"

Izzy exhaled. "Because he's looking for home just like me."

"What? Who is?"

"You once asked me what I wanted to do with Elias. He's looking for home, just like me. He makes me believe I just might be able to have one again someday."

I gently rapped the rail. "His home is in Minnesota."

"If you believe that, you're clueless."

It was silent a long time. "See that mist? That's me." She swept back her hair and caught my gaze. "For years, that's been me. There's no reason for where I've been. None for where I'm going. I go east because you go east. But sooner or later—"

"You'll go home."

"Home?" she asked. "To whom? That's why I'm running. What do you think I did to my parents?"

I frowned. "It was fierce?"

"It was fierce. And it was final."

I thought of her gun barrel in my face. "I'm going to ask. Anything to do with your guitar case?"

She scratched her head. "Dad played guitar. Mom heard him,

and she fell in love on the spot. The two of them were special. Most girls would say I couldn't ask for better parents." She peeked down again.

"Then why did you, you know . . ."

Izzy smiled. "The day I was born, my dad hung a Harvard pennant on my basinet in the newborn nursery, and he gave me the middle name Ivy. By the time I was sixteen, I had met Harvard's president five times, and taken more than a dozen trips to campus. It's why I know the road we're traveling so well. My dad became their largest donor, in exchange for a small guarantee. My acceptance."

"At least he was involved in your—"

"I hate Harvard," Izzy said. "Does anything about me say Harvard to you? Alaska. Now there's a place. There's adventure. Harvard? All so I can meet some wealthy Harvard monkey who cares more about his political correctness than he does about me? Harvard? It wasn't about me, London. He wanted me to marry Harvard. Some dream.

"You, though, you have purpose, a twisted, half-real one, but a shared one, you know? You and Elias—who would have thought? You'll probably end up together . . . Have a real odd kid with a messed-up accent. But life'll be good." She faced me. "Least your dad's life doesn't define yours."

I closed my eyes. "Izzy, I want to tell you—"

"Back to the truck." Elias gestured toward the car park.

I walked beside Izzy, the Great Undoing weighing heavy on my mind. She had no roots. Telling her would be like talking to the wind. It might be safe.

Izzy took my arm, and I pushed down the urge to pull away, as I had so many times before. "That story about Orion." I frowned. "That business about danger in the first Salem and a Hephaestus bloke with the forge waiting in the next . . . Is that real?"

She scoffed. "Is any of this real? We're following the plans of a mentally ill guy who thinks he's on a crusade for a deceased queen. We're looking for some Lightkeeper and following a star map to get there. It's as least real as that."

I quickened my step to reach Elias, but felt Izzy's hand on my shoulder. "But that's okay. I don't mind living in somebody's hallucination as long as it *feels* real. You better love him. You better love him as much as you love yourself, 'cause I'll go to the end, whatever that means, for that." She pulled me near. "But if you don't. If you're just playing ... If you're just doing this to humour him or to add pages to your little diary, then I'm gone."

I glanced up at Elias.

"Do you love that idiot? Either one of him. Don't matter to me."

Love. A word for fools. "I need him. He's my everything right now."

"Liar. You're your own everything. Just like me."

"I need time to sort it out," I hissed.

"Well, jolly good and cheerio." Izzy slapped me on the shoulder, and shook her head.

Love.

I love part of Elias.

I love things about Elias.

I love half of Elias.

I love Elias.

I tried them all, terrified of the one that fit.

CHAPTER 23

Salem, New York.

Beautiful.

"I need to reach the forge. The forge of Hephaestus. Can you direct us to the forge?"

Good morning. Excuse me. May I have a moment of your time ... All very good ways to begin a conversation, but as I watched Elias accost women on Main Street, it struck me how acceptable his ways had become. I had lost all sense of bizarre, and appropriate no longer held meaning for me.

We needed guidance to reach a fleeting memory. Why not get there by following stars and asking to reach a mythical forge?

"The forge, huh? You know you're in New York." A woman frowned.

"I know I'm in Salem."

She seemed to be thinking. Good heavens, this knackered-looking lady was actually attempting to recall the location of the forge of Hephaestus. What a kind soul.

"I don't know anyone by that name, but, wait ... you might be talking about the hippies. The forge of the hippies. I know something about that."

"Where is that?" Elias asked.

"Salem Art Works. Back down the road you followed in. There's a big commune of them. Lord only knows what they do there, what they have there. There might be a forge of some sort."

Elias bowed. "I want to thank you for your help in this time of sorrow for us all. The queen would have been pleased with you."

The queen likely would not have cared.

He took out his sketchbook and quickly completed yet another drawing. He handed it to the woman.

"Why ... why thank you."

"You ... are welcome."

Elias ran back to the truck. "The locals know Hephaestus by a different name: Hippies. Back up the road."

Izzy glanced at me, and I shrugged. "And being here is important? My 'manual' says nothing of this place." I held up my diary, and shook it in the air.

"Perhaps those interpretations have become uncalibrated. Perhaps they no longer align to my map. Izzy brought us to this point." Elias turned. "Izzy, do you have any more to say?"

"Wait!" I frantically leafed through my travels. "In this diary is all we need. See, I have this!"

I glanced down at the page selected at random.

"Forget it," I said.

"No." Elias leaned over. "I want to hear. The stories in that book may still be invaluable."

I shut the diary, but Elias was quicker, his hand slipping between the pages. "Please. Read."

I bowed my head. "I can't. There are no words on the page. It's just an idiotic picture. Nothing like your sketches."

"A picture ..." Elias tugged at the book, and I released it. He opened back up to the spot. I searched for an emotion on his face. Any emotion.

Anything.

"Who are they?"

He placed my precious diary on his lap. Izzy craned her neck to see.

"I told you I can't draw."

"Who are they?" he repeated.

I pointed. "Well, that was the queen. My best attempt at the queen."

Elias nodded solemnly. "You captured her essence."

"So that there, that would be the king. Sean. My dad."

"King Sean. Strange, I never knew him by that name. And the little ones?"

I smiled. "They aren't so little anymore. The tall one is Teeter, and that's Marna."

"And you. Is this you off to the side?" He pointed. "You sketched yourself too lightly. You hardly can see your shape."

"Well, that's how I jolly well wanted to sketch it!" I quieted. "That's how I did it."

Elias softened. "No need to get upset. I understand it's always the artist's choice." He blinked and rubbed his eyes with the heel of his hands. "Is that ..." His finger found it. "Is that another kid?"

Izzy, silent the whole time, now gazed at me. "The one beside you. The one even lighter than you. Who's that one?"

Elias squinted. "There is someone there. I see the outline. No face. No features. Who's that?"

"Nobody to mention!" I grabbed my diary, slammed it shut, pushed out of the truck, and ran forward. I ran until the red brick buildings of Salem vanished from sight; until I was surrounded by beauty and mountains and leaves so vibrant they took my breath away, and the beauty fueled my sorrow.

I reached down and grabbed a handful of the fallen. So beautiful. They fell so early. So soon. Before they had a chance to be seen or loved or ...

My legs churned forward, a new mantra filling my thoughts:

I am not abandoning Elias. It may have appeared so, but it was not true. Nothing about me was true.

I veered into a leaf-filled ditch and panted. Was this place filled with bear and mountain lion? The wondering entered but caused no fear. I alone did that.

Hunted; I felt hunted by a crouching truth that crept nearer by the day. So I would keep on running, because if I slowed, it might catch up. I might just run into myself.

I shivered and wished I was eight again.

• • • • •

"Rough night, Clarita." Izzy's face slowly came into focus. "Help me out, boys."

Strong hands lifted me up, continued to carry me under the arms and beneath the knees. "Gently, into the cart."

"Elias?" I asked.

"We'll get you back to him soon enough."

I stretched my neck to see the unknown speaker, but in the dark, he was simply shadow.

"Well, London, you do have a flair for the dramatic." Izzy sat cross-legged beside me, her guitar case resting on her lap. "Okay. We're set. Easy now."

We lurched forward. I remembered the feel. I had felt it several times in Asia and Africa, where carts were pulled by mule or camel.

I pushed up on my elbows. "What am I in?"

Izzy shoved me back down and covered me with blankets. "Stay down. Get warm. Horses. They're horses. Yeah, it's weird, but just go with it. These guys only get around on bikes or carts—earth-friendly, you know? I didn't figure you'd want to trust your balance."

"And El—"

"Waiting for word. You are mighty fortunate that my tracking abilities are top notch." She handed me my diary. "Beside you on the road. Just think, if I hadn't found you, then you wouldn't have an argument to look forward to, but as it is ..."

"An argument?"

"Oh, Elias is pretty upset. Something about an attack in a tower."

I groaned. "I see."

• • • • •

Two months ago, I thought my trip had ended.

That's when I saw a tower rising in the distance. I ran toward it and knocked at the gate that surrounded.

The door had opened slowly, following the clicks of many locks.

"May I help you, child?"

I looked at the monk, uncertain. It was a strange question, and not the type I was used to hearing. Especially not in Cartagena.

A beautiful city on the Colombian coast, Cartagena had held no warnings in Dad's journal. Yet, trouble found me just the same.

"I'm not sure." I glanced down at my clothing, ripped as it was.

He stepped out beyond the monastery gate, looked both ways, and pulled me inside before relocking the cast-iron lock.

"But you rang our bell."

"I ran into a tiny scrape. I'm Clara Blythe, daughter of Sean Blythe."

The monk's face softened. "There are no tiny scrapes in Cartagena. Sean's daughter. Well. How is the builder of our chapel?"

I said nothing.

"Come, follow me."

We entered the clay building, encountering the faces of several concerned men, one quite young; quite the handsome bloke.

"Manuel, escort our guest to the tower room."

The young monk smiled and led me deeper in and then around and finally up. He opened the door at the end of a long hall and pulled the chain on a single light bulb.

The room was small: just one cot, one dresser, and one chair. One crucifix on the wall.

I dropped my bag onto the floor. "What will it cost me to stay for a night?"

Manuel folded his hands behind his back. "This is not a hotel."

"But everything comes with a price."

"Not the most precious things."

Shouts down below.

Manuel glanced at me. "Who looks for you?"

I said nothing.

"It may help us to know."

A gunshot blast. Clear and distinct.

Manuel's face tightened. "What have you brought on us?" He quickly left, locking the door behind him. I glanced at the crucifix.

"Not friends."

Raised voices echoed beneath my feet, disappeared and then reappeared in the hall outside. They neared, and I removed my diary. When they burst in, I would at least appear at peace. I would not give them the satisfaction of causing visible fear upon their arrival.

And they would arrive. I didn't understand the Spanish spoken two hours ago. That the bloke who promised me a safe room for the night near Bocogrande had returned seeking much more? That had been clear.

That I had fled down Avenida San Martin with torn clothes, severely embarrassing my attacker, now clear as well.

This would not end peacefully.

I prayed.

I stared at the small crucifix and prayed, all the time listening to shouts just outside my door.

I don't suppose it to be your typical prayer:

"Well then, God. My name is Clara. We've not spoken for years. I admit, I am not entirely certain you can help me, hanging on the wall as you are. Your position always seems rather … ungodlike. Right now, I would prefer a Zeus with several thunderbolts."

The doorknob rattled.

"If you saw what I did with Little T, then I suppose we can consider this conversation over. Especially if you've minded me over the years. But perhaps you were busy when I lived on Marbury. And earlier tonight. And yesterday. Perhaps you are feeling generous toward those who should be in the slammer."

I paused, and thought of Dad. "Not that you've shown much generosity toward him."

More doorknob rattling.

"However, I do not have access to Zeus. I seem to be stuck with you."

I then reached for a pen; the next minute blurred, but the one that followed was oddly clear, and I recorded the words I heard in my diary:

And I, my dear Clara, am gleefully stuck with you.

I read the line, so foreign to my world, over and over. I read it aloud and mouthed each syllable. I ignored the row, and turned the phrase over in my mind, until the sentence blocked out the argument outside my tower door.

And when next I looked up from my reading, there was no argument. The night was silent.

I rose and pressed my ear against the wood. No movement in the hall, and I quietly slipped out. Downstairs, there were overturned tables, broken chairs, and smashed glass — and a group of monks at prayer.

"I … I never meant to bring trouble. I heard the shot. Is someone, did someone … Where did they all go? I heard them outside my door."

Manuel alone peeked up. "We are all fine, Clara," he said, and lowered his head.

"Okay then. I'm going to sort this all out on my own. It's best not to bring you into it." I jogged upstairs, grabbed my bag, and turned to the crucifix. "Perhaps you might come in handy."

That night, I stole God from a monastery.

The cart jolted away the memory, and I started and calmed. The crucifix was still tucked in my bag, a relic, a souvenir from an unexplainable scrape.

I clung to the mysterious phrase as I bumped nearer to Elias.

My dear Clara, I am gleefully stuck with you.

Those words; too much to believe.

I'd only heard them once.

Even if they were rubbish, how I wished I could hear them again.

CHAPTER 24

I drifted through many countries that night, the gentle rocking teasing out many memories, but eventually I woke, my body warm and my mind clear. I sat up and eased against Izzy, ever the vigilant mate.

"Morning," she yawned. "You're probably wondering where you are, other than in a back of a cart, so here's what I understand. First, the hippies, though I wouldn't call them that. I also wouldn't call them gypsies or nuts, as apparently many in town do. Artists. That's what they are. This is a communal community of artists. And they'll take us in."

"Without knowing anything about us?" I asked, rubbing my hands over my jeans. I was in tatters. "They aren't monks?"

"None that I've seen, although your antics didn't allow me to explore the place as I'd wanted to. Salem Art Works. That is the name of it. These guys up front? They're working artists here. Helpful, don't you think?"

The sun yellowed the tops of the mountains, and then oranged the middle, and finally purpled the roots. And in a moment imperceptible, morning came, and autumn leaves exploded along the road before me.

"Good timing. Breakfast," one of the guys called as he turned right onto Cary Lane.

Breakfast. When had I last enjoyed a meal? I had no interest in one now. The Great Undoing felt so near to me, like one of the blankets about my shoulders. I threw off the quilt, but still the pain remained, as did my promise. I would tell Elias, my Elias, the next time I saw him. And I would apologise for my behaviour in the tower, for placing him in an awkward position.

The horses stopped, and Izzy hopped out. "Can you stand, Clarita?"

"Of course I can ... stand." Legs wobbled, and I eased myself over the edge, clutching my diary. "So this commune is a rubbish heap, is it?"

"Rubbish?" One of the men chuckled, and pulled the horse and cart away. "Very organised and useful rubbish, which means it isn't rubbish at all."

"Oh, I don't know," his friend said. "Let's say you stacked banana peels in a neat pile. It would be organised and useful in that nobody would slip, but still its nature is rubbish."

"No, its nature is then art."

"Art isn't rubbish."

"But it can be made from rubbish."

The argument soon disappeared from earshot as they walked horses toward a distant stable. "Let me show you around," Izzy said, and took my hand. Together we wandered past a heap of wood, as well as a rusted VW tipped on its side. To the left, a classic silver Porsche, Vermont plates, its interior moulded and ripped beyond repair. And everywhere, shapes. Things.

Sculptures.

Like the garden Jakob had showed me in Minneapolis, huge undefinable sculptures rose from the lawn, presumably complete, absolutely nonsensical. Hunks of metal, and gnarled, rotted wood. Giant obelisks and children's upside-down play sets. A car-sized egg sprouted great fins separated by dinosaur egg-shaped spheres. Abstract sculptures set to enormous scale, bordering on the bizarre.

Except the Porsche.

"So much junk."

"So much art," Izzy said quietly. "My parents' home was filled with pieces like this. So I suggest that until you develop an eye for it, you keep your trap shut. We're guests."

"Welcome." A lady with a Great Dane at her side strode quickly up to us. "And you are Clara. Or Clarita."

I nodded. "I think so."

"I'm Julie. Just first names here. I oversee the Salem Art Works. You need to understand that it is not our practice to accept projects without applications, but when we saw Elias's undertaking, we were quite pleased to provide space and materials."

"Where is he?"

"That was a stipulation made. You, specifically, are not to be told. The property is large, and no doubt you will see him, but while he works, he said that you would cover his share of the communal—"

"No, that's not acceptable. I need to talk to him, and that requires seeing him, which I will be—"

"As I was saying . . ." Julie bent down and stroked her dog. "You will carry his communal load. Cooking. Cleaning. Working. Is this agreeable to you?"

"Blast! I may as well go back to London."

Julie stiffened. "I'll tell Elias that he needs to leave by nightfall."

Izzy grabbed my arm and pulled me aside. "You know what might help you—and take this as a suggestion—think of some-body other than yourself for, oh, a few seconds. And if that's too great a challenge for your self-absorbed brain, remember that this might help soften your future discussion with Elias. And if that doesn't work, remember that I own a guitar!"

"Shut it! This is what I did my whole life! This is what I ran from!" I hissed.

"Again, the liar." Izzy turned to Julie. "She'll do it."

"Very well, Clara Clarita." Julie rose. "I'll lead you to your platform. You'll be sharing a tent with our newest resident artist."

I pointed at Izzy. "We will have words."

I followed Julie to a series of wooden platforms, raised three feet off the ground and placed in a circle surrounding a red fire truck—which hopefully was more art than function. A tent stood on each platform, some fronted by lawn furniture, others lonely and small. Julie led me to a spacious tent. I climbed onto the platform and peeked inside. A girl, slightly older than I, relaxed in a bean bag chair.

Julie appeared at my side, pointing to each of us in turn. "Clara Clarita, Serene. I'll meet you by the visitor center in two hours."

My bag rested beside a mattress on the floor, and I collapsed onto the cushion.

"She isn't bad." Serene grinned. "She's just seen it all. She wants to get the best out of us."

I rolled onto my back. "Well then, what brings you to this freak show?"

She frowned and chuckled. "Same thing that brings us all. The hope for some inspiration. A few months to focus on glass work." She shifted. "And you?"

I yawned. "I was guiding a boy with two identities bent on finding the evil Keeper before the Keeper's efforts destroyed the kingdom of Salem. The queen is dead, I seduced the boy, and now the Great Undoing is coming out in bits, and I need to know how it ends and whether I've mucked it up with the boy. Until then, I'm here in a crazy world of hippies."

Serene thought about this.

"So what's your medium?"

"Excuse me?"

"Glass, pottery, wood, iron, the forge?"

I sat up. "You have a forge?"

"Yeah. In the blacksmith shop. Near the glass works area."

Time to meet Hephaestus.

· · · · ·

I didn't meet him that day.

Instead, I hauled shards of glass to the glassworks, metal chunks to the iron works, moulds from the sand barn to the oven, and clay pieces to the kiln. Then I started on dinner, the only meal that brought the entire community together in the square.

I would show my Elias a new humility. Yes, it was a pain, but he would see how I had changed. He would see, and then he would love me too, and maybe I wouldn't need to go into the past, as we would live in the future, maybe together. Maybe for a while.

I worked the barbecue beneath the makeshift tent. Chickens were roasting. And I made three salads as side dishes, using the final offerings from the communal garden. This would be my finest meal.

Slowly, mouths from across the property appeared, eagerly grabbing my creation. No Elias. One chicken was soon devoured, and my best salad vanished along with the scalloped potatoes. No Elias.

And then, Elias.

He was grimy from forehead to foot, but not his hands. They were clean and spotless. I stood directly behind the barbecue, positioning myself as he approached. He walked slow and smooth, without the erect posture of the Other One. My Elias. We would meet, but maybe a different we. I held my breath as he reached for a plate, reached for a drumstick, and moved on.

No words passed between us. No glances. He sat down among a group of ten young people, and they laughed, and joked, late into the night.

I watched them from a small table in the distance. I poked my food around my plate, but did not eat.

Family. Elias was once again among family. His voice rang clear and joyful, and with every contented note, I sank deeper. I was losing precious time with Elias—the clear one, the gentle one ... the one who needed to hear me say I'm sorry.

Family. I smashed my plate on the table and ran to my tent. "Better still be here. Better still be ... here." I yanked out my laptop, threw open the top, and typed in my web address.

Dad: When did you destroy one you love? Have you done this
recently? Clara? Clara.

I stared at my dad's response and typed.

Me: I seem to do this to everyone I meet. "Come on. Be there."

Dad: You must be my daughter.

I breathed deeply.

Me: I can't come home yet.

Me: Dad?

Dad: It was a lot to ask. Can you tell me about him?

Me: Well, he's American.

Dad: I like him already. Do I get a name?

Me: Um. Elias.

Dad: Is he good to you?

Me: At least half the time.

Dad: Where are you now?

Me: New York.

Dad: Where will you go next?

Me: I'm just following stars and myths and ... I've slipped from reality. I don't know where I'm going. In search of a Keeper. A Lightkeeper.

Dad: You say you've slipped. How far?

Me: Do you remember when you read me Alice in Wonderland? Either Wonderland or the Matrix. I'm not quite sure.

Dad: You worry me. Will you slip so far that I can't follow? Will you come home?

The question didn't feel so heavy, and as Serene entered the tent, I feigned sleep and thought on. Home.

Serene soon slept soundly, her gentle breathing the only sound. Almost the only sound.

A sharp laugh and then distant voices. Voices and drums and a flute. I crawled out of my tent and wandered back toward the commons area, where we had eaten, from where I fled.

Smoke billowed and flames crackled, visible high above the rise of the visitor center. I snuck around the building, and froze.

Fifteen, maybe twenty people danced on the concrete floor in front of a roaring bonfire. Another set flailed around the circle. A gypsy gathering, the music was simple and hypnotic.

"Where are we?" I asked.

Then I saw him. With her. Elias and Izzy held hands and ringed the blaze, their faces alight with light and laughter and each other. I stared, shivering, from a distant shadow, rubbing my own arms, warming my own body.

He was happy. He was more than happy; he was alive. He high-fived others in his furious dance, his awkward, disgusting, glorious dance. Izzy stroked his neck and threw herself into his arms, and then they disappeared around the dark side of the moon, only to reappear again linked to others.

"So this is it, Elias. You've found your home."

And I wanted to hate and I wanted to rage. I wanted to feel the burn of abandonment and the sting of betrayal, but I couldn't. I couldn't hate either one of them.

I laughed.

Not a joyful laugh, a releasing laugh. Tears streamed down, and I crumpled back against the building. I had lost. I had lost Elias to a homeless vagabond who should be at Harvard. For the first time since I left London, I had nothing.

My hands fell to my sides, and I stared up at the sky and the stars that shone brighter than I thought possible.

I turned my back on the one I loved. I needed to be alone. Away from the party. Away from wild and abandoned and warm. I strode a determined path straight toward a cut that led up the nearby mountain.

And I climbed. There was no weaving. All was up. The grade was steep and the path was covered with leaves. I slid often to my knees, scrambling ever higher on all fours. An hour later, I still climbed. The air was thinner, my breathing heavier, but there would be no stopping. I would follow this path, my path to its conclusion.

Then, there it was.

Trees gave way, and a small clearing leveled off. In front of me, one bench. Before it, an eight-foot cross. Was it sculpture? Was it spiritual? It didn't matter; it was in my way.

I gathered my breath and lowered myself onto the seat. Far below me, I could see the flicker of the fire. I could still imagine the sound of their voices, their drums.

Elias's smile.

I turned toward the task at hand.

"Well, here is the problem. You seem to have abandoned me as well, God. At least in the smaller version of you that I stole, you are present and hanging on it."

There should have been a breeze. Something. But this place was still and heavy. Like the underground tunnels, it felt occupied, somehow.

"But I didn't climb this path for nothing. My goal was to be alone, but since you intruded at the end of my road, shall we begin?" I cleared my throat. "Cross, you have lost your God. Now I shall tell you what I have lost. Elias, for one, and after no small expense of time and effort."

I paused, my eyes stinging. Fortunately, I was done crying.

I wasn't done crying.

I buried my face in my hands. "I lost him to Izzy."

I sniffed. "Do you know her? You may want to pay attention to that one, though I think her perhaps one of my better mates. I also lost Mum. I would think you saw that; it was in the papers. She gave nothing to me and I returned the favour.

"My sibs. Most certainly gone as well." I peeked over my shoulder. I could no longer see the fire. "And I think my purpose.

"Finally, I have lost the truth. I had a good grip on it, until apparently a mentally ill mentalist turned up with portions I hadn't been aware could exist. Without the Elias I used so well, I will now never discover if he saw all of the Great Undoing.

"What remains?" I shook my head. "Rather unexpectedly, I still have a father. He wants me back in London. He wants me ... at least now he does, but he doesn't know. Nobody but the mentalist knows. Well, maybe you know."

Guilt. Suffocating and constant; my decade-long companion. I waited for the crushing. The thought of Little T's last day was often the moment when it arrived to torment me. Whenever memories wandered the wasteland of the Great Undoing, I shared a path with my cruelest mate.

Maybe my bench was too small or the climb too steep. Maybe the hill too remote. Guilt was silent. I even tossed him some bread-crumbs and thought of Elias's drawings, of the shadow child Izzy saw. Still nothing.

What was it about this place that could absorb every loss and hold guilt at arm's length?

I rose. "I'm, um, going to go back down. I may return." My hand caressed the bench. "Don't let anyone take my seat."

The walk down was arduous, and my legs felt like lead weights. I fell from trunk to trunk, slowly working down the mountain until finally I emerged by an oversized iron hippo just as the sun hinted an arrival.

I quietly walked to my tent, and re-entered, my mind unusually quiet, and began to hum.

• • • • •

Days fell into rhythms, rhythms that calmed me. Quieted me.

I rose at six, and though breakfast was an on-your-own affair, all week I made sure that there was sausage, bacon, and rolls waiting for any artist who wanted a fine English breakfast. It was only at mealtime that I saw Elias. He came, ate, broke my heart, and left.

I could have spoken. An older version of me would have. But it felt right to wait. I cleaned and hauled and prepared the next two meals, always fading from sight as the groups gathered. There was a small table behind the main building, and that was where I ate after, alone, smiling at the jokes I heard, aching at Elias's laughter. At the small miracle of his being, ever since we arrived, the Elias I loved, only to now be the Elias I could not experience.

But always there was the night. The night was mine. Sometimes to the music of the fife, other times in silence, I climbed a mountain and sat before a Godless cross, my visits lengthening.

My easy rapport with the non-god surprised me, but never

frightened me, and each morning I returned to my tent for a few hours of sleep, a bit less certain of my future, a bit less needing to know.

"You always eat alone?"

Serene plunked down at my dinner table. Night was falling, and I could hardly see her face.

"Yes," I said.

"You don't like people?"

I laughed. "I do … You said you came to get away. For inspiration. Turns out maybe I did too."

"Your friend. Elias. He's the talk of the compound."

"How so?"

Serene shook her head. "He's been given the shed."

I set down my fork. "I'm not certain what that means."

"The shed." Serene gestured beyond Barn 1. "Behind the sand barn. It's the only private workspace. I don't know what he's doing in there. I see him at the blacksmith's. Sometimes at the glassworks. I've watched him pour forms and reinforce metal and shape panels. He's talented."

I nodded. "He is." I looked off. "Is that Izzy with him most times?"

Serene shrugged. "Yeah."

I closed my eyes. "That's all right. So you don't know how long they're planning on staying?"

"Well, actually I do. Tomorrow, there's a big deal in the commons. Elias is going to be showing what he's created. The best art, probably his, finds a place on the grounds, and after that, artists usually go on their way."

"I didn't know."

"Well, now you do." Serene rose and paused. "And now you can do something about it." She winked and disappeared into the night.

I did not climb the mountain that evening.

• • • • •

"Psst! Where you been?"

My shoulders shook, and Elias's face appeared through my blurred vision.

"I've been sitting on that bench for two hours."

"What bench?" I asked, propping myself on an elbow.

He pointed up. "The one way up there."

My fingers fidgeted, and then my body followed suit. "How do you know about that?"

Elias pulled me from the tent into the moonlight. My shorts and halter top did little to warm me.

He stared. "Wow, you really look good."

I scrunched and threw back my hair. "You don't need to pretend, Elias. I know. I've seen. I'm almost genuinely happy for you and Izzy." I shivered. "But it's cold, and I'm not dressed, so tell me how you know about my little trips and then get some sleep. I hear you have quite the show tomorrow."

"Your trips. Yeah, well, about that. I've, uh, I've followed you. And that show—"

"Followed me? You've lurked behind me?" I paused. "Listened to me?"

He kicked at the ground. "Maybe."

I grabbed his T-shirt. "Those words, my private words, were most definitely not meant for these ears!" I twisted his right lobe until he winced.

He massaged his ear. "Some of them sounded like maybe they were. I just wanted to be where you were."

I took a deep breath. "So how many times were you there? Once? Twice?"

He stepped back. "All week."

"All week. All blasted week. Why not just steal my diary and read it cover to cover?"

"I can't."

We stood looking at each other. Serene poked out her head, and we both shot her a glare. She quickly disappeared.

"Clara, I came to apologise, 'cause I took something from you. I get it now. I took your privacy."

I thought about my non-god talks, my non-god confessions. Had I ever spoken of the Undoing aloud?

No. I breathed easier.

"Well then, I suppose, I suppose that I took something from you as well. In the tower. I shouldn't have ..."

"Shouldn't have what?" Elias asked.

"You know very well the what I'm referring to."

Elias raised his brows, waiting.

"I took the advantage. It's one of the ways I've used you. It's what I do."

"Awesome." He grabbed my hand and yanked me away from the warmth of the tent. "You need to see this. Before anyone else, you need to see this."

We ran toward the shed, and Elias opened the padlock. He winked and threw open the doors. One Porsche and one airplane.

"Are they—"

"Finished. Done. Ready to go." He placed his hand on the plane. I rubbed mine on the Porsche.

"You rebuilt it. I mean, inside and out." I peeked inside. New seat. New leather interior. A new dash. "She's fast, isn't she?"

"Very."

"Think we can take her out tonight?"

He looked over at me. "Yeah. Let's try. It'll be her maiden flight."

I pulled on the passenger door. "It's locked."

"I'll help you up on this side."

I walked around and Elias lifted me, turned me in the air and set me in the plane. "Get settled. Belts and goggles."

"Wait. I was referring to the car. I've been in enough tiny planes."

"No worries, mate. Isn't that what you would say? I can fly it. I built it, floor to flaps. I've tested it . . . and Juan isn't here to stop us."

A minute later, the propeller was spinning, and I was freezing.

Two minutes later, we eased out.

Three minutes, and we bounced across the field, gathering speed, gathering strength, bound to the earth, and then, we weren't.

We didn't travel far or high, maybe twenty feet off the ground, just high enough to narrowly miss telephone poles. But I was alive again. And the wind in my face joined the lightness in my heart, because I was with Elias again. My trusting Elias. The Elias who could bring hardened metal to life and make it soar.

He had the same effect on me.

Ten minutes later we set back down, bounced to a stop, and rolled it back into the shed.

"You built an aeroplane." I rubbed my face. "You built a bloomin' aeroplane out of junk!"

Elias helped me out. "They think these are sculptures. But I figured if we are on a road trip, we may as well travel in style." He gestured at the Porsche. "I made a small trade. Should fit three nicely."

"And when are we leaving?"

"Now."

CHAPTER 25

I returned from my tent, my bag slung over my back. The plane was loaded on a trailer, and Elias was once again busy removing the left wing with a blowtorch. Three men eased it down, tucked it into the fuselage, and Elias secured it.

"I don't know how many times I'll need to do that. Hopefully this was it." He breathed deep and reached out the U-Haul keys. "Kirk, the truck stays with you. But I can't help thinking I got the better deal."

A large artist eagerly grabbed the keys. "Are you kidding? Even if it had been working before, we had no purpose for the rusted Porsche. I just hope your guy back in Wisconsin will accept the Porsche in the truck's stead."

"Shouldn't be a problem." Izzy appeared, carrying her guitar case. "He'll be fine with the deal." She smiled at Elias. "It's been quite a trip. Just look at you two now."

I walked toward her. "You're not coming?"

"No. I'm staying here for a while. They don't seem to mind that I'm a nut, or that I don't have it all together, you know? This seems like a good place to figure out my story, and then maybe ... maybe I go home. Tell my parents that Anchorage has a university too."

I blinked. "I thought you said you didn't have 'rents anymore. I really thought you had done the deed."

Izzy laughed. "I love them, you dummy. Who do you think is after me? Not the law. My parents have never stopped looking for me. But Wisconsin can wait a few more weeks." She raised her guitar case. "Every commune needs a troubadour."

"You actually play?" I gave her a hug. "And your 'rents live where we found you?"

"An hour away. Oh, London. Take care of him," she said. "Lots of love there, and it's all for you. Mistreat him and I *will* kill you." Izzy's voice softened. "Even though I love you."

She set down her case and popped the latch, removed a steel-stringed guitar, and she played. It was quiet and beautiful and haunting. She played as we climbed in the car. She played through the starting of the engine.

Izzy played until she was a shadow in my rearview mirror.

I reached the end of Cary Road and paused at the T, glancing left and then right. "I don't know where to go."

"I know."

"Does that bother you?" I asked.

Elias shook his head. "Take me someplace new."

"New. Well, we were west, we can continue east. It doesn't matter, because maybe the real you is finally here to stay. Maybe the Other One is gone."

He gently kissed my ear. "No. I feel it. I'm slipping right now, Clara. Hold my hand."

I did. For an hour, our fingers intertwined. I shared stories of London. Of Marbury street. Of my dad and my mum, Teeter and Marna. He said nothing.

"And there's one more story I need to tell." I took a deep breath. "Because it explains pretty much everything about why I'm here."

His grip tightened around my fingers, and then released. I looked into his eyes.

My Elias was gone.

"What happened to the truck?" he asked.

I shook my head.

"And Izzy. Where is she? Where's the guard?"

"Home. She's going home."

"I see." He bowed his head. "Are you going to abandon me too?"

I took hold of his wrist. "No, Elias. You and I will continue together. We need to leave Salem temporarily. Care to consult your map?"

Elias bowed his head.

What was it like to live with gaps? To be here one moment and gone the next? I once felt sorry only for my Elias, but here, with the Other One, I felt for him too.

"Clarita? This is for you."

He placed the sketch on my lap.

"No, Elias, take it back. I don't need to see it."

Elias slowly removed the sheet. "But it explains ..."

"It's a father running and a child fleeing, isn't it?"

Elias shifted. "What else do you know?"

I forced a smile. "I know that for the first time maybe I don't need to ... know, that is."

"Well," Elias said, and his voice drifted.

Izzy had come and gone, but her words hung with me. I would look after Elias. I would set myself aside, at least until this quest was done. There would be plenty of time to broach the topic of my secret during the return trip.

He cleared his throat. "Orion's clear tonight. Did we find the forge? Did you meet Hephaestus?"

"Yes." I pointed toward the back. "The forge fixed the plane. I flew in it. Amazing skill."

"So still on track. We continue." Elias pointed to the right. "We should head to the east. To the sun. Or in our case to the light to find the Lightkeeper. We stop the evil; Salem is healed."

And maybe you are too.

· · · · ·

Vermont.

New Hampshire.

Our road twisted through beautiful mountains. Not like the Alps, with their crags and peaks. Switzerland caused awe and wonder, its terrain created by an angry God with a sharp chisel. These mountains rolled like waves, smoothed, perhaps, by the flow of prehistoric seas. Gentle. Comforting. We whisked through the dark, through the rise and fall left by deep waters.

Then, we couldn't.

"Elias. Wake up." I shook his shoulder. "We've reached the ocean."

He stretched and blinked. "The ocean. We are far from Salem, aren't we?"

"Yes. We must have crossed into Maine." I pulled over, the turn-off to I–95 looming. "There is no more east. It's north or south from here on. Not much more north either. You have no passport. Canada isn't an option."

Cars rushed by us, and I stared at a distant bay, whose hand reached out and grasped the Atlantic, whose hand reached out and grasped my home. *England.* It called from the other side of that sea. *London.* It had been months since I'd turned to face it.

Elias fought with his star map, twisting and turning it until the direction lined up. "We are out of stars. We're at the edge of the world. This is the horizon."

"Well then, I say we head north."

"Why?" he asked.

"Reach me my diary."

I opened the pages and flicked on the dome light.

"Kabul. Day 102. I bumped into the three on a small street, safe supposedly, but crumbling. I wanted to see this place, this mess of a country. My dad had built a hospital, and I hoped to stay there, but fighting had leveled it. So I turned around, retracing my steps. I walked quickly, my head covered, through the shadows. I was prepared for misery. I was not prepared for this chance encounter.

"Two Americans and a Swede. They called themselves Peacewalkers."

"Peacewalkers?" Elias frowned.

"Uh. Travelers from Salem."

Elias gave an exaggerated nod. "I suppose you've bumped into them during your travels."

"Well, these three used to be five. One perished in Syria. One in Cyprus. They had walked across Iraq and through Iran. They had walked South Sudan and years ago walked Rwanda. Yugoslavia. Libya. Egypt. One walked Vietnam. Wherever there was war, they walked."

I paused. The faces of these three older men were imprinted in my mind like few others.

"Why were they walking?"

"They were praying." I sighed. "To non-god. They were praying for peace, for Salem. I told them they were simply causing more disruption. That if they were ever taken, they would be used and tortured, and the United States and Sweden would be in a quandary of sorts, not knowing whether to attempt a rescue. I told them they were placing their homelands in a scrape."

I looked out the window. "They said they were walking to a different homeland. They had left instructions to be ignored. They believed they needed to pray. There were explosions in the distance, and I suggested perhaps non-god could not hear them over the sounds of war. They lay their hands on my head and began to babble, but I shrugged them off and headed south, back toward the airport.

"They headed north, citizens of two countries, proud of one but searching for another. Searching for Salem."

It was quiet for a while. "I wonder who they were." He folded up his map and tucked it in the glove compartment. "We won't need this anymore. Did they say they had seen the Keeper, the enemy?" Elias said.

"Oh, I am certain they had seen him up close."

"Then north. We'll go north like they did, and we'll prepare."

"Prepare?"

"Pray." Elias folded his hands. "Do you know how?"

"For me, it seems to be an acquired taste." I bit my lip. "Maybe if I'm alone and given the right environment."

"Start."

Elias squeezed tight his eyes and bowed his head. He had assumed the position. This had not been the desired outcome of the story. "I, uh, I shall pray quietly."

"How am I supposed to learn?" he asked without opening his eyes. "Pray."

I exhaled, and forced my mind onto non-god, onto the large cross. "Um, we're in Maine. We are looking for — "

"The Keeper," Elias whispered. "Tell God we're looking for the Keeper."

"I was coming to that," I hissed. "As you just heard, we are looking for the Keeper. If you answer mythological inquiries, perhaps you could show us where to go. The end."

I stepped on the gas and drove into morning, trying to place as many miles as possible between me and my first public prayer. We were close to our destination, I could sense it, and there would be no more slowing now.

CHAPTER 26

Maine took my breath away.

Mountains bathed in colour sloped down on the left to kiss the sea on the right, and in between we zipped forward on this ribbon of tar, tracing the shape of each bay, of each harbour.

And then, north of Portsmouth, I saw it.

The Keeper's Inn.

It was just a small bed and breakfast. A converted white clapboard carriage house. But the sign was clear, at least to me.

I slowed and turned my head. Evil did not emanate from the windows, and the place held no malice. It shook me just the same.

Not as much as the next sighting.

The Keeper's Eatery.

Fifteen minutes separated the buildings, likely unrelated concerns. I scanned the landscape harder. Fish houses. Lobster houses. Lightkeeper mercantile.

Keeper.

That word graced signs and businesses everywhere I looked. If Elias knew what surrounded him, he would be beside himself. Well, beside this self.

"Elias. I know you trust me as your guide."

"I do."

"But this quest. I know so little about this Keeper. Could you clarify anything that might help me as I search? Do you have any more details? Anything at all?"

He removed his sketchbook from his pack. He hunched over a page, and his hands clutched and re-clutched a pencil. Finally, he let his hand go. Minutes later, he reached me the pad. "I guess it's time. I have that."

"It's a lighthouse."

"I don't know. Maybe."

"No, not maybe ... and not a general lighthouse. This is a specific one. We're looking for the keeper of this lighthouse. Am I correct?"

"I don't know."

"It makes sense, doesn't it? And what's this building, this faint building. Is it a building?" I squinted at the structure sketched so lightly it was hardly there. "Is this a mistake?"

"I don't draw mistakes." He folded his arms.

"Right, well, may I keep this? Just until we arrive? I think it may prove quite handy."

We drove on, and for the first time the scenery stole attention from our purpose. There was a piece of England on this coast, with settlements wrapping arms around each inlet. We reached Penobscot Bay, and the towns lining it grew smaller, and quainter. The pace slowed and the air was kissed with salt. Rockland. Rockport.

Camden.

"Stop here." Elias pressed his nose against the glass. "Stop here." He swallowed and glanced around, his head cocked. "That bay."

"Do you remember something?" I asked, and slowly pulled onto a side road.

"I remember."

We had been following idiocy for so long, the presence of a memory, a real memory, felt a certainty that should not be ignored, no matter how faint. I screamed and pounded the wheel. "I knew it. I knew it, Elias. We would get near and you would remember, and then not just part of you but the other part of you, and when both of you remember … Oh, Elias, this is it. I feel it."

"What are you taking about?"

"It doesn't matter. What do you remember? Maine? Camden? Penobscot Bay? A building? A street?"

"A feeling."

I paused. "You remember a feeling? That's it?"

He patted his belly. "I'm hungry. Come on." Elias got out of the Porsche.

"So he remembers being hungry. We stop in Camden because his stomach grumbles." I tongued the inside of my cheek and rubbed my face. "Fine."

We wandered downtown, past the white clapboard inns and flower shops, and into the town's three-story brick heart, my steps a few behind Elias's. There was a uniqueness to his wandering, a route filled with frequent pauses and lengthened looks.

Until we reached the wharf.

Then his feet found purpose, and he quickened his gait. Beyond the harbour; up, over, and around on the road that traced its shape. He veered toward the water again, and then Elias ran.

And stopped.

Laite Beach. Elias stepped gingerly onto the sand-less shore. He crunched over pebbles and shells, dropped to his knees, and pressed his ear against the ground. Dots were connecting—I knew it—and I gave him room, room to walk on the tide wall, balancing as a child. Room to dip his hand in the water.

Thirty minutes later, Elias still stared at the tide, before glancing at a small island on his right.

It happened.

"Curtis Island." Elias pointed into the distance. "See it? That's Curtis Island." He half turned and gazed at the mountain on his left.

"That's Mount Battie. I've been to the top before. From the top you can see everything."

I froze.

The confused one. The Other One. The paranoid Elias stepped into *my* world.

I broke into a run and wrapped him in a hug. "You remember this place! Elias, this is real. These places are real. These memories are real. We aren't in Salem, we're not following stars or myths, but still you remember."

He looked at me, fear in his eyes.

I shook my head. "We found it, a memory that predates your Great Undoing."

"I want to leave." Elias abruptly turned from the sea and climbed back onto the road. We followed its curves back into town. Passed the swaying boats of the Camden Yacht Club and across Frye Street. We split the red brick buildings straddling the road, and peeked into the windows of several chowder houses.

Then the town opened, and the road forked before us. Everywhere floated the smell of fish, and we wandered into Boynton-McKay, and plunked down in one of the high-backed booths.

"Is this all right?" he asked. "I'm so hungry."

"You find yourself and you're still thinking of food?" I rolled my eyes and ordered a bowl of haddock chowder. Elias did the same.

"I do think we're close," he said. "Close to ultimate evil."

I smiled, raised a spoonful of chowder, took aim, and flicked it into his face.

He methodically wiped it off and dumped his bowl on my head.

"You jerk!" I swept thick and creamy off my face. "That was not responding in kind!"

"What you did was not kind!"

A waitress eased over and winced. "Other ways to protest the chowder, though nobody ever has before. You're not from around here."

I grabbed the towel from her hands and wiped chowder from my hair. "I'm certain it's top rate. I'm sorry about the mess. It was a misunderstanding. But you're right, we do need some locals." I stood and stepped into the middle of the eatery, chunky fish drippings falling to the floor. "I'm looking for a lighthouse. I am running out of patience. I smell like haddock. Can anybody help me?"

"Ayup. Which one, lass?" A man wearing rubber overalls slid out of his seat.

I thought and dug in my pocket, brought out Elias's picture. "This. I want this one."

"Well, it ain't Matinicus." A rough voice from behind. "Not Browns Head, either."

"Don't look nothing like Boon or Goat Island."

Soon I was surrounded by ten patrons.

"Seguin?"

"No, fool."

"Ain't the Heron's Neck Light or Owls Head."

I pulled the picture to my chest. "How many of these bloomin' lights are there?"

"Sixty, maybe seventy."

"You know where you need to go?" A rough voice cut through, and the others fell silent.

"If I did, I wouldn't be standing here covered in soup."

An old man smiled, his front teeth absent. He hobbled forward, his face weathered but his eyes clear. "I know a lobsterman. He'll know your lighthouse."

"Thank you. Did you hear that, Elias? This gentleman knows . . . Elias?"

Our booth was empty, save for a sketch on the table.

A head surrounded by a pool of blood.

Yes, that had happened. I picked up the sheet. We were near the end of my story, and as hard as I tried to focus on Elias's quest, panic rose in me again. I was so close to my fear. The next sketch. It would tell all.

I pushed outside, calling, running, calling more. Finally, I returned and paid for the meal.

"You still want to find your lighthouse, lass?"

I felt in my pocket. I had the keys; Elias wasn't going anywhere. I slowly folded the sketch. He wanted me to have it and know exactly what he knew. To that end, Elias would stay and perhaps discover more memories in the process. I hoped.

"Carry on."

I hopped inside a stranger's truck and sunk into my seat. Of all the horrid moments to lose Elias.

"You seem a girl with chowder on her head and a load of cares on her mind."

I forced a smile. "I'm entertaining a few."

"Call me Salt—it's what they all do." He reached out his hand, and though his knuckles were gnarled, his grip was strong.

"Call me Clarita, I guess."

"Pretty name." We pulled onto the windy road that snaked through Camden. He pointed at the harbour. "Walked down there yet? Camden's got a beautiful harbour all right, but it ain't the working man's harbour it once was. Tourists and artists here now. See all them boats? Shrink-wrapped for the season. Got soft up here.

"Now, where we going, a few towns up, the lobsterman still work it hard. Take St. George, 'bout fifteen miles south, it's where we'll find him. He'll know your light, if it is to be known."

I nodded. Something about Salt was comfortable, like Dad's old armchair. "Thanks for your time. Let me reimburse—"

"Naw. A chance for Old Salt to carriage a beautiful young fishsmellin' woman? Maybe some of the local seniors'll see me in action and my prospects will improve."

I laughed and straightened. "Oh, a charming gentleman like yourself?"

"Talk to lobster your whole life, and you almost forget normal human interaction ... There. Lean on over here and take a look. There's a light for you." Salt pointed out his window at a lonely tower, rising in the distance. "Now, that's not yours, but another's been restored. These days, they're all automated. Maintained by Fish and Wildlife. No more lightkeepers. No need." He turned and smiled. "But we lobstermen, can't rid Maine of us. Can't replace a lobsterman with a computer."

We drove through a scenic wonderland, through Rockland and finally into Rockport. The entire way, Salt talked of bait and traps, islands and storms. But these words I caught only in disconnected pieces. My mind was on Elias.

He would not leave a place that he knew. It would eat at him, though it might scare him, but that was all right. He would explore, and I would return with the final piece to his mystery, and perhaps Elias would give the final piece of mine.

His mind might even be whole.

But it was the next step that caused me to stumble. What if he was sound and all I wished for came true? What if somehow this place could do what medication couldn't? What if Elias waited for me?

Wanted me.

So also did my dad.

Elias's path had been clarifying. My own path was becoming murky.

"We're here, lass. St. George. It's where we'll find him."

The road twisted and ended abruptly at the waterfront. Warped docks and lobster traps spread out before me. Salt was right. This harbour was work and sweat and disrepair, the boats that bobbed in the water paint-peeled and pitched tight.

"Tenant's Harbor. On the west end of the Penobscot." Salt hopped out of the truck. "With any luck, we'll find him in. Otherwise, we wait."

We wandered down past nets and repair sheds, toward the colourful lobster boats moored in the harbour. All but one was empty.

Puffins and seagulls flew low overhead and turned east, flying out over the bay. The sky took on the deep shade of London grey, and a rogue memory of my mum pushed in.

"In early, Haley," called Salt.

A gal looked up from the boat, raised her rubber gloves to her hips. She was pretty, working pretty, and she puffed air up and swept back her fringe with the crook of her arm.

"Been some time. Thought you'd grown soft spendin' time wit' all them Camden uppers."

"Oh yes, I have grown soft." He looked at me. "I want to introduce you to my granddaughter, Clarita, from London."

"Hello," I said.

"Well, hell." Haley set to wrapping herring, tossing them into a barrel behind her. "Didn't know you'd ever been across the sea."

"Sometimes the sea just comes to you, then blows back where it come from." Salt grinned.

"Ayup. Reckon it does. But I got seven hundred traps down, and I need to pull up one fifty before the man returns."

"That's who I came to see. I need his eyes."

"Reckon two hours on that." She peeked up at me. "So what's it like in England?"

"Cloudy. Heavy. At least on Marbury Street. The street works the factory. The factory works them until they die, and the next generation takes over."

She looked me over. "You don't seem worked."

"That's true."

Her hands slowed, and she pitched a bait bag into a barrel and straightened. "Years back, Salt and Atticus, they hauled up more lobster than you can imagine. First out, last in. Others saw their buoy colors and they knew to stay away. Ain't so anymore. There's all manner of thievery, especially out past Matinicus."

Salt softened. "That's the island where his reputation, and his moniker, was born. After he took that bullet from another lobsterman, he became Atticus. Territorial dispute, you see."

"Maybe you should spend some time gettin' your hands smelly." She gestured with her head into the boat. "See if any of Salt runs through your veins. You can change yonder."

"No, she can't."

I turned around, and knew at once I was looking at the man.

I had seen old people before. In wheelchairs, or with canes clacking down the street.

But this man was ancient, ancient and terrible. He strode, his legs strong and sure and his black trench coat catching in the wind. His skin was leather, with wrinkles deep and eyes sharp beads. On his head, capturing a white lock, was a yellow bandanna.

More pirate than man, if you asked me.

"Salt. What brings you back?"

"This girl."

Atticus's gaze held me, and I was, temporarily and unexplainably, without words.

"She's his granddaughter," Haley called, without stopping her work.

Atticus smiled. "No, she's not."

Salt smirked. "She needs to find a lighthouse. She has a photo."

Words returned. "A drawing, to be more precise."

Atticus held out his hand, and I removed the sketch from my pocket. He unfolded it, took a one second glance, and handed it back.

"Don't know it."

Salt frowned, and I regained my footing.

"Have you or have you not lived here all your life?" I asked.

"Yeah, ain't nothing new to me."

"I'll wager that you know the location of every dangerous shoal."

"I know where they ain't."

I held the picture in front of his face. "So where is this?"

Haley stared with wide eyes. Salt held back a grin, and Atticus slowly lowered the drawing. "You come to Maine alone?"

"No, I did not. I came with a ... with a friend. Elias."

Atticus took a deep breath, and whispered. "Elias Phinn."

"You know him?" I asked. Elias and his alternate universe had been wholly disconnected along the course of our travels. To discover somebody knew him was unbelievable, akin to a person claiming to live in Salem, and I shook.

"That was Elias Phinn? At Boynton-McKay's? Boy's grown up. Grown strong." Salt grabbed my arm. "Why's he come back? Why'd he come ... back ..." Salt glanced at Atticus, who pursed his lips.

"What does he remember?" Atticus asked.

"Nothing really," I said. "Nothing but this picture and remnants of this place."

Atticus nodded. "Best that's how it all remains. Salt, you old fool." He turned and walked off the dock. The man who knew Elias's past was leaving me. I couldn't let it happen.

"He's not right in the mind!" I called. "He hasn't been right since he was a young lad. Something happened. He's searching for the Keeper. He wants to destroy the evil that comes from this person. I need to know why. Please, we've crossed half the country, and I need to know."

Atticus stopped and slowly turned.

"He wants to destroy him? It's already been done." He glanced at Haley and cursed. "Out. I need the boat. I guess it was going to happen, sooner or later. Time to return to Two Bush Island."

CHAPTER 27

We churned out of Tenant's Harbor, my arms shivering. Not even the lobsterman coat, with a smell that overpowered all leftover hint of chowder, could ease the cold.

Atticus and Salt stood one on either side, but I wanted them nearer. There was a protection in their presence, and I slipped my arm into Salt's.

"Tell her, Atticus. Don't do nothing to show without a tell."

Atticus glanced over at me.

"You don't need to," I said. "You can tell me some other—"

"Elias was six, seven, maybe eight when his father, Elliot, took a job with Fish and Wildlife. It gave him access to all the lighthouses along the coast, but the man's favorite was the light on Two Bush. It's a solitary island, and few know of it, fewer still go near it. Elliot only had to maintain the automatic lamp, is all. But Elliot Phinn had a different love. Them stars."

I slumped down in my chair. "Elias's dad loved constellations."

"To that man, everything important was up, and so he'd hire me to take him out to Two Bush, late at night. As I said, I knew where the shoals weren't, and I'd get him in close. After some effort, he'd climb the light tower with his telescopes and I'd wait near the island."

"There is no good way to climb up on Two Bush." Salt stared out into the bay. "It's a big, flat rock, a plateau wit' cliffs all around."

"Now, I don't know what happened between 'm, that's none of mine ..." Atticus continued. "But Guinevere suddenly stopped comin' round. Figured a divorce, but never pried," he said. "After a bit, though, Little Elias started to come out with his dad, and they'd watch them stars together. Wasn't legal, but I thought it quite a thing for a father to share with his boy. Besides, he paid me well."

I swallowed hard. "It's important for a father to be there for his child."

Salt drew me close.

"That night, sure 'nough, seemed like the others." Atticus's voice seemed far away. "Exceptin' that it was rough. Fifteen minutes turned decent water to choppy foam. I brought out Elliot to Two Bush, except this time he said he'd be spending the whole night, watchin' them stars move. He told me to come out and get him in the morning. No problem there. The life of a lobsterman is a tough one, and I could take twice his money. But Little Elias was waitin' at the pier when I came back, and asked me to take him to his dad. I didn't see the harm in that — couldn't just leave the boy there — and they always went together before, and so I did.

"We reached the island, and the lad clamored up them rocks. I drifted back, waiting, waiting to see him safe into the tower. As the wind's howl picked up, Elias started to run for the door. I saw him stumble down, and I faintly heard his cry, but he was quick back on his feet. He reached the light, threw open the door, and disappeared." Atticus sighed. "I set to leave, but then again I heard his scream. It was a different sound. It wasn't right. I still dream it." Atticus swallowed and looked off. "Elias came bolting out of the lighthouse with his undressed father in pursuit. A woman poked her head out of the door, and I saw right off it wasn't Guinevere. Little Elias must have caught his father in the act."

My knees buckled, but Salt held me fast. "Can you handle more?"

"Carry on," I said quietly.

"The boy reached the rocky cliff line just as his dad caught up. And I heard all the excuses a man tries to give. Elliot tried to grab his son, I imagine to buy more time to right the unthinkable, but little Elias's heart must've already broke, and he pulled free and shoved him. Don't reckon a little kid can shove too hard, but I also don't reckon Elliot was expecting it. With all the spray on those rocks, Elliot slipped off that cliff and fell." Atticus sighed again. "He hit his head square on a rock. I checked him. He was dead, by his own doing and by his son's hand. I left him and the woman, and Elias and I sped away that night. That boy didn't cry the whole way back. He didn't speak. He was ... different. I waited a day to tell authorities, until Elias left town with his grandpa ... I waited until he was in the clear. No boy needs to have that kind of guilt tied to him the rest of his life. Accidently killing his family? Where would he put that?"

"You don't," I said quietly.

"Now the woman ... how she got off the island and who she was? Still a mystery."

The salt breeze blew stiff across my face and my lips felt suddenly dry. I felt dry.

"He killed his dad. He killed the Keeper."

"Man was fishing in foreign waters. There ..." Atticus pointed. "Two Bush."

I shook. I would have to face it, but I couldn't, not without Elias. "Turn around."

"But your lighthouse." Salt stared at me. "It's right there, lass."

"Turn around!"

We swung around the island in silence and returned to the harbour. I hopped off the boat and stumbled on the dock and ran toward Salt's truck, stopping only to gasp on the way.

I threw open the passenger door, denting the silver Camry parked beside it, and climbed in.

Minutes later, Salt eased in beside me. "You all right? I gather Elias didn't share this incident with you."

"Who?"

"Elias."

I burst into tears. Not tears, sobs. Wrenching sobs that ached in a stomach already pained. I grabbed on to Salt and squeezed, without time or place interrupting my thoughts.

"Wait! Yes. Yes he did ..."

The sketchings.

A stormy night.

A horrid fall.

Looking down at a woman.

A horrified Elias fleeing from his father.

Elias's father surrounded by a pool of blood.

"He's been trying to tell me all along. Trying to let me in. But his events and my events ... they matched so closely that I just assumed ..." I rocked and shivered. "His emotions must match mine as well."

I would not hide mine any longer.

Salt stroked my hair. "Sad story, to be sure, but I'm not following."

"See, that was also me. I did it too. It was my fault ..."

He squeezed his forehead, and rubbed his stubble. "Your fault?"

"Don't you see? It has to be, or nothing makes sense!"

Everything in me screamed run, as I had so many times before, as I'd been doing since leaving home. But this time I would not run from, I would run to, to the one who did not hold my secret but knew my heart.

Dash back to Camden. Find Elias and tell him of my Great Undoing. He alone will understand.

The truck would be much faster.

"Salt, take me back quickly. I need to find him."

Without a word, he pulled away from the harbour and onto the road. My leg bounced, and my mind raced.

Elias, please be by the car.

· · · · ·

Not even the car was by the car.

Elias had moved it. Somehow, he had started it, which only my Elias could do. I searched Camden, revisiting the route we had taken.

He was not at Laite Beach.

He was not by Camden Harbour.

He was not by the café.

Night fell, and I wandered back to where the car had been parked, peering at the old carriage houses that lined the road.

Finding Elias would be impossible.

Or not.

Lit up by a house light, and fluttering in the breeze, a single sheet of paper hung a few houses down from where I'd parked. I walked up the drive and removed the picture. A perfect self-portrait of Elias, above an arrow pointing to the carriage doors.

I walked into the garage, and quietly shut the door behind me. Elias sat on a cot, near the Porsche and the aeroplane.

I took my seat beside him.

"It's a strange world we live in, Elias." I breathed heavily, trying to sort my surroundings, but caring very little. "To travel to the other side of the world and find all you've fled from is actually waiting for you. To think I was helping you, and now you're my last hope."

"I know this town, Clarita."

"You're not listening to me. I'm trying to tell you something important. Something really important. And if you don't listen … I need you to listen."

"It started coming back at the beach —"

"Shut it! Are you going to accept my apology or not?"

Elias folded his hands.

I did the same. "Do not ... say ... a word. Not until I'm finished. I do, I want to hear everything you found, but if I don't get this out, I will explode." I rubbed my face. "I need to tell you about my mum."

"I know all about the queen." Elias sounded agitated. Definitely the Other One.

"She's not a queen! She's not ... a ... queen ... At least not when I was younger." I swallowed hard. "At that time she was just a woman, with a husband, living in London on Marbury Street, with a ten-year-old girl and a three-year-old son named Teeter and another just born, Little Thomas. And I was the girl. It was me."

I paused, uncertain if Elias would interrupt, but he sat quietly, and I continued.

"Dad brought Mum home on that day. She'd been at the doctor who was examining Little Thomas, Down's baby that he was, with Teeter and I in tow. There was such a storm! So much wind. So much chill.

"Dad wasn't even supposed to be there — none of it would have happened had he stayed at work — but Mum fell ill in the waiting room. Suddenly, she was vomiting and so dizzy she could hardly stand. She always was weak that way. Someone called Dad, who left work early, arrived and helped her and Little T into the car, and drove us all home to our flat. 'Help your mum get inside while I park.' Those were his words. 'I'll bring Little T.' But Mum insisted on carrying Thomas. She grabbed him from the car seat and I took hold of her, and we slowly navigated the ice patches on the walk. Dad hesitated and zoomed off, and we stumbled on, reaching the steps."

Now would be a good time to stop. I quieted beside Elias, who bumped me with his shoulder.

"Keep going, Clarita."

One minute, and several deep breaths later, I obeyed.

"I took my eyes off the ground and reached for the rail, and Mum ... she slipped. It happened so fast. She was screaming and falling and reaching Little T toward me. I let go of her and grasped my brother. I felt him—my arms caught him—but he fell through. He fell through my arms and landed ... and landed on his head on the pavement. Elias, the ice was thick, and I didn't see it ... I just didn't see ... Why couldn't I hold on to him?"

My tears returned, and I pleaded in silence for Elias to hold me, but he didn't listen to the words I didn't speak, and I rocked until I found my voice.

"I led her right over the patch, and that's where she fell. Mum screamed and crawled toward T. Dad's shouts came nearer, and Teeter and I ran into the flat. I ran to my room and locked the door and looked out my window. Little T lay in a pool of blood and Dad draped his sobbing body over T's tiny one and Mum hit Dad, and I blinked and the coppers were there, trying to pull Mum off Dad and Dad off T. But Dad wouldn't go. He couldn't let go of the son I dropped, and he slugged the copper, laid him right out, and just like that he was on his stomach, his wrists bound in darbies. Mum was hysterical, still screaming at Dad, that it was his fault, that all this was his fault, and all I had to do was run down and tell what happened. That it was me. It was all me and my carelessness and my weak arms. But I couldn't move, and I watched my family splinter; Dad carried away by the cops and Mum and T whisked away in the ambulance. I heard Teeter wailing, and I became his new mum that night." I paused. "Only Mum came back. And only half of her. Her mind, her body were never the same."

Elias touched my face, and then his own. He softly began to cry.

"Clarita." He drew his legs in and rocked. "You didn't try to hurt him. Right? I mean, that was an accident."

"Of course it was." I wiped my eyes with the heel of my hand, and rubbed my tattoo.

"But accident or not, the world changed. I destroyed them all, from when I dropped my brother to when I stood silent as they took Dad away." I leaned over and caught his gaze. "I need to know. Only you can help ... How do you deal with the guilt?"

Elias did not speak. For weeks, he blabbed from morning until night, and now I needed from him one word, one word from this boy who knew the pain of it. The truth of it.

One word to change my life.

"Please." I winced. "Haven't you ever been part of an accident with huge implications? A large, life-changing variety of accident?"

He paused mid-rock. "What do you know?"

"Elias, I know that this Keeper, this quest, this is what remains of your father. He was a lightkeeper."

The carriage house light flickered, and in the glow, Elias's face changed. He looked helpless, just as I felt, and I reached out to him.

"You saw something, and there was an accident, and your father fell and hit his head. I know who you are looking for, but he's gone. I know the lighthouse in your mind. I've been to Two Bush Island."

Elias stood, his body stiff and his hands clenched. His face showed no emotion.

"It was no accident."

His words swirled about me. "What are you saying? You were eight. You were only eight. You had no intention ... you couldn't have."

He grabbed a small sketchbook and tossed it onto my lap. I slowly opened it.

There it was. The man from the east wall of his room. A woman in undress. The two together. Across his father's photo, a giant red X. Around the woman, a red circle.

I dropped the sketchbook, slowly reached for my bag, and backed toward the door. "Why did we come, Elias? What are you looking for?"

He did not flinch. "The woman. She may still be here."

"And if she is?" I fumbled with the door latch.

Elias was silent.

"Say something," I stammered. "Elias ... tell me we're just following stars. Tell me this isn't why you came."

He took a deep breath. "Fine. It isn't why I came. It's why we came. We'll finish it. Together."

I turned and threw open the door and fled into the night.

"Clara! Clara, it's me! Clara, I'm just back! Don't leave me."

A faint call reached my ears, but it meant nothing.

God, what have I done?

CHAPTER 28

DAD: You've called his mother?

ME: No, I just got out of there.

DAD: The police? Do they know?

ME: I don't even know. I don't know anything. I don't know who
     he is.

DAD: You, where are you?

ME: Camden, Maine.

DAD: Where in Camden, Maine?

ME: Dad, what does it matter?

DAD: Where?

ME: Mount Battie. I climbed Mount Battie. There's a little lookout up
     here, and I was hoping maybe he'd be here.

DAD: Elias?????

ME: No. God. I know it sounds stupid, but I think I bumped into
     God on a mountain a few days back, and I didn't know where
     to go, so I thought maybe ...

DAD: Is he there?

I looked around. From where I sat, I could see mountains reaching into the sea, and islands floating in the glistening bays. White-sailed ships caught the last hint of daylight, and a cool breeze blew.

ME: I think so.

DAD: Then stay right there. Elias Phinn. Minneapolis. I'll take care of notifications. Clara, you can't see him again. You know that, right?

DAD: Right?

ME: I'll stay right here.

"Right. Stay right here," I repeated and shut my laptop. "You're about to have Elias arrested. On this trip, half of me used him. Half of him used me. We're not so different. Would you throw your own daughter in the slammer? If you knew I saw you out the window and let you take the blame, would you arrest me?"

I took a deep breath. The lookout included a tall, circular monument, constructed of fitted stone. Four thin steps led up to the tower, and open arched doorways allowed you to walk right through it. It would provide shelter for me tonight.

I opened my bag and threw on two more sweaters. I inflated the camping cot, and lay down in the monument.

"Well then, God, here I am. It would be nice for you to make a more certain appearance, especially tonight. I have some items I need to discuss."

The wind rustled the leaves.

"Fair enough. I shall consider that your entrance. I don't know but that I should be furious and terrified of Elias, but I'm not, not right now." I stood and paced the clearing. "Dad says I can't see him, and that is likely best, it's just ... he alone explains my last weeks.

I'm in the middle, not a crossroads-type middle, but a no roads-type middle, and the truth, the truth is I'm not frightened because I no longer know Elias. I'm frightened because I no longer know me. That's it, I suppose." I sighed. "That probably was not a very good prayer. Quite rambling, little focus. Oh, and I am presently taking orders from my father in London. It seems quite ridiculous, given my past months, but yet quite warming at the same time." I thought. "All right, now I think I'm really done."

I remained with God on Mt. Battie for the remainder of the night, as well as the next day. Several hikers invaded my mountain, but none stayed long, and as night began to fall, not only was I famished, I also realised I couldn't stay there forever.

Elias's last words replayed in my mind. They had not been the words of a madman, or a killer. They had not carried the cadence of the Other One.

I plopped down beside my bag and removed Dad's journal. Anything to rid my mind of Elias. I flipped to the last entry.

Entry 300

It's been awhile since I've written in this old thing. I guess I thought my adventures were over. I thought that when I started a family, the excitement of the hunt would fade. But I'm looking at him, and I think my true search is just beginning. He is so different than Clara, a girl so much like me. He's not like Teeter either. He's not loud or demanding. He is my Little T, human and perfect. Does he see me? Does he know me like the others? Maybe not. Maybe he never will, if the doctors' drivel means anything. Maybe he'll struggle, struggle to understand, to connect, to learn. But I see him in my arms, his eyes looking everywhere but to me, and I know there is another part. A hidden part only I know,

245

buried beneath. What the doctors don't understand is none of T's baseline measurements matter. Who doesn't get emotionally stuck? Who doesn't have a struggling half and a loving half? As for T, I'm not going anywhere. I'll always love both of him, and he'll always love both of me.

I slammed shut the journal.

My Elias. The last words had been his. I had promised him I would not leave, but in my horror, I did. The only way to make it right was to break another promise.

"Sorry, Dad, I need to find him." I jumped to my feet. "You can blame yourself for this one."

What would I do when I did? It didn't matter. It was time to stop running.

I bid God farewell and began a slow descent, arriving back on Laite Beach around noon.

It took some looking, given the wildness of my departure, but soon I located his last known location: the carriage house, its doors standing open, and the interior empty. I ran to the residence and pounded. Slowly, the door opened.

"Salt?"

He stepped out slowly. "You okay, lass? I did look for you. You went searching and he came just after. I let him park in the garage—"

"Yes, I know. Where is Elias now?"

"I'll answer that, but what's going on, Clara? Why were the authorities parked in Tenant's Harbour?"

Dad.

"How would I know?"

"Ayup." Salt stepped out onto the porch. "So I'll start over. Elias became more and more frantic here, and I hauled him and that plane to Rockland. Boy cares deeply about you, wouldn't stop babbling about his Clara. But I reckon you know all that. Bottom line was he needed a space to work, and I thought Tenant's boathouse was perfect. Plenty a room in there, and you knew the place. Wasn't sure where you were and figured you might find your way back there. But as I said, the harbour was crammed with police, and Atticus was being questioned. I quietly took Elias to a less stressful spot to work."

"Work on what?"

"That plane. Seems like a big hobby, but he was so tense. Talking about it calmed him. Didn't see no harm in it, least until you showed up."

My heart slowed, as if it was beating in molasses, and I willed my breaths. "Is there an airport near there?"

"Knox County Regional. Where I left the lad. I'll go pick him up this evening."

"I don't think he'll be there this evening." I grabbed his arm and tugged. "We need to go now."

Salt rolled his eyes. "Do I look like the ferry service?"

"No, no you don't."

"Come on, lass."

Minutes later, we entered the airport and the private hangar area.

"He's in this one here." Salt tugged on a giant door. "Got a friend who works in aviation, and it seemed a good alternative—"

It was, of course, empty.

· · · · ·

Atticus stood on the edge of the dock and stared out to sea.

"It's a round world. You live long enough, you see it, the coming round of things." He glanced over his shoulder. "Elias wished you were with him."

I stopped, one foot on the dock, the other on the earth. "Where is he? What is going on?"

Atticus turned. "Mine to show, though I take no pleasure in it. It's gonna hurt." He gestured toward the boat, and along with Salt we eased out toward Two Bush. Nobody spoke. Words weren't needed. The sky was clear and stars shone above us, Orion bright in the eastern sky.

The sea was a window, reflecting the lights but allowing me to glance below. It was empty. There was nothing beneath the surface. No life. No ... life. When finally we lapped up in the shadows of Two Bush, I knew.

The three of us climbed up the rocky crag and onto the flat that was the island. No tree or bush grew there; it had been razed flat, except for the lighthouse shining in the near distance, pointing safety to all who drew near.

Almost all.

I walked toward the far end of the island, toward a twisted sculpture, glistening in the beacon's light. It was metal. It was cordoned off with police tape. I paused, and then I ran.

"Elias! Elias!"

And my foot struck it.

The piece of the fuselage, the words written:

Clara

A Light in the Sky

I lifted it and held it up to the moonlight. It was real. It felt real. It had been real.

I spun around and raced back to Atticus. "Bring me to him! Where'd they take him?"

"What do you see?" Atticus dropped his gaze. "Think a boy could survive this?"

"Maybe!" I shoved the man, and marched toward Salt to shove him, but my arms, they didn't work, and I paced. "Maybe, maybe he could, right?"

"Clara." Salt opened his mouth and let it fall shut, only to restart. "Okay. Maybe."

I staggered toward the wreckage, perched precariously near the cliff. "It's not completely destroyed. It didn't burn." I spun around. "Have they found him?"

Atticus slowly removed his handkerchief. "I did. By the lighthouse."

I wandered toward it, toward the entry, and my hand raised to my mouth.

The door was covered with drawings.

Of Elias and his father holding hands.

Of Elias and his father looking through a telescope.

Of a small Elias and his father locked in embrace.

And in the center of the door, Elias and me. Holding hands, staring at each other.

Oh God.

"The police are thinking he crawled from the crash clear to the lighthouse. I watched a plane fly low right over the dock, go quiet near this island and I just knew. I chugged out and found him right where you stand, collapsed by the door, pushpins and blood everywhere on the ground," Atticus continued. "There was a drawin' book filled with more pictures beneath his head. But he stuck some up before he ... Boy must've been bent on trying to hang the important ones."

I dropped to my knees and lay down. Salt lowered himself beside me and stroked my head. Tears flowed easily, as did time. I don't know how long I cried.

"He didn't draw, Salt." I sniffed and pushed myself up. "My Elias didn't draw. Only the ... only the Other One, and he wouldn't have hung these. He hated the Keeper. He hated ... his ... dad. Unless, the two, in the end, unless the two became one."

He did.

I stared up at Orion, and whispered. "We did it. Elias, you did it. In the end it was just you."

Atticus cleared his throat.

"I . . . I need the other sketches," I said. "The ones he didn't put up. Please. Where's the book now? Take me to it—"

"Figured they might hold interest." Atticus reached into his trench coat and removed the sketchbook, gently placing it beside me on the ground.

"I reckon you are goin' to want some time alone."

"Thank you," I mouthed, and grabbed the book and drew it close. "Would you mind coming back for me in the morning? I'll be here."

Atticus smirked. "Don't mind taking your money twice."

What was left of Elias and I spent the night together.

The book was tattered, but still beautiful, filled with scenes from the entire trip, proof again that a mind at war had truly made peace in the end.

I relived it all, let myself feel it all. The wild ride down the dirt mound in the Elias. The fight at Kira's university. The antique shop, Kenton in the tunnel, Izzy cleaning her gun.

I winced at the partially clothed Londoner sitting in a tower, giggled at Elias's mad fire dance, and wondered why I could feel so full sitting before an empty cross.

But I spent hours with the final three pictures:

Elias standing triumphant in front of the finished plane.

A young, horrified girl staring out of a window, and a proud dad staring back up.

And a kiss.

Once again, he had peeked inside my bag, and once again he had catalogued the weightiest items at the end.

I stood and walked toward the darkness of the cliff. I lay on my back and listened to waves crash beneath me. I laughed and cried and stared up at the crescent moon, while Orion's starlight, and perhaps even the keeper of the lights, watched over me.

"Dear Elias, you're not getting away from me that easy. I can keep my eye on you just as easily from London."

And the stars twinkled brighter than they had before.

EPILOGUE

"Clara. Wake up. We're here."

I blinked in the morning light, and Dad gently placed his hand on my shoulder. I rubbed my hands over my denims, took a deep breath, and looked around. Izzy was still slumped in her seat, asleep. We'd planned this road trip for months, ever since our move to Salem, Ohio. But I knew I'd return long before that, ever since I tried to explain to Dad the whole of why I left in the first place, with no success. I gave myself a year, a year to get to know my FFA. Maybe in that time he could love me as he had. Maybe enough to accept the entire truth.

But those words left unsaid—the load I promised both Kira and Izzy I would on this day lay down—grew heavier by the minute.

"I thought this would be easier." I bit my lip and swept back tears.

Dad forced a smile. "I'm sorry Guinevere didn't want to come to our memorial," he said softly.

Guinevere. News of Elias's passing should have buried our relationship as well, but how profound her forgiveness had been toward me. "She couldn't." I swallowed hard. "Two Bush has taken too much from her."

I stepped out of the Camry and walked down to the dock and stopped.

"Go on. Show me where, then make your peace. It feels good, you know." Izzy nudged me with her guitar case. We stepped into Atticus's boat and he headed out without a word.

A half hour later, we stood on Two Bush Island, blanketed by a heavy calm. I walked quietly toward the lighthouse, and stopped on the patch of dirt that fronted the door. Izzy stared for a minute. "Yeah, okay."

She opened her case and removed her six-string, then played a song both beautiful and sad. I took hold of Dad's hand, walked slowly to the far cliff, and we plunked down together. We sat for hours, my dad and I, staring out at Penobscot Bay and beyond, beyond toward what had been home, to Marbury Street and a life that now seemed so far away. I pressed hard into his shoulder, soaking up the feeling from a different life, a new life, wondering why I'd run from it so long.

The guitar music stopped, and I glanced over my shoulder. Izzy raised both palms and eyebrows, and then pointed dramatically at Dad. I swallowed and rejoined the Bay.

And Dad sang.

Softly, like he used to sing. And in the spaces between his words, mine left unspoken grew hot. I could hold my secret no more.

"I could have told them, Dad!" I blurted, and buried my head in my arms. "I saw it all happen with Little T. From the window? I saw it all. They carried you away and I said nothing. I could've. They needed to know it was me who did it. Me. Clara. I dropped him. That might have changed everything. I mean, you might not have been jailed and Mum might not have lost hope and I ..."

Dad reached over and touched the tiny 3 on my hand. "Such a nice remembrance. Oh, my Clara, I saw you. Your scared little face. I always knew, and I never blamed you. Your mum never did either. Truth is, I blamed myself."

My breath caught, and a weight floated upward, and I inhaled free and clear, knowing that something foul had died. I was Clara, small and simple, and a path home stretched before me.

A path named Peace.

Elias had shown me the way, and once more I glanced up, this time at brilliant blue.

Down below, Dad would journey beside me. Above, both Elias and Little T would always be with me.

Though we weren't on a mountain, I risked one short prayer. "Take care of them better than I did."

And a gentle salt breeze kissed my lips.